A DARK AND DEADLY
DECEPTION

**Center Point
Large Print**

A DARK AND DEADLY
DECEPTION

ELEANOR TAYLOR BLAND

CENTER POINT PUBLISHING
THORNDIKE, MAINE

This Center Point Large Print edition
is published in the year 2006 by arrangement with
St. Martin's Press.

The text of this Large Print edition is unabridged. In other
aspects, this book may vary from the original edition. Printed in
Thailand. Set in 16-point Times New Roman type.

ISBN 1-58547-768-0

Library of Congress Cataloging-in-Publication Data

Bland, Eleanor Taylor.
    A dark and deadly deception / Eleanor Taylor Bland.--Center Point large print ed.
    p. cm.
    ISBN 1-58547-768-0 (lib. bdg. : alk. paper)
    1. MacAlister, Marti (Fictitious character)--Fiction. 2. Police--Illinois--Chicago--Fiction.
3. Actresses--Crimes against--Fiction. 4. African American police--Fiction. 5. Motion picture
industry--Fiction. 6. Chicago (Ill.)--Fiction. 7. Policewomen--Fiction. 8. Large type books.
I. Title.

PS3552.L36534D37 2006
813'.54--dc22

                                                                    2005036283

IN MEMORIUM

My brothers-in-law, Sterlin Bland and Lee Bland.

My "Little" nephew Carl Douglas Richardson, whom
I miss terribly and dearly love.

Louis J. Boryc, and his beloved Tara, who will
always be in the hearts and memories of those who
love them.

Daniel Drew, mayor of Waukegan. So many of us
will always remember you.

I BORE YOU UP ON WINGS OF EAGLES
AND BROUGHT YOU HERE TO MYSELF.
—EXODUS 19:4

Welcome John Carlo, Megumi, John Paul, and
Jackson.

A BABY IS GOD'S OPINION THAT LIFE SHOULD GO ON.
—CARL SANDBURG

Congratulations to Pat and Judy Clyne on their fiftieth
wedding anniversary.

A special thank-you to my agent, Ted Chichak, whose support and encouragement are appreciated more than I can say; my editor, Kelley Ragland, for her enthusiasm and support; and to Toby Yuen, copy editor, whose job I seem to have made easier this time, and whose thoroughness and competence were greatly appreciated.

I would also like to thank family: my sons, Kevin and Todd, whose constant and unconditional love and support mean more to me than I can say; my grandchildren, Anthony, LaTa'Ja, Todd Junior, An'Tonia—time passes so quickly and you are growing up so fast. I am most grateful for the time we spent together while you were young; also my four-footed grandchildren with fur, Geronimo and Maxie, Teddy and Sydney, my little angels in disguise.

To my dear and special friend Nanette Boryc, who not only encourages me, but insists that I write, and does a fantastic job doing all of my Internet research.

Three very special people have recently come into my life: my cousin George Gershefski, whom I spoke to for the first time this year; my "Polish" cousin Lou; and my sister-cousin, Phyllis. I am so grateful and blessed to have found them.

To everyone at the Waukegan Public Library, especially the research librarians, for their cheerful assistance.

I especially want to acknowledge Chief Biang, Deputy Chief Yancey, and Commander Richard

Davis; through their leadership and example, our Waukegan Police Department exemplifies professionalism and compassion. I would also like to acknowledge Chief Gallager and our fire department—firefighters and paramedics. Every time I hear a siren or pull over for an ambulance I know that whenever necessary they will put their lives on the line to save others, and always do everything medically possible to save a life.

To the Robert Sabonjian Lake County Board, for those moments of sanity and common sense, for courage and persistence in pursuing the dream.

Superfans: Dee and Jamie O'Meara; Augie, at Centuries and Sleuths; and Judy Duhl—our writer's group will never be the same without Scotland Yard Bookstore.

For technical assistance: Charles Schaller, former consul, United States Embassy, Bucharest, Romania, and his wife, Pat; Danny Diaz, City of Waukegan; Wayne Munn, Carnegie Restoration Committee; Patricia Jones, Waukegan Township supervisor, for bravery, determination, and also the tour of the Genesee Theater; Daniel Foust, licensed clinical counselor; Teddy Anderson, Waukegan Downtown Association; the staff at Haines Museum; the staff at Staben House and LaCasa; Maxie's Writing Studio; Mary Ann Curtis, Catholic Charities; Frank Phillips, Meals on Wheels; Mary Bolin, food pantry coordinator; also, AnnMarie Stohl, Marcia Portnoy, and Lucy Rahn.

FRIDAY, MARCH 19—LINCOLN PRAIRIE

Aloud snap awakened him. Wood scraped against brick. Another branch from the elms planted close to the house must have broken. Thomas Newsome pushed the heavy blanket aside and, mindful of the stiffness in his hips and knees, pushed himself up from the armchair. Leaning on his cane, he shuffled to the window and pulled back the heavy velvet curtain. The wind had picked up. Snow, large flakes falling thick and fast, whipped past the leaded glass, moving horizontally. Winter, the stripping away of things past, a time for the seed to lie fallow within the frozen earth: his favorite time of year. Like the animals that slept through blizzards, and cold, and rivers dammed with ice, he, too, chose to hibernate, staying inside with a fire in the hearth but wakeful—watching and waiting, for what he didn't know.

Loath to turn away from the storm that raged outside, he stood there until the cold from bare glass and the chill from a draft began to permeate his bones, stiffening his joints, making his back ache. He sighed. Today was his birthday. He was seventy-nine years old. Perhaps there wouldn't be many more winters. Perhaps soon, he would lie beneath the snow awaiting resurrection. He turned from the window and went to a tall, narrow cupboard. He touched the dark wood, older than he was, and scarred. The veins on the backs of his hands stood out like cords. He rubbed the knots in the wood with fingers that had never known a callus.

There were no tremors in his hand now. Was it the medication? Or . . . the Theotokos—Mother, Madonna, Birth-Giver of God. He opened the cabinet, looked at the icon placed at eye level.

The icon was small, five inches by eight. A border of blue-and-red paint that might once have been bright was now dull and scarred. Bare wood was exposed where the paint had chipped or peeled. He thought the light surrounding the Madonna's face and head must have been gold. Now it was a mottled brown-green. Her face was the color of old parchment. Her dress made him think of a brown wool coat he had worn as a boy.

"Mama," he whispered. "Mother."

She was a tormented mother, looking toward some distant place far beyond his line of vision. There was no Christ child in her arms to love, no crucified Christ to mourn. She leaned forward, lap empty, arms empty. Her hands palms up, a silent plea or a mother's prayer? The anguish in her eyes was too deep for him to fathom or to even begin to understand. "What do you see, Mama?" Again he asked that question, again the answer came, "I see forever."

SUNDAY, APRIL 25—BUCHAREST, ROMANIA

Vladimir entered the sacristy alone. Even now, after thirty-four years as a priest, he liked to linger after vespers. It was the last prayer of the evening and the first prayer of the new day, a quiet celebration of the end and another beginning, as if they were one, a promise that existed beyond the confines of mortality.

Vladimir extinguished the last candle. He took deep breaths as the scent of smoke mingled with the aroma of incense. He listened to the silence until it became a prayer, a meditation. No, this was a respite. He would not think about the Romanian senate's decision to allow a cathedral designed a hundred years ago to finally be built. He would not consider the financial concerns involved. He would not ponder the reports of miracles bestowed by the Virgin of Germany, when her icon visited the Romanian church in Berlin. Many had come in pilgrimage to their Theotokos—their Mother. Many had touched the drops of myrrh that flowed from her image. Vladimir believed that the most meaningful healing was that of the soul. He knew that for many, the certainty of physical healing would be as fleeting as the religious fervor awakened by Her visit. He also knew that for those few, there would indeed be a miracle. But now there were more immediate concerns.

Tomorrow he would meet with Josef yet again to discuss this visit to Canada and the United States. Meetings had been arranged with Bishop Petre in Michigan and Archbishop Gabriel in Illinois. What remained to be decided were which churches and missions he would visit. This was a tedious task for Josef. These were decisions rife with political implications for Vladimir. Balance, Josef kept saying, balance. Peace, Vladimir thought, peace. This was not just about the unification of all Orthodox Romanians. This was not another attempt to clarify ecclesiastical relationships. If peace and unity and a charity that exceeded justice could not flourish within the Church, then where in this universe could it even begin to grow roots?

Vladimir massaged the dull throb stirring at his temples, then bowed low to the image of the Christ. Not a crucified Christ, not a risen Christ, but the battered, beaten, broken body of the Christ who died for the sins of the world. He looked at this Jesus until all other thoughts faded and a quiet joy and gratitude began filling his heart. Now, in these moments of prayer, he was not Vladimir, Archbishop of Bucharest, Metropolitan of Ungro-Wallachia, patriarch of the Romanian Orthodox Church. He was just Vladimir, the servant of God.

C H A P T E R

3

WEDNESDAY, MAY 5—LINCOLN PRAIRIE

Detective Marti MacAlister waded through the water that had overflowed the banks of the Des Plaines River. Just a few days ago she would have been able to drive down this street to get to Gurnee Mills or Six Flags Great America. Now this road and all nearby roads were flooded and closed to traffic and the river hadn't crested yet. Cloud cover made the sky look like a solid gray mass. The air was dense with moisture. Soon it would rain again. Not the usual thunderstorms, just a drenching deluge that would last for several hours and raise the water level even higher.

She had borrowed a pair of boots from a fireman on standby. They were a little too big and she was surprised by how heavy they were. She made her way to the railing at the side of the road, where a bridge allowed the river to flow beneath the street. Standing there, she looked north. The placid, slow-moving Des Plaines had become a swift-moving stream rushing toward her and spreading east and west as it overflowed its banks. Water covered what had been a grassy floodplain and slapped at the lower branches of a stand of burr oak.

Less than half a mile away sailors from the nearby naval base, local residents, and other volunteers were filling sandbags. The locals seemed to have become accustomed to the occasional flooding, but this was the worst it had been in fifteen years. The curious, or perhaps those with homes too far away to be threatened, stood alone, arms folded, or in groups of three or four chatting and gesturing toward the houses that were in danger. Marti couldn't hear what anyone was saying.

Her husband, Ben Walker, a fireman paramedic, was in the water wearing a wet suit, working to free the body that had become trapped in the thick branches of an uprooted tree. Ben's partner, Allan, waited alongside in a small boat. Evidence technicians were in a second boat, taking pictures. Two techs wearing diving suits were in the river looking for anything that might have belonged to the victim or provide information as to who she was or how she died. Just beyond the water's edge, uniformed officers kept onlookers away.

Water swirled as Marti's partner, Matthew "Vik" Jessenovik, came over and stood beside her. He was wearing hip waders.

"I see you came prepared," she said.

He was four inches taller than her five feet ten and looked down at her as he spoke. "These belonged to my old man."

"Took you long enough to get here." Usually, when they were called at home, he was the first to arrive. "Sleep in this morning?"

"I took Mildred to the Sunrise for breakfast."

Marti smiled. Vik's wife had multiple sclerosis. Eating out could only mean she was feeling good.

Vik nodded toward the recovery team and the forensic techs. "Just what we need," he said. "Another body."

"Things have been slow," Marti reminded him. They had been working on cold cases for over a month and Lieutenant Gail Nicholson insisted that they work on the three cases least likely to be solved. Neither of them liked the lieutenant, nor did she pretend to like them. They were here as members of the Northern Illinois Regional Task Force, which was under Frank Winan's command. This would take precedence over the Lincoln Prairie cold cases.

"Male or female?" Vik asked. "Or do we know?"

"Woman."

"Do we know anything else?"

"Not yet."

"Why doesn't that surprise me. Anything that did go in with her is probably miles downstream by now. Just our luck that tree snagged her or she would be, too."

"Is that a complaint?"

Vik considered that. "Nah. Thanks to whoever it is or whoever did it, we should be able to tell Nicholson to shove it for at least a few days. Who found her?"

Marti pointed toward two boys. Neither looked older than twelve. The younger boy had short blond hair. He was wrapped in a blanket. A woman, also blond, was at his side. They were standing in a grassy area that wasn't underwater. The woman was rubbing his hair with a towel.

The boy who looked to be the older of the two had a mullet cut, short on top with the long hair in the back pulled into a ponytail. He and a man, who also had a mullet, were almost close enough to the water's edge to wade in. The man refused to move back when one of the uniforms suggested it. He kept leaning down to speak to the boy and jabbed the boy's shoulder with the heel of his hand whenever he caught the boy looking away from the felled tree, where Ben was working to free the body.

"The blond was going for a Huckleberry Finn ride in an inner tube," Marti explained. "The one with the ponytail was on one of those inflatable rafts. It capsized, he swam for the tree, saw the body, and almost drowned getting away."

"Stupid, both of them," Vik said. "We could be fishing them out." Despite the gruffness in his voice, Marti knew how he felt when kids witnessed a homicide or found a body. "Not too many vultures out today," he added, nodding toward a lone reporter who was scanning the scene with a video camera. A bag with a tape recorder was slung over his shoulder.

Marti was keeping an eye on him, too. When he had enough film he'd begin interviewing for voice-overs. Once he identified her and Vik as homicide cops he'd be all over them. Otherwise there was just one local newspaper photographer with a camera and telephoto lens.

"The governor's not flying in by helicopter until tomorrow to check out the flood damage," Marti reminded him.

"And meanwhile, what's one more body?" Vik grumbled. "A live politician, now that's news."

Marti wasn't sure how long Ben had been in the water when he signaled Allan to bring the boat closer. She knew he was tired. They had stayed up late last night, more interested in each other than in sleep as vanilla-scented candles burned down and flickered out. As the boat moved in, someone in the small crowd gave a loud, nervous laugh. Someone else gave an equally loud shush. Marti turned to look at the two boys. The blond boy's mother shielded him from what was going on. The other boy was shivering, but did not look away.

"Macho," Vik muttered. "That kid's seen more than most adults out here."

By the time the boat reached the edge of the river, the body was covered with a blue plastic tarp. Two firemen brought a stretcher and carried the body to where a gurney waited on dry ground. They transferred the body and wheeled the victim to the ambulance. Marti and Vik did their best to avoid the onlookers as they made their way to where Ben stood, still dripping water. The three of them entered the ambulance. Ben pulled back the tarp, exposing her face. The woman's skin was the color of pecans. There wasn't much damage to her face. Her eyes were open and a startling shade of brown at least two shades lighter than her skin. Her hair was permed. The hair on the left side was pulled behind her ear and secured with an ornate barrette. It had come loose on the right side and a black mesh hairnet clung to wet strands. Marti guessed her age as mid-thirties.

Ben lifted the tarp to give them a look at the body. The trench coat the woman wore had been lavender. Now it was covered with silt and mud. It was belted and buttoned, but Marti could see that the woman had on a soggy, pink angora sweater. There was no obvious body trauma. Marti looked at Ben.

"Back of the head," he said. "There's a lot of damage to the skull."

"Enough to kill her?" Marti asked.

"It could have."

"Maybe she was knocked against something while she was in the water," Vik commented. "The river is moving pretty fast."

"That'll have to wait for the autopsy," Ben said. "But she took a hell of a blow, maybe more than one." He turned the woman's head to one side. "See where the skull is caved in." Bone fragments were tangled in her hair.

Marti looked up to see the reporter from the *News-Times* standing a few feet from the ambulance taking pictures. She motioned him away. "Now that they've got digital cameras," she said, "there's no telling how long he was standing there or how many shots he got."

"You can't hear the film advance or the shutter close

anymore," Vik complained.

"I wouldn't worry too much just yet," Ben said. "The way the *News-Times* is *not* reporting local news these days you'll probably have to get the *Chicago Tribune* to read about a body being found in the Des Plaines River in Gurnee." He pulled off vinyl gloves. "It's just another day, another body to them anyway. Why can't we get to that level of indifference?"

Marti shrugged, preoccupied with who the woman was and how she got here, and wondering who would have to be notified of her death.

As Marti approached the blond boy, she could see that he was crying.

"What's your name, son?" Vik asked.

"Tyler." He sniffled.

"Are you his mother, ma'am?" he asked the woman. She nodded.

"We'll need to talk with him as soon as possible."

"You're not taking him to the police station?"

"Of course not," Vik scoffed. "Just give us your address and we'll be there within the next half hour."

They lived about half a block away.

As they turned toward the duo with the mullet cuts and ponytails, Vik said, "Tyler will remember most of what he saw. We could run into a problem with this boy's father telling him what to tell us and what to keep his mouth shut about."

"Why?" Marti asked. "These kids didn't do anything that bad."

"This one did. He got scared. These macho types don't do that."

Water squished beneath their feet as they approached.

"Yeah, so what do you two want?" the big guy asked. He wasn't wearing a jacket. Softball-sized biceps stretched the sleeves of a T-shirt with the legend "Bikers love Bitches" on the front. The boy's chin jutted out as his father spoke.

"Where do you live?" Marti asked. He was not a typical Gurnee resident.

"What's it to you?"

"Is this your son?" Marti countered. She wasn't in the mood to deal with a wiseass.

"You thinking about taking him in?"

Marti looked at the boy, then stared at his dad. "If that's what you want."

The man glowered at her, then said, "Lake Forest."

Marti waited.

Before she could count to three he added, "We're spending a couple of days with the relatives so the wife can go shopping at the mall." Muscles tightened as he folded his arms. "My boy don't usually hang with no wimps. Wasn't for that one over there," he nodded toward Tyler, "thinking he saw a snake in the water and freaking out, none of this would have happened."

That was not how the boys had explained things to the first uniform on the scene, but Marti didn't see any point in calling him on it.

20

"What's your name?" she asked the boy.

"Cecil Slocum Jr.," the man answered. "C. J. for short." He spoke with such pride that Marti expected him to say, "chip off the old block," but he didn't.

"Cecil Slocum Jr.," Marti repeated.

Vik coughed. Marti knew he was stifling a laugh.

She looked at the boy. "Hi, C. J."

He swallowed hard, but didn't answer until his father hit his shoulder with the heel of his hand. Then he said, "Yeah."

Marti spoke to his father.

"If you'll give us your family's address we'll meet you there as soon as we can."

"What, no handcuffs?" Dad looked disappointed. "And just so you know," he added, "I'm assuming that the lady in the water fell in somewhere and drowned, but just in case it was something else, C. J. here is real good with a twelve-gauge. We go hunting most every weekend in the fall."

Marti didn't respond although that undoubtedly meant Dad was good with a gun, too. She would make a note of it. She watched as father and son turned and walked away with identical swaggers.

As Marti and Vik walked toward their vehicles, they agreed that they would talk with Tyler first. His version of what happened seemed most likely to be accurate.

Tyler and his family lived in a Victorian in one of the few older parts of town. Unlike the newer subdivisions—what Marti's mother liked to call cookie-cutter houses because they were all variations of the same floor plan—these houses had what realtors liked to call character.

Marti and Vik followed Tyler's mother into the sunroom. It was like entering a garden. Hanging planters with philodendrons and Boston ferns, daffodils blooming in clay pots. They sat at a table with a Scrabble game set up. Tyler and his father were drinking cocoa. Usually, Marti and Vik would have declined, but today they sat with the family and accepted steaming mugs of hot, sweet chocolate. It wasn't that cold outside, but it was damp, and when the wind kicked in it had a bite to it.

"C. J. saw her first," Tyler said, without being asked. "He started yelling and hollering and I tried to get over to where he was 'cause I thought he was stuck in the tree or drowning maybe." He held the cup near his face but didn't drink. Marti waited.

"He made me promise not to tell anyone he was scared, but he was. Real scared. More scared than me. I thought she might still be alive at first, but the way her face was down in the water there was no way she could breathe. And she wasn't moving, except for when the water pushed her. Otherwise I would have tried to help her get out." He put the cup down, looked from Vik to Marti, and added, "I learned how to do CPR in Boy Scouts. I would have helped her if I could."

Marti let Vik ask him a few more questions about

the approximate time and what the weather and the river had been like.

"Cold," the boy said, and shivered. "I never remember seeing the river that high. The grass made it look kind of like the Everglades, but it was more like white-water rafting once we went in. C. J. hadn't ever done any rafting. He's never even been in a canoe. I told him he should use the inner tube, but he had to have the raft, and he couldn't wear a life jacket—that was for little kids."

"Who was out there when you went in?" Vik asked.

"Nobody but the people just around that curve in the road filling sandbags. That's why we went in so early. So nobody would see us and tell."

"Were there any cars parked nearby?"

Tyler shook his head.

"Did you see anyone anywhere near the banks of the river or maybe on the bridge?"

The boy hesitated. "There wasn't anyone close by. Once we got in, I could feel the current moving real fast. I wanted to get out, but C. J. headed right for the middle. I told him we needed to keep to the edge, but he didn't listen. So mostly I was watching him and trying to get him to come back where it was safer. Then he fell off the raft and was yelling to me to come help him."

"Tyler took seventh place in the four-hundred-meter freestyle at the Junior Olympics," his mother explained, and added, "Nationals."

"Ma," Tyler said as if he was embarrassed, but then

23

he gave Marti a quick, shy smile. "The current took C. J. to that tree. He started yelling that he was stuck, and then he really panicked and started screaming, 'Rats! Rats!' If anyone had heard him, they sure would have come. I swam over to help him. I was real scared he'd drown."

Marti was impressed because Tyler took responsibility for what he did and didn't blame it on C. J. She knew from experience with her own two twelve-year-old boys that even smart kids could do things they shouldn't because of a taunt, or a dare, or sometimes just male bravado.

By the time Marti and Vik drove two blocks to talk with C. J., the houses had gone from turn-of-the-century clapboard with gables and porches to sprawling brick and aluminum-sided ranches built in the fifties and sixties. Green shutters framed the windows where C. J. was visiting. Most of the tulips that grew on each side of the walk had been trampled. A customized Harley-Davidson was parked in the driveway. It was pink, with lots of chrome. Marti could hear the children's voices before she reached the front door. She wasn't sure if they were arguing or playing, but they were loud.

As soon as she rang the bell a woman yelled, "Just quiet down! Right now! Do you hear me?" There was no noticeable change. "Did you hear what I said?" the woman called as she opened the door, then, "You're not the police, are you?"

"Yes, ma'am," Vik told her.

"Oh." She sounded disappointed. "Cecil said you might want to talk with C. J., but you're not even in uniform and there's only two of you. Do you have one of those big sticks?"

Vik shook his head.

"A whistle maybe? Do you have anything that will get their attention? Cecil's boys are real hellions." She looked over their shoulder. "You don't even have a real police car. I bet you can't even lock them in the backseat. Can you do anything to get them to shut up for a few minutes? I can't hear myself think. Not that I've got any time to think with them here." The woman was about four feet eleven and couldn't have weighed more than a hundred pounds. Her hair looked like she had combed it with a rake and then stuck her finger in a light socket. She ran her fingers through it as she spoke.

"Give that to me now!" a boy yelled. That was followed by a girl crying, "No! No-o-o-o-o! M-o-o-o-m-m-m-m-m-y, Jimmy's going to hit me."

The woman shook her head. She looked close to tears. "You might as well come in," she said as she opened the door wider.

It sounded like the yelling was coming from the basement. There was a crash, a moment of silence, then a loud thump followed by an even louder argument.

"You're not the boss of me," the woman muttered. "They win the lottery and think they own the world.

Why don't I just see if I can get C. J. to come up here."
She left Marti and Vik standing just inside the door.
Marti looked at her watch and waited fifty-three seconds. The woman and the children were all yelling now. She motioned to Vik to walk ahead of her. Halfway down the stairs, Vik bellowed, "Police. Freeze or you're all under arrest!"

Three boys stood stock-still. They all had mullet cuts and ponytails. One little girl about four rushed over to the woman and wrapped her arms around her denim-clad legs. The other girl, maybe seven or eight, stared at the boys, mouth open. In the sudden silence a cat meowed.

"Did you lock Whiskers in the liquor cabinet again?" the woman asked and rushed over to release a calico kitten.

"Sit!" Vik ordered. "Now! All of you! Go over to that couch and sit down." When they hesitated, he added, "Forthwith!" Everyone obeyed.

"Where's Mr. Slocum?" he asked.

"Where do you think? Over at a bar on Forty-one, same as always, tossing down a few cold ones with his biker buddies."

Vik looked at C. J. for a moment, walked over to him, and said with unexpected gentleness, "Come on upstairs, son. We need to talk for a few minutes." He glared at the other children for what seemed like a full minute, then said in a low but menacing tone, "The rest of you will remain seated. You will not argue. You will not scream. You will not wrestle. You will not

26

whisper loud enough for me to hear you upstairs. And after I leave, if you start in again your . . ."—he turned to the woman.

"Aunt Daisy."

"Your aunt Daisy will give me a call and I will return." He looked at each of the boys in turn. "Maybe you'd like to spend the next couple of days in a locked ward or a room with bars on the window."

As Marti followed him upstairs, she whispered, "Forthwith?"

He put his finger to his lips and pointed at C. J., who was walking ahead of them.

Upstairs, isolated from his brothers and without his father, C. J. became a scared little boy.

"I didn't kill her," he said.

"What makes you think someone killed her?" Vik asked.

"My dad said so, but I didn't do it. I didn't do nothing but find her." He hung his head. "And I didn't mean to do that."

"Why don't you just tell us what happened."

Looking up, C. J. said, "That Tyler. He's such a baby. And all this water. Everywhere, like an ocean. School's closed. Streets are barricaded. Nothing like this happens where we live. And it's so boring when we have to come here. Girls." He gave Aunt Daisy a look that was more disgust than annoyance. "If I *ever* have a sister . . . So why not go sailing? Of course nobody had a boat. I could handle a boat. And Tyler—he gets in the water and he's all scared. 'Don't go in the middle.' 'Stay near the edge.' 'You'll drown.' 'There might be water moccasins.' He's a wimpy little kid, just like Dad says. Water moccasins." His voice sounded scornful, but he looked at Vik. "Are there? Water moccasins?"

Vik shook his head.

"Yeah. Right. Like Dad said, Tyler's a wimp. I mean what's the point of doing something if you're not going to have fun." His chin went up as if he was daring someone to disagree.

"Anyway, I'm out in the water having a good time; the wimp is near the edge being a baby as usual. Then he yells, 'What's that?' I steer the raft over to find out what he's talking about. Then this stuff is touching my arms. Hair, just hair. I thought it was a dead rat or something until I saw the barrette. Then I knew it wasn't nothing but a dead body. I mean, like, a body, big deal. So I tell Tyler and of course he gets real crazy, screaming and yelling. Swimming over so he can hide behind me like it'll come to life and grab him. Then he panics like a little kid. If it wasn't for me he would have drowned."

Vik asked him a few questions, confirmed that he hadn't seen anyone either, no cars, nothing of interest.

"I mean, would I have gone out there if anyone else was there?" C. J. asked. "What's the fun if you're going to get caught?"

"Did you see anyone farther away? Down the street maybe. Any emergency vehicles?"

"Man, there wasn't nobody out there but me and

Tyler. Nobody on the street. Nobody nowhere. Just those dumb guys way down by the church filling bags with sand. Like that's gonna stop that much water."

"Did you check to make sure nobody was nearby before you went for a swim?"

"Nah. But Tyler did. I figured as long as there weren't any cops around nobody was going to mess with us. Besides, I don't even live here. Who's to say I can't go out on the river and have a little fun? Man, I just wanted to get a little action. It is so boring here. Like having Great America up the street is such a big deal. You know how many times I've been on those roller coasters?"

Neither Marti nor Vik mentioned anything about C. J. going hunting with his father and firing weapons. As they left, they looked into the den and saw Aunt Daisy lying on a couch with a damp cloth on her forehead. The house was still quiet.

Outside Marti asked again, "Forthwith?"

"Yeah. That always worked for Mildred. I don't think Krista and Michael knew what she meant."

Forthwith. Based on the reaction Vik got from those kids, she was going to have to remember that.

As soon as they walked into the station, the desk
sergeant pointed in the direction of Lieutenant
Nicholson's office.

"Damn," Vik complained as they walked down the
corridor.

"Got that right," Marti agreed. The cold cases they
had been working on had not required too much face-
to-face contact with the lieutenant, but every time they
got a task force case, she couldn't leave them alone.
Vik thought it was curiosity, something he attributed
to all females. Marti thought Nicholson was just being
deliberately disruptive.

They stopped at the lieutenant's closed door. As
always, Vik knocked; then they waited the requisite
three minutes for the lieutenant to respond.

Even after working with her for almost nine months,
Marti had no idea why Nicholson did that. She liked
to imagine the woman taking a quick shot of Jack
Daniel's, but her breath never smelled of alcohol or
breath mints.

The lieutenant was a petite woman in her mid-for-
ties. As always she was dressed in a conservative suit,
gray today, with a white blouse and matching gray
heels. She never wore slacks. Delicate features in a
heart-shaped face were framed by short, naturally

curly hair. Gail Nicholson could have passed for white if it wasn't for her chestnut-brown skin.

According to Vik, the male officers Nicholson worked with would have considered her a real looker if she gave them even an occasional smile. Every time Marti saw her, her expression was stern. The frown lines around her eyes looked permanent. She came to work early and left late. Her secretary swore that the only personal calls she had received since she arrived last October involved finding and purchasing a town house.

"Just so there is no confusion," Nicholson began, looking at Marti, "this new case changes nothing."

Nicholson had not recommended them for the Regional Task Force assignment. She never made any direct reference to the fact that Marti and Vik were responsible for all regional homicide cases. She had never verbally acknowledged that those cases took precedence over hers.

"You are still working on *my* cases. I expect consistent, methodical progress and I want those cases solved, not filed again. I specifically want you to work on that case with the skeletal remains. Sixty years is much too long for a case to go unsolved."

"Unless you've only known the case existed for nine months," Marti reminded her. There was a complete skeleton in the morgue that was brought in ten years ago and still remained unidentified. Marti didn't see any point in reminding Nicholson of that, or suggesting that might be the more logical case to work on.

31

"I understand your reluctance to take on a case this difficult, MacAlister. It does beg the question of whether a case is solved based on ability and intellect or luck and coincidence."

Marti remained silent. In her opinion, all the lieutenant brought to the job was contempt and a lack of leadership ability.

"Lieutenant . . ." Vik began.

Marti added ego to that assessment when the lieutenant said, "Jessenovik, I suggest you look to the Emmett Till case. This case is our equivalent."

"I also expect a daily online report by 10 A.M. on all activity completed the day before," the lieutenant continued, "a complete schedule of all pending court cases, and a log indicating the amount of time you spend on the cold cases and this new one."

"The task force case," Marti said.

As soon as Marti said "task force," Nicholson clenched her hand into a fist. Her mouth looked like she had just drank vinegar. "Let me put it this way, MacAlister, the time spent investigating the three cold cases will remain at its present level, but utilized to investigate the skeletal remains case. No overtime will be approved while you are working on anything else."

Vik was gnawing on his lower lip to keep from smiling.

Marti didn't say anything else. When Nicholson nodded toward the door, they left.

"Not bad," Vik whispered as soon as the door closed behind them. "That crack about ability and luck was blatant sarcasm. Sounds to me like you're really getting to her."

Technically, Marti and Vik did not have to take any orders from Nicholson until the task force case was resolved. Until now, there hadn't been any significant conflicts and those parameters remained untested.

"If she thinks I'm going to start working sixty-hour weeks because of *her* cold cases she can think again."

"And the skeletal remains?" Vik asked.

"Intriguing, aren't they?" she admitted.

They could smell the coffee brewing when they reached their office, but Slim and Cowboy, the vice cops who shared their space, weren't there. Desks had been squeezed into the room to accommodate Lupe Torres and Brian Holmberg, the two uniforms the lieutenant had assigned to Marti and Vik on a time-available basis for homicide investigation training. Marti and Vik still referred to Lupe and Brian as their replacements, but the annual homicide rate rarely exceeded twenty and they hadn't worked with either officer in almost a month.

Vik banged his empty mug on his desk. "She is a pain." As he stood up he gave his chair enough of a shove to bang against the wall. "Emmett Till." He stomped over to the coffeepot.

"Look at it this way, Vik. Sooner or later she is going to run up against Frank Winan. If she chooses to push it now, let her," Marti said.

"But Emmett Till? What's that case got to do with a

bunch of old bones?"

"Nothing. This case is all about where our bones were found. She's talking publicity."

"Downtown renovation," Vik scoffed. "If it's headlines she's after, the odds on getting any out of this are nonexistent. Unless one of us kills her."

"Maybe she's getting desperate," Marti suggested. "And even though we don't know how long the bones were there, Dr. Mehta did confirm that it was a male."

"Right." Vik threw up his hands. "We can't even find a forensic scientist willing to take the time to tell us anything else. Nobody thinks it has any priority except Lieutenant Lemon."

That was what everyone called Nicholson behind her back. The nickname had multiple connotations, everything from her facial expression to the size of her breasts to various sexual innuendoes.

Marti smiled. "She could be reaching the point where she can't handle our working a case that she can't control." Still smiling, she put in a call to Dr. Mehta. Marti had not been happy when Dr. Cyprian, the former coroner, retired. But Dr. Mehta was just as conscientious and professional, and even better, he seemed more relaxed and had a sense of humor. "Tomorrow morning at the earliest," he said when she asked about the autopsy on the victim retrieved from the river. "We still haven't positively I.D.'d three of the victims from last night's vehicular accident."

"Great," Vik said, when she told him. "Now we don't have any excuse for not getting Lieutenant

34

Lemon's reports to her on time today."

Marti felt a familiar lurch in her stomach, followed by the usual churning. "That does take care of today," she echoed. There was always tomorrow, and another complaint, another demand, more criticism. There always was with Nicholson. She began checking missing person's reports. They needed an I.D. on the dead woman ASAP. There was no way she wanted a task force case filed, but not closed.

Meanwhile, she needed to organize the little information that they did have on the three cold cases, and make copies of what they had on the skeletal remains so they could bring Lupe and Holmberg up to speed.

It was raining when Marti got home. Supper was ready, but she told everyone to eat without her while she took a shower and then filled the hot tub. Her stomach was alternately churning and taking acid baths since her encounter with Nicholson.

Ben came in while she was soaking.

"You okay?" he asked.

"Now that you're here."

"Nicholson?"

"Who else?" She opened her eyes, saw how tired he was, and said, "You look exhausted."

"Ummm." He undressed and sighed as the hot water covered his shoulders. "We need to talk later. Important," he said, then, "Later. It'll keep." He dozed for a while, then dried off, got into bed nude, and fell asleep while she was massaging his shoulders.

Marti wanted to wake him to find out what he wanted to talk to her about and ask if he had eaten, but did not.

C H A P T E R

5

BUCHAREST, ROMANIA

F ew people took notice as Vladimir, in the backseat of a small car, rode through the streets. Spring had come to Bucharest. Rain gave way to brilliant sunlight; thousands of flowers were blooming in the Cismigiu Garden. They made him think of the sunflowers his grandmother had loved and the roses his mother had planted around their cottage in such abundance.

Vladimir closed his eyes for a moment when the car turned onto Unirii Boulevard. He saw it not as it was now, with blocks of concrete apartment and office buildings, but as it had once been. He could still see the iconostasis in a small church, long desecrated, where fountains now spouted water. He could still recall the dozens of houses and monasteries, butcher shops, and bakeries bulldozed so that one man's obsession could become this monument to madness.

Today, as he often did, he remembered his dearest friend, Andrei, who had died this past winter. He closed his eyes, seeing not the Palace of Parliament just ahead, but Andrei's house. They were poor folk, and as a boy, Andrei's father had helped his father and his grandfather build it. It had been a small house with a beamed ceiling. Age and dampness warped the kitchen floor. The wood planks slanted toward the door that opened onto the vegetable garden.

There was always a pot of soup simmering on the cast-iron, coal-burning stove. Vladimir's favorite was mamaliguta, a thick corn porridge. Even now, with Andrei's mother dead more than thirty years, Vladimir could remember the aroma. Always, he compared the mamaliguta he was served now with that prepared by Andrei's mother. Always, he was disappointed.

Vladimir glanced at Josef who had squeezed in beside him. Nicolae sat up front beside the driver. None of them spoke, Josef no doubt intent upon his task for this trip, discussing the problem of pollution in the Danube River caused by the Iron Gates dam and its effect on the Black Sea. It was something the Americans were well familiar with.

Nicolae seemed equally preoccupied with the details involved in working out an agreement between American and Romanian scientists. Both countries wanted to work together and explore the Movile Cave in southeastern Romania. Now that the Americans were successfully exploring Mars, that part of their mission also seemed possible. The cave ecosystem, supported entirely by chemosynthesis, was considered the closest model on this planet to life as it could have been on Mars.

Vladimir considered his mission the most challenging—how to help the thousands of orphans whose fate depended as much on politics as generosity. Adoptions by Romanians living in Canada and the United States would depend on the Romanian government's cooperation. Meanwhile, back home, thousands of children languished in orphanages. Thousands of children lived in the streets. At the very least, they needed smaller group homes. Ideally, families in Romania who were able to love and care for them should adopt them. His mission was to solicit the financial resources necessary to support Romania's efforts to keep the children in their own country and provide for their needs.

He leaned forward, nudged the driver, and said, "Go to where the children are." He knew that the driver was always instructed by Josef to avoid the streets where the children were so that he would not see them. There was no Palace of Parliament for the children. The larger institutions where orphans were warehoused were slowly being closed. He was told that fewer of those who lived there were malnourished and neglected. He was frequently assured that they were receiving health care and a basic education.

But he did not have to look further than Bucharest to know that children slept in doorways and scavenged food from garbage cans. For two blocks, he saw them, some with bare feet, some with festering sores. One boy stopped digging through the garbage long enough to look at him. Vladimir could see that the boy's body

38

was too thin to ever have known a full belly. His clothes were ragged. His hair untrimmed, unwashed. His face dirty. Vladimir felt tears warm on his face.

"Stop," he said. "Give him money for food."

The driver complied. Usually, seeing this unexpected generosity from a stranger, more children would crowd around the car. Today they did not. It was the day the garbage trucks came. Vladimir had heard it called the day of treasures. People who lived on or near Unirii Boulevard and the palace threw away much of what they did not want or no longer needed. Not just food, but clothing and other necessities for survival might be found.

Vladimir wanted the children to have families. He and his two brothers and four sisters had shared a small house with their parents and grandparents. His father worked in the vineyards. His grandparents tended the vegetable garden. He and his brothers milked the goats while his sisters gathered eggs from the hens. His mother did the laundry and cooked their food.

They listened to stories of war and revolution, miracles, and answered prayers at his grandmother's knee. They prayed to the icon of the Theotokos—who his grandmother called Little Mother—every day. They went to the small church with the pictures painted on the outside. When they went inside for the liturgy, Vladimir wondered at the mysteries the priest performed behind the iconostatis as he peeked between the openings trying to see. This was what he wanted for Romania's orphans.

Romania was largely self-sufficient, but still a poor country, still more agricultural than industrial. He was most hopeful of persuading Canadian and American churches and families to ease the additional financial burden for those Romanian families who would willingly accept another child if they could afford to.

C H A P T E R

6

THURSDAY, MAY 6—LINCOLN PRAIRIE

The autopsy on the female found in the river didn't begin until 10 A.M. Two women were leaving the building as Marti and Vik arrived. One was a teenaged brunette with blond highlights; the other was older, a brunette with gray streaks in her hair. They were clinging to each other and sobbing.

Marti tried not to think about the collision scene, or the two cars all but welded together by the heat. She tried not to wonder which victim had just been identified. Three bodies had been badly burned and the other two, both thrown from the vehicles, were mangled with a few body parts no longer attached.

"All it takes is one driver over zero-point-zero-eight percent," Vik commented. "That, a couple of cars, a stop sign someone ignores. Damned shame."

There had been no witnesses, at least none that survived. Once the identities were confirmed, and the reports on the physical components of the accident completed, Marti and Vik would have to reconstruct as much of what preceded the accident as they could. Assessing responsibility would be the task of a coroner's jury.

The autopsy room still smelled like roasted meat. That combined with the usual odors of disinfectant and body fluids made Marti reach for the Vicks VapoRub. She shared it with Vik. Compared to the car crash victims, the woman found in the river looked almost like she was sleeping. Marti wanted to take off the hairnet, unclasp the barrette, and brush the tangles from her dark, wet hair.

Dr. Mehta, the new coroner, was from India, two inches shorter than Marti's five-ten, with curly black hair and dark eyes. Unlike Dr. Cyprian, the medical examiner they worked with before, who was always calm and inscrutable, Dr. Mehta telegraphed many emotions. Today he looked tired, and sad. Identifying the car crash victims and confirming their identities with the next of kin must have been difficult. Now he spent a long time examining the head wound and checking the X-rays that had already been taken. "Blunt trauma to the head," he said finally. "Three wounds."

"It looks like one big hit," Vik said.

Dr. Mehta disagreed. "No, cylindrical weapon; stick, pipe maybe. Two blows here." He pointed to the back of the head. "If you look at the outer right edge, and then the outer left edge, you can see the differences. The indentation on the right is deeper. The left side was not struck with as much force."

"Which do you think came first?" Marti asked.

"The left, especially if she knew it was coming, or even if she was conscious and able to run or move away from her attacker. It was sufficient to knock her unconscious. The blow to the right would have been easier to deliver with that amount of force if the body were inert."

"And the third blow?" Vik asked.

"It's not that close to these two," Dr. Mehta said. "There was bleeding, but the skull is intact."

"You think it happened while she was in the water?"

"It wasn't caused by the same thing as the other two."

"Were the two blows sufficient to kill her?" Marti asked.

"We'll see. They did cause major trauma." A few minutes later he said, "There's no premorbidity bruising except for this circular bruise on her upper right arm and the bruise and abrasion on her forehead."

"Someone grabbed her," Vik said.

"Perhaps. There are no other signs of a struggle."

Half an hour later, Dr. Mehta looked up from the autopsy table. "She was alive when she went into the water. Rigor was not advanced enough when we brought her in for her to have been conscious when she went in. There was no struggle to breathe or attempt to swim. The lack of significant abrasions on

42

the parts of the body that were exposed could indicate that she went in at or near the center of the river where the water was deep."

"But she did go into the water after she was hit," Marti said.

Dr. Mehta shrugged. "It seems unlikely that she was hit after she went into the water unless someone went in with her."

"And she was hit with something like a stick or a pipe."

"Something smooth."

"Not a tree branch."

"That's possible."

As they walked back to the office, Marti said, "They'll rule it a homicide. We can't call it premeditated, not yet anyway. It could have been the result of an argument."

"Maybe she broke up with her boyfriend."

"That doesn't explain anything. A lot of women manage to do that without ending up dead."

"This one could have had a bad temper, or panicked."

"Let's just stick with what we know," Marti said.

"Which is not a hell of a lot," Vik complained.

Lupe Torres and Brian Holmberg were waiting for them when they returned to their office.

"We thought you might like some hot pizza," Lupe said. "But since you took so long . . ." She shrugged.

"Cold is better than nothing," Vik said, helping himself.

Marti had forgotten all about lunch. She wasn't hungry.

Lupe and Holmberg were in uniform. Marti could remember Lupe as a young officer. Now, after almost seven years on the force, there were small changes. Lupe smiled as often, but the smile didn't always reach her eyes. The badge and the gun had become part of the job, not just symbols of authority. Most important, Lupe handled the job with the ease and confidence of someone with twice as much as experience working the streets.

"Time on your hands?" Marti asked.

"Try body found in river," Lupe suggested.

Holmberg added, "Need a couple of assistants, gofers, or research experts?"

"We could use all three," Marti told him, "but not for the drowning case, at least not yet."

Holmberg smiled. "But you do have something for us to do other than street patrol and being Officer Friendly."

"Weird case," Holmberg said after Marti and Vik brought them current on the case involving the skeletal remains. "I'd like to know who he is, what happened, why."

Holmberg had a degree in criminology, but had been on the force for less than a year. He was tall and lean with all of the charm that went with good looks, but he

wanted to be a good cop. He already had a solid reputation among the senior officers.

"Right now we're having a problem getting a
forensic anthropologist out here to look at him," Marti
explained. "We've gone through every missing
person's record in four counties—including Cook—
without coming up with anything."

"They didn't have the databases that we have now,"
Holmberg said.

"There might not be any data if our guy died in the
thirties or forties," Vik added. "Times were different
them."

"If anyone would know about that, it's you," Marti
agreed. Vik was approaching fifty, but he seemed
older. His craggy face, beak nose skewed by a high
school break, wiry salt-and-pepper eyebrows that
almost met across the bridge of his nose, and his
height all contributed to what Marti called his vulture
look.

"With the Depression and then the war," Vik went
on, "it wasn't that unusual for someone to just up and
leave. No job, no place to live, broke, alcoholic, whatever."

"Kind of like now," Marti reminded him.

"Kind of," Vik admitted. The sour expression on his
face was the only indication that he was disappointed
that after all these years, those things hadn't changed.

"Does this mean we get to see the place where the
skeleton was found?" Holmberg asked.

Lupe added, "There hasn't been anything about it in

the newspaper lately, and even when there was, they never included any pictures."

"Some guy named Wayne Munn is putting together a slide presentation on it," Holmberg said.

Marti looked down at the empty file folder on her desk. It was labeled "Drowning Victim." "I suppose we can take you on a private tour." Once they saw the place they would be hooked, just as she was. If it wasn't for that little meeting with the lieutenant, she would put in whatever overtime it took to get both cases solved. As things stood, not working this case was the only way, figuratively speaking, of giving Nicholson the finger.

The house where the skeleton had been found was two blocks from the precinct. It wasn't raining when they went outside, so they decided to walk.

"Town's changing," Vik said when they reached Geneva Street. He frowned as he looked at the new marquee on the Geneva Theater.

"It looks just like the old one," Marti said.

"Only if you see pictures taken in black and white," Vik disagreed. "I do not remember red, white, and blue lights."

"They are not red, white, and blue."

"Red, blue, orange, yellow, purple, what's the difference?"

"Vik, if you would just go inside . . ."

"Yeah, yeah, I know, better seating, portable bars, lots of bathrooms upstairs and down and . . ."

"Chandeliers," Marti said. "The most beautiful chandeliers I've ever seen."

"And not one bad seat," Holmberg added. "The perfect sound system; and so far, great programs. You should have seen *Riverdance*."

"Whoopie," Vik said, and dismissed it all with a wave of his arm. "It's not like the old days."

"No, it isn't," Marti agreed. "They don't sell popcorn anymore." She knew it was more than that for Vik. Although going inside the renovated theater could not erase his memories, the changes were irrevocable, and to Vik, any changes that involved his past siphoned off not who he was, but how he had become who he was.

The building was less than a block from the theater. The owner of the place had halted renovations when the skeleton was found. He was there to let them in. The place was for sale again, but so far there were no takers.

Marti stood outside looking up at the façade for a few minutes. Someone had bricked in all of the windows that had once been part of the second floor. Even close up, the work was seamless. She couldn't tell the original brick from that used to seal off the upstairs.

"Can you see any difference in the materials?" she asked.

"Uh-uh," Vik said.

"Does that mean the same person or company that changed the building also built it? Or that the same company made the brick maybe?"

47

"I have no idea. Stephen did construction work. I'll ask him about it."

Vik was not much of a handyman, but his son had worked for a contractor while he was in college.

"The same family owned the place for ninety-three years," Vik explained to Lupe and Holmberg.

"Did you know any of the original owners?" Marti asked, suppressing a grin.

"Best I can tell you is that sometime during the late nineteen-thirties or early nineteen-forties the house was inherited by two sisters, Rosie and Rachel. One of the girls got engaged during the war . . ."

"World War Two?" Marti asked.

"Right. The guy she was engaged to jilted her. The other girl married a Navy pilot, got pregnant before he got shot down. I think both sisters left before the baby was born. Moved someplace east, Massachusetts, Connecticut, maybe Maine. Rented out the building. I can't say why they didn't just sell the place. Rented it out. Damned shame about their great-grandson."

Lupe wanted to know what happened to him.

"He's the one who sold this place. Nobody would have found the bones if he kept it in the family."

They went inside. "We need a history on who rented this place," Marti told Holmberg. "The sisters changed real estate agents seven times."

The current owner had decided to renovate and discovered that what he thought was a one-story property with a high ceiling was not that at all. The renovations had stopped when the bones were discovered and nothing had been done since.

"There were two floors," Vik explained. Now that the walls were stripped they could see where the stairs had been. A gaping hole and a sturdy ladder provided access to the upper level. As they climbed up, Vik said, "Everything is just like it was when they sealed it off."

There was an apartment on the second floor with three rooms and a bath, as well as a dentist's office and a beauty shop.

Holmberg walked ahead of them. "You have got to see this," he said. "Old Sparky in triplicate." He pointed at three metal hoods topped with circular gas burners that provided the heat.

"Are they hair dryers?" Lupe asked.

They dangled from the ceiling like light fixtures, but were high enough for someone to sit beneath them without coming into contact with a metal hood or gas flame.

"I wonder if anyone ever got their hair singed," Marti wondered aloud. "It's a wonder the whole place didn't burn down."

"Females," Vik said. "The only damned fools stupid enough to sit under something like that just to look pretty."

Marti thought of her father getting a shave at the barbershop years ago. The barber did sharpen the razor on a leather strop, but for once Vik was right, there was nothing comparable to these dryers.

Vik hesitated for a moment, waiting for a comeback;

49

when there was none, he pointed to the woodwork. "Nice moldings. The owner says he's going to make a table out of one of the doors."

Inside the apartment, Marti felt as if she was standing on the stage of a turn-of-the-century play. All of the wood was hand-carved. All of the light fixtures on the ceilings and walls were surrounded by plaster with elaborate curlicue designs. "Too bad the wallpaper can't be salvaged." It was water-stained and brown with age, but there was nothing she could buy today that would equal the delicate floral designs. She could visualize this living room wallpaper—a pale green with wildflower bouquets—in her dining room.

Vik opened a closet door. "This is where the skeleton was found."

Holmberg squatted and touched a dark stain. "And they found a bullet. Just one?"

"Umm humm," Vik said. "And a complete skeleton. Some of the bones had separated, and mice gnawed at some of them, but they were all there."

"All this time and an anthropologist hasn't looked at it yet?" Lupe asked.

"Dr. Mehta confirmed that it was an adult male," Marti told her. A preliminary exam by Dr. Mehta indicated that the victim was male, based on the suborbital crest—the ridge of bone above the eye sockets—and the size of the nuchal crest at the back of the skull. Dr. Mehta also concluded that the victim was an adult, because of the development of the rib ends, but was unable to give an approximate age. Other than that, the bones had not yielded any of their secrets. "A forensic pathologist at Northwestern, Meline Pickus, worked with us on a few cases, but she's retired now and lives in California. I've talked with the doctor who replaced her, Nina Rose Peterson, several times, but she's working two hot cases in Chicago that involve children and can't give this any priority."

"Last time we talked with her," Vik added, "she thought she might be able to come up the end of this week, but we haven't heard anything since."

"Is that all we've got?" Holmberg asked. "One bullet and damaged bones?"

"Bug residue," Vik told him.

"And very little dust," Marti added. She found that interesting, but had no clue as to what could be inferred from it. "No clothing fibers. No buttons, no belt buckle."

"He could have been one of the dentist's patients," Vik suggested. "Do you suppose that, say, by nine-teen-thirty or nineteen-forty dentists had progressed beyond 'give 'em a shot of whiskey and pull the tooth with pliers'?"

"We don't know when he died," Marti reminded him.

Ignoring that, Vik went on. "Could be that our guy went to the dentist—who maybe was experimenting with something like . . . I don't know . . . laudanum . . . and whatever it was, gave our victim an overdose, and got rid of the body."

"That doesn't explain the bullet, Jessenovik."

"Maybe that was how the dentist tried to cover up the crime."

Holmberg winked at Marti. "That is one hell of a hypothesis."

Vik didn't notice the wink. He shook his head. "Hypothetical is about as close as we're likely to come to solving this one."

When they went outside it was raining. None of them had brought an umbrella, but Marti didn't mind getting wet. After being in that building, rain seemed like the next best thing to a quick shower.

"Check out all the traffic," Vik said.

Marti looked both ways. "There isn't any."

"Right. And that's with the Anstandt Expressway shut down because they're shooting car chases again for another movie."

Vik was always complaining about how unnecessary the four-lane, two-mile expressway was.

"Tells you something about how much we need the Anstandt, doesn't it?" he went on. "And now this." He waved toward the Geneva Theater. "Downtown revitalization. Hah! Political jargon for another Anstandt. One theater gussied up and another one burned down. . . . And crowd control once or twice a month—two uniforms on horses. Politicians. You've got to watch them all the time. They took care of this part of town a hundred years ago when they industrialized the lakefront. Even the idiots in Chicago and Milwaukee were smart enough to leave the land by the lake alone."

7

They were getting ready to call it a day when the desk sergeant called. "I might have something for you. Someone called in from the company that's filming on the Anstandt. Wanted us to run a check on a missing cast member. Woman thought we should check all the area hospitals for her since she wasn't familiar with the area."

"You've got to be kidding."

"The missing person is female, an actress, and working in those chase scenes they're filming on the Anstandt."

"What's the caller's name?"

"Tansy Lark."

Marti had mixed feelings as she hung up. She wanted to I.D. the drowning victim, but she liked the feeling of knowing she and Vik were in charge of that case, that there would be no interference or directives from Lieutenant Nicholson. She had to keep reminding herself of that when she was conducting an investigation under the lieutenant's command. She relayed the sergeant's information to Vik.

"Tansy Lark," he said. "Sounds like a nutcase who's already flown over the cuckoo's nest."

"Have you ever been on a movie set?"

"I don't consider the Anstandt a movie set."

"Just get a couple of the victim's morgue shots out of the coroner's folder, Jessenovik."

"Right. It'll be just our luck that this case will be closed by tomorrow and Lieutenant Nicholson will be asking for hourly updates on the old bones case."

The weather had turned mean again. The rain was steady, the wind off the lake cold. Thunder rumbled. Marti counted to ten-Mississippi twice, then watched lightning do a jagged dance several miles away. The Anstandt ran along the base of a long bluff that had once extended to the lake. Onlookers, behind barriers at street level, huddled under umbrellas and looked down at the action. Or the lack of it. Nothing was happening that Marti could see.

"Looks exciting as hell," Vik said.

"Literally," Marti added.

An off-duty officer manning one of the barriers recognized her and Vik. He pointed south, away from the large boards with floodlights that were staggered along both sides of the Anstandt, and let them pass.

Walking south, they reached a curve in the road and saw a bus, a trailer, eight Porta Pottis, and half a dozen vintage cars all well out of camera range. One of the cars had been reduced to salvage. Two men were standing in the rain, smoking.

"Can either of you tell me where I can find Tansy Lark?" Marti asked.

"Trailer," one of the men said. "Over there." A cigarette dangled from his mouth and he sounded like he was trying to do an imitation of Edward G. Robinson.

As they walked toward the trailer, Vik said, "Must be a method actor." He spoke loud enough for the man to hear him.

The wind shifted, blowing rain in their faces. The trailer door was ajar. Marti knocked and entered without waiting to be invited. The interior looked like it was a combination coffee bar and office. The odor of cigarette smoke was so strong Marti felt her sinuses getting clogged. A woman sat at large wooden desk. She looked like an aging Barbie after her breakup with Ken. Expertly applied makeup and fine lines that the foundation didn't disguise: long blond ponytail secured with a rubber band with dark roots just beginning to grow out; eyes such a startling blue that she had to be wearing contacts. She was red-faced with anger as she screamed into a cell phone.

"Now, Devorah! Now! If you can't get your ass up here in two hours I swear you'll never work again!" She reached for a silver cigarette case as she listened, then said, "Savannah isn't here! I need someone now! Do you want the job or not?" She picked up a cigarette lighter and flicked it as she listened again. "Good. Take a cab to the Metro station right away. There's a train leaving for Lincoln Prairie in seventeen minutes. It'll get you here in an hour and twenty minutes . . . What? A cab to Lincoln Prairie? Look, honey, I'll be sure to let you know when you become a star. This is a two-to-three day job at scale with a free trip to Las Vegas and L.A. for more location shots thrown in.

Now move your ass. I'll send someone to meet the train."

Smoke wafted in Marti's direction as she took two deep drags on the cigarette. "So, what can I do for you two?"

"We're police officers, ma'am," Vik said. They showed the woman their I.D.s. "Are you Tansy Lark?"

"Yeah, look, hold on for a minute will you. I've got a crisis here." She made another call. "Look, we've got a replacement for Savannah." She spoke in a calmer voice but still sounded angry. "There shouldn't be a problem with the wardrobe; just pull whatever you've got." She paused, listened, then said, "I don't give a damn how reliable Savannah is. She isn't here now. I don't go into production overruns for has-been actresses in bit-part, nonspeaking roles."

"Now," she said, looking at Marti, "I called you people so you could check out the hospitals . . ."

"That's not our job, ma'am."

"Then what the hell is your job and why are you here?"

Before they could answer her, the cell phone trilled the theme song from *The Sound of Music*. Miss Lark picked up, listened for a minute, then said, "Look, just make sure that the reporter who came out here yesterday doesn't have any stills of Savannah and if he does, make sure he doesn't use them."

The chair squeaked as the woman leaned back and let out a deep breath. When Marti started to speak, she held up her hand, and closed her eyes. "Devorah, wardrobe, PR," she said, then, "Hotel room." She consulted a sheet of paper, punched in a phone number, and said, "Midway Productions. Room 206 is assigned to a Savannah Payne-Jones. Change that to Devorah Vaughn."

Eyes closed, she repeated the "Devorah, wardrobe, PR" mantra, added, "Hotel room," then, "plane reservations," then "tomorrow." She thought for a moment, then looked up at Marti and Vik.

"Look, I've got a production schedule to stick to. Is there some law against you making those phone calls?"

"We're cops, not private investigators," Marti told her.

"Private . . . no, they cost money. I just need to know if she's been in an accident or something in case there's an insurance liability. Just what . . ."

"Look, miss," Vik interrupted. "We'd like you to look at a photograph, tell us if it's the woman you're looking for."

"A photograph? A mug shot? Of Savannah?"

Vik handed her the photographs.

Lark's eyes widened, as she looked at one, then the other, then looked at them again. "It is Savannah. But, what's wrong with her? She doesn't look like herself at all."

"That's because she's dead, ma'am," Vik explained.

Tansy Lark's eyes got very wide. She began gasping for breath. Before Marti could ask what was wrong, Lark reached into a drawer, pulled out a paper bag, and began breathing into it. In a minute or two she seemed all right.

"Savannah Payne-Jones. Dead. I've used her in bit parts for years. Never anything big; she didn't have the voice for it, but she could say more with gestures and facial expressions than a lot of people could say with words." She looked down at the pictures, pushed them away. "Don't tell me what happened. Don't tell me anything. I do not want to know."

"We'll need you to identify the body," Vik explained.

"Look at her? Like that? Dead?"

"Yes, ma'am."

Tansy Lark's ponytail whipped from one side of her face to the other as she shook her head. "No. Sorry. I don't identify dead people." She reached for the phone and made two calls in quick succession. Nobody she spoke with wanted to identify Savannah either.

Miss Lark checked her watch, tapped long nails painted orange and yellow on the desktop, thought for close to a minute, then dialed, waited, and identified herself. "I'm sorry to bother you, sir, but we could have a major PR crisis here. Savannah Payne-Jones is dead, sir. How do you want to handle the press release?" She listened, then turned to Marti. "How did she die? Was it an accident? An overdose?"

"We can't say at this time."

Tansy relayed that to the "sir" on the other end of the line, then handed the phone to Marti.

"Sir" identified himself as a well-known movie pro-

58

ducer. Even Marti had heard of him. He said, "The film crew can finish up there tomorrow night. Can you hold this until then?"

"I'm sorry, sir, but . . ." Marti began.

"Sure, sure, I didn't expect the police to cooperate. Put Tansy on the line again."

Tansy lit another cigarette as she listened, then said, "Yes sir, we do have film of her from last night."

When she hung up, she said, "I can't believe this! Looks like Miss Savannah might get what she's always wanted. Star status. For a day or two anyway. Great PR for the film." Tansy Lark had gone from anger and hyperventilation to near euphoria. She did a tap dance, flipped through some papers, found what she was looking for, and made another call. "Yes, sweetie, Savannah Payne hyphen Jones. I know you've never heard of her. Nobody else has either, but you will see to it that they do in tomorrow's early edition. She's dead. Suspicious circumstances. The film we shot of her yesterday will be included in the movie."

She looked at Marti. "Where did you find her?"

"In the Des Plaines River."

"The one that's flooding. Yes!" Her smile was huge as she spoke into the phone. "They found her in the river, sweetie, the one that is flooding this part of the state. The governor is coming tomorrow. Play it up. It'll be great for the locals. I can be at the morgue in about ten minutes to identify the body. Make sure someone is there to take pictures." When she hung up,

59

she said, "The identification will have to wait a while. It'll be thirty minutes before the photographer can get there."

"Ma'am, the sooner we can identify her . . ." Vik began.

"I know, I know, but she is dead. It isn't like timing will make a difference to her anymore. Who knows, this might even put this town on the map."

"Where was she staying?" Vik asked.

"That motel not far from the Navy base, right off of that highway that comes in from the city. The . . . ummm . . ."

"Shady Lane Motel," Vik ventured.

"That's it."

He called in and had two uniforms dispatched to prevent entry into the room and requested evidence techs.

"Oh, what luck!" Lark exclaimed. "I can't believe this."

"Did she rent a car?" Marti asked.

"Who? Savannah? Maybe."

"Was she local?"

"Oh no. She lives in L.A."

"Did she have any friends here? Was she meeting anyone after work?"

Tansy Lark sighed and shook her head. "You two don't know anything about this business, do you? It's nothing like what you see on TV. We were just doing some location shots here. No happy hours, no cast parties. Just rain, bright lights, and the same boring ride down that road until they got it just right. The guy directing this shoot doesn't even yell 'Action.' " She pulled a manila envelope out of a drawer, checked the contents, then said, "Well, I can give you next of kin."

"That's great, but we can't notify anyone until we have a positive I.D."

"And we need that ASAP," Vik added.

Miss Lark reached for the photographs. She closed her eyes, took a deep breath, then looked at them. "Okay. Okay." She checked her watch. "How long will this take? Oh, damn . . . What was Savannah wearing when you . . . found her?"

"A lavender trench coat," Marti said. "A pink angora sweater, and a black skirt."

"Damn. The coat would have been hers, but the clothes . . . I don't suppose we could pick up the skirt and sweater when I go to . . . identify her."

"Sorry, no."

"It was such a small part. Oh, well, that's wardrobe's problem."

She reached for the cell phone again. "Check yesterday's takes on Savannah and last night's shoot. See what she was wearing. A Devorah Vaughn is on her way here to replace her, so wardrobe will have to match it. Makeup will have to check it out, too. Don't shoot any more with Devorah than you have to. And under no circumstances do we want to see Devorah's face." She frowned, then snapped, "That's your job. Just do it."

It took Tansy Lark less than ten seconds to identify

Savannah Payne-Jones. She didn't hyperventilate. She did manage to look grief-stricken when the photographer snapped her photo as she left the viewing room. As Marti and Vik were escorting her from the morgue, Miss Lark stopped, turned to them, swallowed hard, and said. "Her voice just wasn't right. But she could act. She really was a damned good actress. And just kept at it, just wouldn't give up. This could be the most press she's ever received and she won't even be here to enjoy it." She dabbed at her eyes and turned away.

When Marti and Vik arrived at the Shady Lane Motel, an ambulance was just pulling away. Uniformed officers escorted two sailors and a civilian to waiting black-and-whites. Inside, an Elvis impersonator swiveled his hips on a stage not much bigger than two pallets pushed together. He was singing "Don't Be Cruel" with more enthusiasm than talent. From the looks of it, the audience was almost evenly divided, hookers and servicemen.

The evidence techs were finished with room 206. Except for the residue from taking fingerprints, there was no indication they had been there. The room was small with a single bed. The curtains matched the faded geometric-patterned bedspread. An orange-and-yellow shag carpet was stained and matted in places.

Savannah Payne-Jones hadn't bothered to unpack. Enough jeans, T-shirts, sweaters, and underwear for three days were in one small suitcase along with a pair of athletic shoes. Makeup and other personal items were in a carry-on. A Gideon Bible was in the drawer of a nightstand decorated with cigarette burns. A telephone with a local directory was on a desk. The desk wobbled when Marti touched it.

"No purse," Marti said. "She must have had it with her. And she was wearing the clothes she was working in."

"That tells us a whole lot, MacAlister."

"Maybe they'll be able to figure out where she was when she went in."

"'They' meaning your fairy godmother on drugs?" Vik asked.

The kids were in bed when Marti got home. She brought Trouble, their guard dog, in for the night and set the alarm system. Then she thought about Ben. He had something important to tell her. She had forgotten all about that until now. He was up for a promotion. It had probably gone through. She wouldn't wake him if he was asleep. He could tell her about it in the morning.

They lived in a quad-level house. Marti paused at what her two boys called "the middle place" and looked in on them. Bigfoot, their beta dog and house pet, slept at the foot of Theo's bed. Theo was her son by her first marriage. He had kicked off his blanket and was sleeping in an oversized T-shirt. He still looked so much like his father that she almost caught her breath. The model plane they were working on when Johnny died now hung from the ceiling over Theo's bed.

Like his father, Theo could be silent when there was something he needed to say, but at twelve, with Ben's encouragement, he was talking more. Sometimes he even let her in on how he felt or what he was thinking. He mumbled something now as she covered him with the blanket, then with both hands under his cheek, was still.

Mike, Ben's son by his first marriage, had his blanket pulled up to his chin. He looked as much like Ben as Theo looked like Johnny. Fair skin, round face, soft features. Mike used to be a short, chubby bully. Now, seeing him stretched out, Marti realized how tall he was getting. He was slimming down and instead of wearing an angry scowl or pout, he laughed a lot and told silly jokes.

She looked from Mike's face, relaxed with just a hint of a smile, to Theo's, somber brown planes and angles, widow's peak, narrow chin. She thought of all the wounded, neglected, betrayed children she had seen over the years. Children she could neither shelter, nor love, nor protect. How lucky she was.

Upstairs, she looked in on Joanna. She wouldn't have the boys with her forever, but with Joanna, she was really running out of time. Joanna would be a senior in high school come fall. Practical Joanna, sensible, calm . . . secure here at home with Momma's guidance and Ben's protectiveness. She was so confident, so self-assured. How would she fare in the much larger world of college, then work?

Joanna was also a slob. Marti resisted the urge to pick up her sweats and jeans and create order out of the chaos of textbooks and notebooks and papers on her desk; the jumble of lotion, makeup, and cologne on her bureau. What would she do when she could clean this room and stand within its empty order and wait for Joanna to come home from college, and make a mess of it again?

She could hear Momma's light snore as she passed the closed door to her room. The hallway light was still on, as was the lamp by the bed in the room at the end of the hall. Ben was wide-awake.

"I was waiting for you," he said. He had something to tell her. He didn't look pleased. He must not have gotten the promotion.

"It's late," she said, glad that he wasn't sleeping.

He moved over as she sat on his side of the bed.

"Remember that test they did at the health fair at church?"

"Mine or yours?" She had let them take her blood pressure, just a little above normal, test her for diabetes, negative. Ben had a PSA, and a . . . a PSA.

"The PSA?"

The prostate test, or as Ben called it, "the Past Sixty Angst test." He laughed when he said it. He was only forty-five.

"I got the results the day before yesterday. It's fourteen."

A hot acid bath began in the pit of her stomach.

"What does that mean? What should it be?"

"Three, maybe four."

The acid rushed up her esophagus. She swallowed, tasted bile. "Then it's . . . you've got . . ."

"Antibiotics. I'll take them for another eleven days and get tested again."

She put her head on his chest and he patted her back. The acid bath inside did not abate.

"And?"

"And we handle that if and when it comes."

"What do we tell the children?"

"Nothing right now."

"Ben, they've already lost one parent."

His hand moved up and down her back in a slow, even rhythm.

"Right now it's just an abnormal test that could be caused by a minor infection."

She tried to focus on that. The acid felt like it was burning holes in her stomach.

"I can't lose you," she said. "I can't lose you, too."

"I didn't want to tell you yet," he admitted. "But I didn't want to keep it to myself for two weeks either."

She felt the weight of his hand. He was comforting her. He needed her to comfort him.

"I will always be here," she said.

She slipped her feet out of her shoes and got into bed beside him without undressing. They held each other without speaking. Neither of them slept until daybreak.

C H A P T E R 8

FRIDAY, MAY 7—LINCOLN PRAIRIE

As soon as roll call was over Friday morning, Lieutenant Nicholson walked over to Marti and Vik. "My office," she snapped. "Now!"

As she turned and walked away Marti said, "Coffee. Now." Instead of going to the lieutenant's office, she went to traffic division, got a Styrofoam cup, and filled it with what was in the coffeepot. "Yesterday's," she said after she tasted it. She gulped it down even though it was cold.

"An early morning session with Nicholson is just what I need," she said as they walked down the hall. "Any idea of what her problem is this time?"

"No, but if looks could kill, you wouldn't be here right now. Everything okay? You look like you need a day's sleep."

"I'll tell you about it later."

Vik knocked on the lieutenant's door. Nicholson's usual three-minute response time went on for five minutes.

"Do you think this means she's really, really, really mad?" Marti asked.

"It could mean that she's changed her mind," Vik said. "Maybe we should just go to our office and get some work done," he suggested.

67

"Come in," Nicholson called.

"Too late," Vik grumbled.

"MacAlister," Nicholson said before the door closed behind them. "What is the meaning of this?"

"The meaning of what?"

The lieutenant glared at her. "I ask the questions around here."

"Then perhaps you could explain further," Marti suggested trying to keep the sarcasm out of her voice.

Vik, aware that she was about to lose her temper, took a step closer and nudged her. "Ma'am," he said.

The lieutenant refused to be distracted. "I received a call from the *News-Times* yesterday confirming an interview you are going to give them."

Marti didn't know what she was talking about.

"Why wasn't this cleared with me? MacAlister?"

"What interview?" Marti asked. "When?"

"When . . . when . . ." the lieutenant sputtered. "What do you mean when? This isn't even a question of *if.* I give all interviews. You're subordinates. How dare you agree to talk to anyone about anything without clearing it with me first."

Marti decided that since she was just a subordinate she wasn't required to respond, and said nothing.

"Do not ever, under any circumstances, ever agree to an interview, a press conference, or any other communication with any news agency. Ever. As for that picture of you in yesterday's *News-Times*, I called the editor and told them never, under any circumstances, were they to do that again."

68

When neither Marti nor Vik said anything, Nicholson waved toward the door. "Get out."

Marti slammed the door as she left. "What is she talking about?"

"Hell if I know, MacAlister. Maybe she's losing it."

"I'd like to lose her."

"For a minute there I thought you were going to slug her."

"If they ever drum her out of the department, which I seriously doubt, I will." She didn't say anything else until they reached their office. The aroma of coffee—real, fresh, special blend—wafted out to greet them.

Slim, one of the two vice cops they shared space with, held a cup out to her as she walked in. "I heard old Lemon Puss was riding your butt after role call."

"You have redeemed yourself for every rotten thing I ever said about you," Marti told him, as she accepted the coffee.

Tall, lean, with a smooth caramel complexion, he gave her a lazy Cupid's-bow smile.

"If you could just do something about that Obsession for Men you have to shower in every morning."

"Man, Big Mac, just when I think I've got you in the palm of my hand you go and say something like that. So, what's up with Lemon Puss now?"

"I haven't a clue."

Cowboy, Slim's partner in vice, leaned back and put his booted feet on his desk. "That time of the month."

Marti believed him. She was certain everyone in the precinct knew exactly when that was for all female cops.

69

Cowboy took off his five-gallon hat, revealing hair so blond it was almost white. "She is one mean mama when PMS hits."

"If that's the case, she's on the rag all the time," Slim said. "Almost makes you glad that Marti's her prime target."

"Watch your mouth," Marti told him. "You have to live with me."

Slim favored her with another slow smile.

"And you know how far that will get you, big boy."

"By the way, nice picture of you and your old man in the newspaper yesterday, Big Mac. Not bad knowing a celebrity. How about mentioning me and Cowboy to your connection, whoever it is."

"What picture?"

"You didn't see it?"

"No." She hadn't had time to read a newspaper since the Sunday edition of the *Chicago Tribune*.

"And I thought you were being modest. I just happen to have six copies. I was thinking of asking for your autograph."

When Marti looked at the front-page photograph taken while she and Ben were walking toward the ambulance, she knew why the lieutenant was angry. The caption read:

HUSBAND AND WIFE TEAM WORK
TOGETHER TO SOLVE CRIME

Homicide Detective Marti MacAlister and her

husband, Fireman Paramedic Ben Walker, consult on the drowning victim Walker pulled from the Des Plaines River. MacAlister, a well-known Lincoln Prairie police officer, also heads up the Regional Task Force's Homicide Division. Walker recently received recognition from the city for rescuing two children and their dog from a fire that gutted their home.

"I *have* got something *important* for you, MacAlister," Cowboy interrupted. "A little lady by the name of Sara Jones has called from California at least five times asking about her mother."

Marti checked her voice mail. There were three additional calls from the same person. Jones lived somewhere in L.A. County. The sheriff's department there must have notified her daughter last night.

"Anyway, last time she called, she said she was on her way to the airport, so I guess you'll be meeting her before the day is out."

Marti tasted the coffee, resisting the impulse to say "umm." It was cool enough to sip. When the cup was empty, she refilled it. Then she looked at her in-basket. It was overflowing. When she sorted through everything she had three typed memos from Lieutenant Nicholson, complaining because Marti wasn't responding to her e-mails. Marti didn't think the lieutenant was "losing it," but there was the possibility that her apparent indifference to Nicholson's deliberate baiting and negative attitude was beginning to

71

get to her. That and the newspaper article must be what had her so close to the edge this morning.

"So. How's Geronimo?" Marti asked, changing the subject.

Cowboy had all but adopted the pit bull for a few weeks last fall and now the dog's owner, a Desert Storm vet, took care of the rental properties Cowboy owned in exchange for free rent in one of Cowboy's apartments.

"Dog's doing fine. And Fred's got himself a girl-friend."

"That's good to hear." She listened to Sara Jones's messages again.

"Are you sure this is my mother?" Then, "Nobody will tell me what happened to her." Then, "The coroner's office says it is her. I'm taking the next flight out of here."

All of her cases ended like this: dead victim, bewildered, heartbroken relatives, and friends. Maybe she should have been a vice cop. They got to have a few happy endings. She thought of Ben for a moment, and the results of the PSA, and called to tell him about their picture in the newspaper. The guys at the fire station were already teasing him about it. She looked at the photo again, then tried to put the possible implications of the PSA test out of her mind as she read through her incoming reports.

Slim and Cowboy were heading out the door as she began checking out car rental dealerships.

"You know, Jessenovik, maybe that Tansy Lark wasn't so far off. We are getting ready to waste the rest of the morning on the phone trying to find out how Miss Savannah Payne-Jones got around town, and maybe even where she went."

By eleven o'clock Marti knew that Jones had not rented a car. Jones took a taxi to and from the motel and the Anstandt. The last cab she had called from the shoot site had dropped her off in the parking lot of a restaurant just east of Route 41. That would explain the clothing Jones was wearing when they found her. The eatery was about three blocks from the Des Plaines River and six miles from where she was found.

"Be good to get out of here for a while," Vik said, a comment that was unlike him. "Don't check your e-mail before we leave."

"Nicholson?"

"Three e-mails demanding yesterday's time logs and reports. She's threatening suspension. Yours, not mine."

"Let's get the hell out of here."

The phone rang just as Marti was reaching for her jacket.

"Marti! Ed Gilbreth here." He was a staff writer at the *News-Times*. "I called your boss and your husband's boss, thought I might do an article on the two of you."

So that was what the interview was all about.

"Is there anyone else I can discuss it with, Frank Winan maybe?"

"That's a great idea," Marti told him. She knew

Frank would say yes and having the head of the task force okay it would really tick Nicholson off. Then she thought of Ben. If nothing else the attention, or notoriety, according to how the guys at the fire station might see it, might take his mind off of the PSA results and pending retest.

The restaurant where the taxi had dropped off Savannah Jones was constructed with real logs. It was a low-slung rambling building that sat back from the highway and was partially obscured by tall pine trees. A chalkboard menu advertised the soup of the day, vegetable beef, and three entrees. There wasn't much of a lunch crowd. Several elderly couples sat in the booths that lined the walls. Half a dozen old men sat at one of the round tables, and further away, four woman chatted over tea and fruit plates. Their thin white hair was tinted blue, teased and stiff with hair spray.

The owner, Frank Phillips, was also the chef and on the premises every day from opening until close. They struck out when Vik showed him Savannah Jones's morgue shots.

"No," Phillips said, shaking his head. "We don't get many black customers here. Just locals mostly. This is a family place. A few customers wander in off the highway every now and then, but we sit far enough back off the road so as not to attract much attention."

Phillips looked at the photographs again. "Dead, isn't she? Too bad. Nice-looking woman. You didn't find her near here, did you?"

"No, but a cab dropped her off in your parking lot Tuesday night."

"Like she was meeting someone, maybe," Phillips said. "Hmmm. Spaghetti and lasagna are the specials on Tuesday. Big hit with the kids. I can't remember anyone coming in alone or acting like they were waiting to meet someone. Of course it was busy, and noisy. I'll ask around, check with the wait staff when they come in. Most folks who come here are regulars. They'd remember if they saw any strangers."

Outside, last night's storms had shifted to persistent drizzle. The Des Plaines River was expected to crest within the next twenty-four hours and at levels that were lower than expected. Even better, the weather channel was predicting sunshine in the three-day forecast. Gravel crunched as they headed back to their car.

"Well," Marti said, "according to the cab driver, Jones got out at the far end of this parking lot and she was still standing where he left her when he got back on the highway."

There was a forest preserve about a mile and half away, but they drove to the nearest bridge first. The road was closed and water covered the pavement. It wasn't deep so they drove around the barrier.

"No boots," Marti muttered as she stopped at the bridge and got out of the car. The water didn't quite reach the top of her service shoes. The railing gave a little when she leaned against it. She took a step back and looked down at the swirls and eddies as the usually languid river rushed southward.

"They're going to hate us for asking," Vik said. "But we need a couple divers to go in here. I can't see her walking to the forest preserve and the next bridge is too far away."

"Assuming she came here at all."

"I know, but it's that or somebody hit her someplace else and dumped her."

"Or . . ." Marti began.

"Or any of a dozen other things could have happened."

"Might as well go with what we've got," Marti agreed.

To their surprise, one of the divers did come up with a piece of the hairnet that had been caught on a beam supporting the bridge.

"That doesn't mean she went in here," Vik cautioned.

"Of course not. She could have been just passing through."

They sent the divers to the forest preserve the river flowed through and ordered a search along the floodplain between the preserve and the bridge.

"Places along the edge where the water is stagnant or moving slow," Marti clarified. Anything that went into the swift-moving water would be miles from here by now. She felt an unfamiliar reluctance to return to the precinct. It had to be those damned reports. Or it was the lieutenant.

D elilah Greathouse pushed the curtains back so that she and Cornelius Jefferson could look out the kitchen window. Not that there was much to see, just a few patches of grass, a picket fence with half the pickets missing, and two muddy plots that got the sun all day, where Cornelius put in her vegetable garden.

"Seems like it's been rainin' for at least forty days," she said. "Must be about time for old Noah to show up on the ark."

Cornelius was looking out the window, too. He didn't answer.

The Eldercare lady from Meals on Wheels had just delivered their midday meals. Delilah pulled back the foil that covered hers. "Umm. Got us some meat loaf and mashed potatoes today." It was one of her favorites. "Gravy, too."

Cornelius bowed his head. "Gracious Lord, we give you thanks for the food we are about to receive for the nourishment of our bodies. Amen."

"Got some applesauce and canned pears. You want my green peas?"

When Cornelius didn't answer this time she reached across the table and rapped his knuckles with a spoon. "Turn your hearing aid up!"

"You been runnin' off at the mouth again, old woman?" he teased.

"You want these green peas or not?" She pushed the foil container toward him. While he scooped them out, she added, "Garden's got to get planted soon as the rain clears up. And we got to talk about what you're gonna plant. Them Santa tomatoes we put in last year wasn't what I expected."

"Sure wasn't," Cornelius agreed. "I thought they'd be big, fat, and got them bunches of little grape-looking things instead."

Delilah stood up and reached for her cane. "With them and the cherry tomatoes you put in I didn't hardly have enough good-sized tomatoes for canning," she added as she reached the stove. "Water's hot." She poured some from the pan into two cups. "Got your choice today, coffee or tea."

"Tea," he said. She took a tea bag, too. This was a five-week month. No reason to run out of coffee before they got their Social Security checks again. She put a spoonful of sugar in each cup.

She and Cornelius were neighbors better than sixty years. He lived right next door. Now his wife and her husband were both dead. All they had was each other. "I though maybe I'd make some corn bread and some pinto beans with a little smoked meat for supper."

"Be nice to have some greens with it," Cornelius suggested.

"Maybe." That sounded good to her, too. She tended to hoard what she canned so it would last from one summer to the next. Greens always tasted so good though when you sopped up the pot liquor with corn bread. "Maybe," she said again.

Cornelius smiled, knowing that meant yes.

"Garden's going in late this year, what with all this rain," she reminded him.

"Remember when we'd have weather like this and there'd be ponds in the fields, Lila?"

"Ain't no more fields, at least none that you can see from this window. All the land what's left is over by the school."

Cornelius chuckled. "Them bullfrogs would go to croakin' and the kids would be catchin' them pollywogs. Mothers be hollerin' when they tried to bring 'em home."

"And everyone on the face of the earth was trackin' in mud."

"Shame about that woman what drowned in the river," Cornelius said.

Delilah knew he was talking about something else because she was getting cranky. Wasn't no good, old days, no matter how hard he tried to get her to think so. In spite of herself, she asked, "What woman?"

"If you came over and watched the evenin' news with me, Lila, you'd know."

"Ain't nothin' on that television worth watchin' no more. Them talkin' books they bring me from the library and my radio suit me just fine."

"Interestin' though," Cornelius went on, "her being an actress and all, and a colored one at that."

"Not that pretty one what used to be on the show about them folks what lived in the projects in Chicago?"

"No, wasn't her."

When he didn't add anything else, Delilah said, "Well, who was it then? What they bringin' a colored actress here for anyway?"

"Can't say why. Her name was Savannah Payne-Jones. Pretty name. Can't say I ever heard of her though. They didn't show no picture."

"How old?" Delilah asked.

"Newswoman said forty-three."

"Oh." That was way too young to be her daughter, Tamar. "Might of been a picture in the *News-Times*." Not that he could see good enough to read the paper, or she could see any better. Needed eyeglasses, both of them. "Old Helen still gettin' the newspaper?"

"Now, Lila, Tamar left home the summer of forty-four. We both know you ain't gonna be reading nothin' about her in the newspaper or hearin' nothin' about her on the news, not after all these years. Wartimes them was when she left, Lila. Schools here was still separate for coloreds. Besides, wasn't nothin' here for her to do even if she did get a high school diploma. She didn't want to do hair and there wasn't much else for her back then, lessin' she was somebody's cook or maid."

Delilah stared out the window, blinking fast so she wouldn't cry.

"Now you listen here, Lila Greathouse. You didn't try to do nothin' more for your daughter than your mama did for you. You wasn't but fifteen when you married a man twice your age. You and your mama both wanted the same thing, woman. For your only child to be safe, to be taken care of. Only difference was that your mama knew she was dying."

"Asher was something, wasn't he, Cornelius." Asher had been Cornelius's boarder, not his son. "Handsome man, that Asher." And not but two years younger than she was. Someone she might have married if Mama hadn't died when she did. Was that why she wanted Tamar to marry him? Because *she* couldn't? Or was Cornelius right? Did she just want Tamar to be safe with someone who could take care of her? "Asher was a fine young man," she said, more to herself than to Cornelius. "He was going to make something of himself, start his own business. He was saving to buy a home for him and Tamar."

"So he said, Lila, so he said. I never did see no pay stub nor no bankbook. Asher could have been doin' anything way off in Michigan. All we know is what he wrote and told us."

"And Tamar sure did write to him. For a long time I thought Tamar would at least send me a postcard," Delilah admitted. "Maybe even a letter."

"Most likely got herself one of them factory jobs somewhere, same as Asher got himself work in that car factory in Flint. Jobs where they work you all day, pay you as little as they can get away with, and you come home tired and get up even more tired the next mornin'."

Cornelius had worked for the Newsome family for years; hard work, carrying, moving, lifting, digging, gardening. He put on their new roof by himself and built that garage as well. Then he hurt his back real bad chopping wood. Newsome Senior let him go with one week's pay and hired two men to replace him.

"Lila, you know and I know that Tamar and Asher didn't come back because there wasn't nothin' here for them to come back to."

Nothin' but us, Delilah thought, but the words would have stuck in her throat if she tried to say them out loud.

"What did any of us have here in Bullfrog Bog, woman? 'Wipe the dust from your feet,' the Bible says. They did."

"The Bible also says, 'Honor your father and mother and you will have length of days.'"

Cornelius cocked his head to one side and looked at her. He broke out in a grin. "You quoting the Bible to me, Lila?" Then his face got serious. "I think that after all this time both Tamar and Asher have gone home to the Lord, else we would have heard from them by now."

Delilah wanted to cover her ears every time he said something like that. Asher wrote Tamar while he was in Flint. Almost every day there was a letter in the mailbox from him. After Tamar was gone she read them letters. Time she was done reading she knew why Tamar had to go. Now she tried to ignore what Cornelius had said about them both being dead and busied herself clearing the table.

"Ain't like we was the only ones, Lila. Look at Mr. Newsome, Lord rest his soul."

"Lord rest his soul indeed! Lord keep his soul in hell for what he did to you!"

"His son took off almost the same Tamar and Asher did. That's about as close as you can come to hell without dying. I don't know that anyone's ever heard from his boy either."

Cornelius was a Christian man, too quick to turn the other cheek. She had worked for the Newsomes, too. Soon as she couldn't carry them baskets of wet laundry up them stairs and hang 'em outside to dry, she was let go, too. And there was no week's pay neither. A pretty, young light-skinned girl took her place. Could have been Tamar if she hadn't already left town.

"Newsome's son come from money, Cornelius, and he was white, and he was a man. Newsome Senior knew just where he was. He just couldn't talk him into comin' home."

Tears stung her eyes. Tamar would be but seventy-two now, born like she was when Delilah wasn't but fifteen. "All I ever wanted for her was for her own good."

"That's what most folks want for their children. Trick is, lettin' them find it themselves." Cornelius came over to where she was standing. "Here, woman. Let me wash them dishes." He patted her shoulder. "Come on now, Lila. Ain't nothin' much happened like we wanted it to since we been born. We got to be grateful for what we have left, not what He's taken from us."

Wasn't nothin' left, Lila thought, but she didn't say it out loud. All what she had ever been given was taken from her the day Tamar ran away. "You're always going to be a preacher's son, ain't you, Cornelius?"

He gave her hand a pat, then a squeeze. She snatched her hand away but, in spite of herself, she felt comforted. Wasn't nobody left but Cornelius.

Delilah walked over to the window. Days like this, when there wasn't no sun shining, no flowers blooming, no birds singing, and there sure never would be no more bullfrogs croaking, she felt like she'd be better off dead than living, but she wouldn't scandalize poor Cornelius by saying so.

C H A P T E R

10

A young woman Marti assumed was Sara Jones was waiting for them when Marti and Vik returned to the precinct. There was no mistaking her resemblance to the woman they had pulled from the river. She was young, with skin the color of pecans and brown eyes several shades lighter. Her hair hung to her shoulders and was curled under at the ends in a casual flip. They would have to take her to the morgue. Even that would be better than dealing with the lieutenant.

"Miss Jones," Marti said, walking over to where she sat near the sergeant's desk.

The young woman stood. She wasn't more than five feet three and couldn't wear a size larger than a five. The woman in the morgue was at least four inches taller, but almost as slim.

"I'm Detective MacAlister. This is my partner, Detective Jessenovik."

"Detectives? What happened? What happened to my mother?" Her voice was calm, too calm. Her eyes were filled with panic.

"First, we have to be certain that this is your mother," Marti explained. "Then we can talk."

Unlike most visitors to the morgue, Sara Jones didn't turn away when the curtain was pulled back. She looked at the woman on the gurney for what seemed like several minutes with her fingertips touching the glass. Then she said, "I want to see her, touch her."

It was an unusual request, but Marti didn't know when they would release the body to a mortician.

"Are you sure?"

"Yes, she's my mother."

Sara's voice was steady. Marti didn't expect any hysterics so she agreed.

Once in the viewing room, Sara looked down at her mother, touched her finger to her mother's lips, leaned over, and kissed her on the forehead.

When she came out, Sara said, "I don't suppose I can have her jewelry now?"

"Jewelry?" Marti asked.

"Yes, it isn't expensive, just yellow zirconia in a fake gold setting. It was a matching set, ring, brooch, earrings."

"I'm sorry," Marti told her. "There was no jewelry."

"There had to be. She would not have left it in a hotel room or traveled without it or taken it off unless she was taking a shower or going to bed. There was a clause in all of her contracts saying she would wear some if not all of it."

"Why was this jewelry so special?"

"Her voice," Miss Jones said. Tears came to her eyes. "She had thyroid cancer years ago. They got it all out, but they damaged her vocal cords. She couldn't talk loud or yell. She couldn't sing. Ma spoke above a whisper, but not by much." She swallowed hard. "I think the jewelry . . . I think it made up for that somehow. I think it was her way of having a voice." Tears streamed down her face.

Marti gave her some Kleenex.

"Do you have a picture of this jewelry?"

"Not with me, but whoever is shooting the outtakes should have one of her stills. That jewelry might not have cost much, but it belonged to my grandmother." She dabbed at her eyes, then added, "I guess we have to go back to the police station so you can tell me what happened. When I went in to her, I could tell from the way they positioned her that something was wrong with the back of her head."

Marti and Vik took Sara Jones to the Barrister instead of the precinct for a late lunch. Jones ordered the fruit plate with cottage cheese. Marti wished she had that much discipline as she ordered her usual, shepherd's pie. After Marti explained what they knew so far, or at least as much as she could tell her, she said, "Miss Jones, Sara, how old are you?"

"Twenty-three."

"How long can you stay here?"

"Until you find out what happened to my mother and who did it. I'm a teacher. Math and science. A substitute can handle my classes until I get back."

"Would you be agreeable to staying with one of our church families? I would rather take you to my pastor's house, have them arrange something, than leave you in a motel." The pastor had seven children. The oldest girl was attending a local Christian college. She was a little younger than Sara, but not by much.

"This might not be a good time to be alone in a strange place," Marti added. Despite her composure and obvious maturity, Marti didn't think Sara should have to deal with this by herself. There was no telling what they might find out about Sara's mother.

"We're all family at my church," Marti added.

Sara hesitated, then nodded.

Marti gave her one of her business cards and put her cell phone number on the back.

As soon as the two detectives left, Sara took her cell phone out of her pocket and punched in Akiro's cell number.

"Akiro," she whispered when he answered. "I'm in Lincoln Prairie."

"I can come if you need me."

"No, I'm safe, staying with a minister and his family. Come after you wrap up things at the dig, if they haven't found whoever killed her by then."

"You're sure?"

"Yes. They just found her. In the river. . . ." Her voice broke, but she tried to hold back the tears. "I told them I would stay here until I could bring her home." She pulled out a Kleenex and wiped her eyes. "They won't let her go until they know who did it. Akiro. Why would they kill her?"

"I don't know their ways, Sara. It makes no sense to me. I just want to be sure you're okay."

"I'll call you every day, okay."

"And I'll come—next Friday I think, unless something comes up. You're sure you're safe?"

"Yes," Sara lied. "I'm sure."

There was a message from Nina Rose Peterson, the forensic anthropologist, when Marti and Vik returned to the precinct. She finally had time to look at their skeletal remains. Marti put in a quick call to Lupe and Holmberg. Peterson had already started examining the remains when the four of them arrived at the morgue.

Peterson was a tall slender woman with light brown hair. She wore wire-rimmed glasses and was holding a femur in one hand and a tibia in the other.

"I'm going to pack him up and take him with me," she said. "We might be able to use him for research."

"Are the bones that old?" Vik asked.

"Whoever this was, he wasn't that old, but his bones—from what you tell me—he could have been in the closet for fifty to sixty years. He could have died during the Depression, or the Second World War. And just looking at his skull I can see something very interesting. See the eye sockets?" She pointed. "Somewhat rectangular and wide apart, characteristic of an African American, but the nasal aperture," she pointed again, "is very narrow as is the palate, which are distinctive Caucasoid features. This man was of mixed race, which makes the information we might be able to glean from his bones even more interesting. Back in those days, women and minorities weren't important enough to be included in research studies. We're discovering a lot of things posthumously."

"What about skin color?" Marti asked.

"I can't even make a guess," Peterson told her. "He could have passed for white. He could have been dark-skinned."

Marti thought of Lieutenant Nicholson—Caucasian features, brown skin.

"Can you tell us how old he was?" Holmberg asked.

"Well, he was definitely an adult, and looking at his rib ends, I'd guess not over thirty, but I can't be more specific until I've had a closer look at him. I'd rather not estimate height or weight either. We have computerized methods that are much more accurate. And if you do have missing persons' records going back that far, my guess is that your chances of finding him are slim to none. The population was so migratory from the Depression until after the war that an awful lot of people went unreported."

Marti also knew that if he looked like and lived as an African American that would make it even less likely that anyone would have reported him missing.

Peterson packed up her instruments. "If you do come up with some data we could try matching him with, let me know. Meanwhile, I'd prefer to indicate 'unknown' on my data base and fill in verifiable information as I go along."

"Will it take long?" Lupe asked.

"Oh, no, not the basics at least. This young man is much too interesting to work with in my spare time. And I've got a couple of lab assistants as well as some graduate students who will be delighted to meet him."

Vik raised his wiry eyebrows in a gesture that would usually be followed with, "We've got a live one here." Dr. Peterson didn't seem ditzy to Marti though. If anything, Marti was impressed by her enthusiasm for her work.

"We haven't been able to get going on this yet," Lupe said as they left the morgue.

With typical enthusiasm, Holmberg added, "But we

are going to start first thing tomorrow."

"You're going to get started first thing in the morning," Lupe told him. "I'm sleeping in."

"In fact," Holmberg went on, "I'm going back to the precinct so I can get started on it right now." He jumped over a puddle and hurried on, walking ahead of them.

"No second shift for me today," Lupe said. "I'm going home." She crossed the street and entered the parking lot.

"Let's put in a call to Mark Dobrzycki," Marti suggested to Vik as they walked slowly back to the precinct. The rain was hesitating between drizzle and downpour and the forecast for sunshine was postponed.

"The FBI guy? Why?"

"Just to be sure he knows about Savannah Payne-Jones's death. She was an actress. She was traveling interstate. There weren't any drugs in her system or any indication of drug or alcohol abuse, but this could have been done by almost anyone. Maybe she didn't pay off a gambling debt or she borrowed money from the wrong people. Maybe she just saw something she shouldn't have. There are records and information that he can access faster than we can, should the need arise."

"MacAlister, are you feeling okay today?"

Marti thought about Ben but didn't say anything. "We need to see Miss Tansy Lark again, check out those stills of Savannah Jones, and hope there's a good shot of that jewelry," she said. "The only thing we've got right now as a possible motive is somebody wanting that jewelry."

"It could be caught in an undercurrent and halfway to the Mississippi by now."

Tansy Lark had her head down on her desk and was napping when they arrived.

"Looks like the manic phase is over," Marti whispered, then, louder, said, "Miss Lark!"

She came awake all at once. "Yes? Now what? What is it?" She sat straight up, then said, "Oh, it's you two. Now what do you want?"

Vik explained about the pictures.

"Well, if we do have anything . . ." She went over to a file cabinet and spent about five minutes flipping through loose papers, folders of various colors, and manila folders. "Here," she said and pulled out a shiny blue folder.

Inside there were several shots of Savannah in profile and one full face. Even dead she looked as youthful as she did in the photos. It was hard to believe she was in her forties.

"Do you recognize this jewelry?" Marti asked.

Tansy reached for her silver case and took out a cigarette. "I never paid much attention but I would assume it's the jewelry she puts in her contracts." She looked at the photos. "Old stuff, isn't it? I wonder if she had it on for the shoot. It would have been perfect. *Deadly Deceptions* is a takeoff on a forties gangster movie."

"Can you find out if she was wearing it Tuesday night?"

"I'm not sure about the ring or the brooch, but if she was wearing the earrings we might have a shot of that. I can find out for you, but not right this minute. The guy who handles that won't be here until about six."

Marti took one of the profile shots and the full face. Back at the precinct, she asked for enlargements of the jewelry. As she ordered Chinese and settled in to wait, she wondered what Momma had fixed for supper. She hadn't eaten with the family since Monday.

Come to think of it, it had been two days since she had talked with her kids. Joanna was between basketball and softball season and would be spending more time at home. The boys were getting ready for a camping trip. Marti had planned to drop in at Staben House to see her sister-in-law Iris and her niece, Lynn Ella. They had attended church with the family on Sunday and stayed for dinner, but Lynn Ella was still being tutored and was as shy as ever, except when she was around Ben. Marti wanted to see Lynn Ella more often, spend more time with her.

And she needed to spend more time with her own children. Before they grew up, before they went to college, before they were on their own. Now. She needed to be with them now while she could snatch a few more memories to store up. Now while Ben was with them. No, Ben was always going to be with them. He was going to be just fine. The antibiotics would take care of everything. There wasn't anything to worry about at all.

Ben had been awake and waiting for her when she came home last night. They lit candles and got into the hot tub together, and, as tired as she was, she listened to him as he talked. He told her about things that happened when he was growing up, things like being bigger than all of the other kids, and having to walk—good weather and bad—to get to the Catholic high school he attended when there wasn't enough money for bus fare. And his first job, sweeping out the barbershop, more because his father had been laid off than because the barber needed his help. Ben would be all right. He had made it through 'Nam. He would be fine. He had to be.

C H A P T E R

11

She took out the jewelry and looked at it. She had waited so long for this, and now it was hers: the ring, the brooch, and one earring, gold with yellow stones. Everything had happened so fast, it wasn't until she got home that she'd realized one earring was missing. She held up the ring. The way the facets of the stones caught the light. It was like looking at a star twinkling in the moonlight.

Glancing at it laying on the car seat as she drove home, she had been disappointed. It looked like cheap costume jewelry, old and clunky. But close up, it was unlike anything she had ever seen before. She slipped the ring on her finger. It felt heavy. The swirls in the design made it look feather light.

Reluctantly, she took off the ring and put it in a little velvet bag along with the brooch and the earring. She put that bag in the back of a bureau drawer and took out a matching one. She rubbed her finger against the second bag's blue velvet nap, then shook its contents into the palm of her hand. Cuff links. Green stones. Maybe emeralds, maybe glass. Nothing fancy about the setting, but his. She took out the pocket watch, set it, and wound it. It still worked. She could not remember his face, or even his scent. But she could remember holding his hand, remember him letting go of her.

C   H   A   P   T   E   R

12

SATURDAY, MAY 8—LINCOLN PRAIRIE

It was just past sunrise when Thomas Newsome awakened. Rain tapped against the windows but there was no wind, and now the rainfall was not enough to make the river keep rising. Not that he could see the river from here. Nor did he want to. He could remember other floods. Each time they said this one was worse, but he wasn't sure about that. He remembered Gurnee when it was still a town, with farms and barns and acres of soybeans and corn; even a few cows and sheep and goats. Now there were just acres of stores and restaurants. He didn't go there anymore. He didn't go anywhere except to the doctor's office. Nothing was like it used to be, but knowing that wasn't as difficult to get used to as disliking what everything had become.

He was dozing off when Harriet brought his breakfast. Back when they had full-time help, there would have been a knock first, but Harriet, his daughter-in-law, just barged in, just like she had barged into his son's life, rear-ending his car back when the roads around here had two lanes. Now, with his wife dead and his son dead, there was just the two of them. Unlike him, Harriet was still in good health. It had been a terrible thing, burying his son. Too bad it hadn't been her. He was certain she would outlive him. And, she was so damned cheerful all the time it was annoying.

"Come on, Dad," Harriet said. He hated it when she called him that. "I know you're not asleep. Here you are."

He heard the tray hit the table but didn't open his eyes.

"Fresh-squeezed orange juice, your egg soft-boiled, and your oatmeal just the way you like it, and guess what, I warmed up a little applesauce as well."

She did take good care of him, Thomas admitted. If only he liked her. But he did not. There wasn't any particular reason why he didn't, at least not that he could think of. Maybe it was because she had not only failed to produce any grandchildren, but outlived his son as well. None of that could be undone, so therefore none of it mattered, but he didn't have to accept any of it and "go on." What did that mean, go on? Keep breathing? When your only son died, you didn't just go on; part of you died with him.

After he had eaten and Harriet had barged in again and removed his tray he got up, showered, and dressed. He was reading all of Dickens again and particularly enjoying *Bleak House*. Perhaps enjoying wasn't quite the right word. The story spoke to how he had begun to feel about his own life in the years since Tom died.

He tried not to think of Tom's death as a punishment, but it was. There were so many wrongs, those of his father, those of his son, and his.

Come Memorial Day he would make his annual pilgrimage to the family plot. There would be six of them buried there eventually. His parents, his wife, and his son were there now. One day, perhaps soon, he would join them. He rather suspected that Harriet would live forever.

His oldest brother had not survived the Normandy invasion and was buried in France. Then there was Edmund, his younger brother. Nobody knew what had become of him. Edmund's disappearance was as much a puzzle as the way his father had died—in a storm while moving a downed wire. Why would his father have gotten out of the car and touched it? His father would not have even been on that road that night, were it not for him.

Edmund and Dad. Why was it that his sins of omission hung more heavily on his soul than those he had committed? The road not taken. The things left undone. The words not spoken. The feelings never revealed. And now there would only be a priest to confess to, a priest to forgive him. What wouldn't he give to have Edmund and Dad here, to have just one more look at them, and just one brief moment to talk?

Thomas opened the cupboard where he kept the Theotokos. He looked at the pain in that mother's face. Over the years, he had come to believe her pain was far greater than his own and to find some comfort in that. But now he wanted peace, forgiveness, both harder to come by. He opened a drawer, took out a page from Monday's *Chicago Tribune*, and put it on the table beside his worn leather copy of Dickens. Then he opened another drawer and took out a wooden chest about the size of one that his mother's silver table service was kept in.

This chest had a hinged top and was made of oak with elaborate scrollwork on the sides. Within the latticed edges of the top the twelve apostles stood, each with his own symbol, each stern-faced with the hard, steady gaze of one who judges. The Theotokos sat in the center, holding her child. This mother was serene. Above the heads of the carved figures the risen Christ ascended. Angels, blowing into long wooden balciums and playing stringed gardons, rushed to greet Him.

Thomas opened the chest and took out the manuscript attributed to Eugène Ionesco. The jewelry was at the bottom of the box. Heavy silver and gold pieces, most with zirconia. And the cuff links. He reached out to touch them, then drew his hand back as if they were hot and would burn him. It was only their secret that hurt now. He imagined his father standing in the road, reaching down to pick up a live wire. The cuff links were the cause of it. He didn't know what had happened that night, but even if it was divine retribution, the cuff links were the cause of it all.

Neither the box nor what was kept inside belonged to him. Nor was the icon of the Theotokos his to look at every morning and pray to at night. They were just something else to atone for.

Soon he would remedy that, even though they were not that valuable or of any importance. The patriarch was coming. He would arrange to return all of this to him and make his confession. Then, if his rest in the next world was still not assured, perhaps as he waited to take his place in the family plot, he could, at last, find peace.

Thomas Newsome was asleep in the chair by the window when she returned to his room. His book was on the floor where it must have fallen. Sometimes he just pretended to be asleep, but now he was sitting with his chin on his chest and his mouth half-open, drooling. He caught his breath for a moment, mid-snore. She stood still and waited, just in case this time the strangling sound meant he was taking his last breath. He hesitated, then exhaled.

The thick carpet muffled her footsteps as she walked to the built-in cupboard. She opened the door, pulled out the bottom drawer, and opened the chest without removing it. She took a quick look at the old man, then returned the manuscript page. She had taken it to the museum curator yesterday. Without doing whatever tests they could do to authenticate it, or translating it from Romanian or French to English, he had been quick to tell her he could sell it. He had quoted her a price that she suspected was half what he could get for it, but she accepted. It was more than she expected.

He shrugged when she showed him a piece of the jewelry and asked about a price. "Not that much," he told her. She knew from the expression in his eyes and the way he held it in his hand a moment longer than was necessary that he was lying. She would have to find out more about the jewelry before she made arrangements to sell it. She would have to find out very soon.

She didn't think the old man was getting senile. He had been living in the past ever since Tom died. Then again, she had not expected Tom to die of a heart attack at thirty-eight either. The old man could just drop dead on her, too.

Now there was that newspaper clipping he kept in the cupboard. His Beatitude Vladimir, patriarch of Budapest, was coming to visit a Romanian Orthodox

Church in Skokie. Thomas Newsome, who had attended Presbyterian services on those few occasions when he went to church at all, now had a sudden interest in the church of his ancestors. She had called to see if this Vladimir would be leading any liturgical services and written down the time and date, 11 A.M. next Sunday, the sixteenth.

Her mother had "made her peace with God" and died in her sleep four days later. She wasn't much older then than the old man was now. With that in mind, she was going to suggest that the old man go to this Vladimir's liturgy next Sunday. Maybe, like her mother, he, too, would make peace with his God and die. Then these treasures, which he didn't even have the common sense to value, would be hers. She weighed a piece of the jewelry in her hand again. The sixteenth. Now that she had a plan, she would have to find out what this was worth and find a buyer as quickly as possible.

C H A P T E R

13

Marti awakened to chaos. The Boy Scout weekend camping trip had been rained out. Fifteen Boy Scouts were camped out in sleeping bags when she got home last night and, from the sounds of it, all of them were awake now. She looked at the clock. It was five twenty-five in the morning. The sun wasn't even up yet. Eyes closed, she reached out for Ben. He wasn't there. The sound of a television blared for a moment, boys laughed. Someone ran up or down the stairs. She pulled the covers over her head.

Two hours later, Marti awakened again. This time she got up. The noise was coming from the kitchen and the dining room. She stopped at the kitchen and watched as Ben flipped pancakes and Allan, his partner in scouting as well as in rescues and fire-fighting, brought them in stacks to the table. The Boy Scouts, all twelve and thirteen years old, were eating the pancakes as fast as they could be delivered.

Theo and Mike were at the dining room table, along with their next-door neighbors and best friends, Peter and Patrick. Marti looked at the four of them, surprised to see how much they had grown. Peter's hair was a darker shade of brown now; Patrick was still blond but the taller of the two. Theo had always been slimmer and taller than Mike, but Mike was losing weight and they were about the same height. She could tell they were getting interested in girls by the way they acted when they went to Joanna's games, nudging each other and whispering when the more physically developed members of the teams were playing.

Momma had always insisted that the children would ultimately get into relationships that were most like those they saw at home. Marti's first husband, Johnny, had such a dysfunctional family that Momma warned her against dating him. But Johnny spent a lot of time at her house and a lot of time in the church. He wanted his family to be like hers, not his. Sometimes it took a lot of effort, but together they had made that happen.

Things were easier between her and Ben. She thought it was partly because they each had been married before and lost a spouse. Momma said it was because they were more mature the second time around. Their family life had been similar. His parents were a lot like hers. Best of all, she and Ben valued companionship and affection as much as they enjoyed good sex and they talked a lot—when they weren't too tired.

Ben caught her eye now and winked. It was a little signal between them that meant he was okay. She winked back, less at ease with this waiting for the next PSA test than he was. He fixed her a plate with pancakes and sausages, spreading butter on the pancakes the way she liked them, and pouring just the right amount of maple syrup. Theo gave her his place at the table.

While the boys cleaned the kitchen and loaded the dishwasher, she asked Ben about Joanna.

"Believe it or not, she is spending the weekend with Sharon and Lisa."

"How are things going with those two now that Lisa's decided to try living at home?" Sharon was her best friend, but not the smartest. Sharon and her daughter, Lisa, who was much more sensible, always had problems getting along. Lisa had been living here until a couple of weeks ago.

"Momma's taken them a batch of cookies a few times," Ben said. "So my guess is that things are still a little shaky. But so far, they seem to be trying."

The older Marti got the more her family grew. First Sharon and Lisa after Johnny died, now her sister-in-law Iris and nine-year-old niece, Lynn Ella.

"Too bad things didn't work out with Sharon tutoring Lynn Ella," Marti said.

"Everything seemed to be okay until Lynn Ella started counseling at LACASA."

The Lake County Council Against Sexual Assault worked with rape and sexual abuse survivors. Lynn Ella had been in foster care most of her life. The women she had been placed with tended to be physically abusive and the men those women associated with tended to be kind, although the things they expected Lynn Ella to do in return for that kindness no child should be expected to endure. Marti was beginning to wonder if that wasn't at least a part of Sharon's problem also. Sharon always made such terrible choices when it came to men and she always called each of them "Mr. Wonderful."

Marti put her arm around Ben's waist and leaned her head on his shoulder. She couldn't imagine life without him. She needed him too much. Dear Lord, she prayed silently, Ben has to be all right. Please don't take him away from us.

When Marti arrived at work, the coffee was hot and Holmberg's computer was on, but he wasn't in the office. She had an e-mail from Nina Rose Peterson. Their skeleton was definitely biracial. He was twenty-eight when he died and five feet nine inches tall, his approximate weight one hundred and sixty pounds. A bullet caused the marks on the ribs. The trajectory indicated that the bullet went through his heart. There were also indications that the victim did heavy manual labor. Marti was surprised that they could get that much information from a bunch of old bones.

"How long has he been dead?" Vik asked as Marti read off the information.

"Says here fifty-five to sixty years."

Vik made a quick calculation. "Military records," he said.

"What?"

"Let's go out on the Internet and see what kinds of military records are out there."

They tried every cue word they could think off without coming up with anything. When Lupe and Holmberg came in, Vik was cussing in Polish.

"What are you two up to?" Holmberg asked.

Marti let Vik explain.

"You're not going to find anything out that way," Holmberg said.

"Why not?" Vik challenged.

"For one thing, sometime in the early sixties eighty percent of all World War Two records were destroyed in a fire at a military facility in St. Louis."

Vik didn't say anything.

"They wouldn't release those records over the

105

Internet anyway. You might be able to find out something if you filled out the right forms with the right information. What you know now sure wouldn't be enough."

"We just wasted an hour," Vik complained.

"So much for that," Marti agreed "Do you have Lemon Face's permission to work overtime today?"

"Paperwork," Lupe explained. "Holmberg here has done a lot of field training on the mean streets of Lincoln Prairie. And the weather isn't keeping any of the local pushers, addicts, pimps, or hookers inside."

"Then there's traffic violations, parking violations, curfew violations," Holmberg added. "Jaywalking, car hijacking . . ."

"Let's not get carried away," Lupe suggested.

Marti and Vik brought them up to date on the skeletal remains case first, then filled them in on what was happening with the Savannah Payne-Jones case. Marti showed them the stills of Savannah and the close-ups of the jewelry.

"Then Jones wasn't a random victim," Lupe concluded.

"No way," Holmberg agreed. "She took that cab to meet someone and whoever it was wanted that jewelry."

"Too bad these photos are in black and white," Lupe said. "The jewelry doesn't stand out, it just dates her. The details aren't that good in the blowups either. It looks like costume jewelry from the twenties or thirties."

"Voilà!" Holmberg exclaimed when he went through his in-basket. "Some of the rental records for the building where the bones were found have been delivered."

Marti didn't ask Holmberg how he had managed to get them so fast. The sergeant said he'd worked until ten last night.

He flipped through a couple of pages, then said, "These are the most recent rentals. They won't tell us what we need to know, but it's a beginning."

He read for a few minutes, with Lupe standing beside him reading along.

"So," Lupe said. "In the past eleven years, the property was empty for three years, and rented by five different people in eight years. If anyone thought there might be a false ceiling and a second floor, there is no mention of it here."

"We've got no bone dating on the skeleton," Holmberg added. "I haven't found any leads on missing persons yet. I haven't figured out how to access any records there might be of structural changes to the building."

Marti put in another call to the original owner's great-grandson, who lived in Connecticut. He had inherited the property from his mother and held on to it for ten months before putting it up for sale.

"As far as I know, we have no living relatives in Lincoln Prairie," he repeated. "My mother never spoke of Lincoln Prairie at all. I'm sure she never went there, never saw the property. My mother and her sister inherited it from my grandfather. They left before the war was over, right after my father got killed."

"Was your father from Lincoln Prairie?"

"No, Iowa. I keep in touch with my relatives there. Look, you're asking about a place I've never seen except for a Realtor's photo. It's just a building. I have no connection with that place or that city. No memories. There's no nostalgic value, nothing. That's why I sold it."

"Have you had time to go through your mother's papers?" Marti asked.

"There's nothing that's not a legal document. The only documents relating to renting the building are the agreements between her or my grandmother and the agents handling the rentals. There's nothing saying who the place was rented to. There are papers referencing one insurance claim. Someone lost control of a car, jumped the curb, and hit the building."

"What year?" Marti asked.

"Nineteen seventy-eight."

"Why don't you send me copies of whatever you have. Can you fax it?"

"I'll have my daughter take care of that tomorrow."

As soon as Marti hung up, she called the local museum, a converted Victorian on Sherman. They were photographing and making videos of the second-floor building the way it looked now; maybe they'd have some old photos. John Doggett, the curator, answered the phone. Marti explained what she needed.

"Nothing comes to mind," Doggett told her, "but, we do have a large collection of photographs. I'll start looking through them today."

"If you find anything on that building, and you can give it even an approximate date, I'd appreciate it."

When she hung up, Holmberg said, "You're going to get a progress report every time I work on this. I might never have thought of the museum."

"We can't go to Connecticut to look at whatever papers the great-grandson has," Marti told him, "so we have to assume he knows what he's looking at, at least until we get the copies. As for the museum having photographs, that's a long shot."

"Too bad this isn't the task force case," Vik said. "What do you want to bet we'll wrap up the drowning victim's case tomorrow and be the lieutenant's target of choice again?"

"Jessenovik, you are the only person I know who can turn the best possible outcome into something negative. I don't think I like it any better when you're optimistic than when you're a pessimist."

After Lupe and Holmberg left, Marti and Vik agreed that they had put in enough time on the skeletal remains case. Marti checked her e-mail again. There was one from Lieutenant Nicholson demanding yesterday's reports and the reports from the day before immediately. Marti filed two scanty reports that she felt sufficiently summarized where they were, then suggested to Vik that they go talk with Sara Jones.

109

S ara was staying with Marti's pastor's family. They followed the pastor's wife into the kitchen and accepted cups of coffee and a plate with homemade cookies and thick slices of banana bread. The room was nothing like Marti's kitchen, which was light and airy with hanging plants and wind chimes and bird feeders hanging just outside the windows. This room would have depressed her if it wasn't for the colorful kente cloth place mats on the long mahogany table and the pale gold walls that offset the dark brown cabinets.

Sara was standing at the counter nearest the sink. She was working on a science experiment with the pastor's ten-year-old daughter. Except for forensics, Marti liked most things scientific to have some element of mystery. It didn't bother her at all that she could recite and explain Newton's third law of motion without understanding a word of it. As she listened to Sara explain this experiment, she had no trouble recognizing the chemical changes Sara was describing, nor did the child. Part of her wished a teacher like Sara had taught her chemistry. Part of her liked looking at creation with awe and not having a clue.

Experiment complete, Sara sent the little girl off to

play, poured herself a cup of coffee, and joined them at the table.

"Are you okay here?" Marti asked.

Sara nodded and reached for the sugar bowl.

"You're sure."

"I . . . need to be here, where my mother is . . . until I can take her home."

Marti thought back to the day Johnny died. She could not leave his hospital room. She watched as the tubes were removed. Then she refused to let them cover his face, take him away. She sat there with him, alone, and she believed he remained in that room with her until he could leave her and she could let him go. That was not going to happen to her again, not yet, not now. Ben was going to be fine.

Marti forced herself to pour cream in her coffee to cool it, even though she didn't like it that way. She took a sip, then asked, "What can you tell us about your mother's jewelry?"

"Not much. It was my grandmother's. I got the impression that it had been in the family even longer than that, but nobody ever said and I never asked."

"Have you always lived in L.A.?"

"Yes, but my mother was born back East, somewhere near Boston." She frowned. "She talked about going to the beach, digging clams, the smell of saltwater, but she never mentioned the name of the town."

Marti took out her notebook, wrote down the victim's name and approximate place of birth.

"And your father?"

Sara shook her head. "I don't know anything about him at all. They weren't married. Mom was taking acting classes in New York. She quit and moved to Los Angeles. I always thought there must be some scandal involved, that maybe my father was a married professor or something, but Mom never said and somehow I always knew that I wasn't to ask."

Marti thought Sara was calm, too calm under the circumstances. She didn't know if that meant Sara was just one of those people who didn't show much emotion, at least not when with strangers, or if she was still in shock, or if mother and daughter were not as close as they seemed to be. In her experience, if there had been an argument or any kind of discord immediately preceding her mother's death, Sara's reaction would have been the opposite.

"Did you ever wonder why your mother didn't tell you much about her family?"

"Of course I did. It was like . . . like . . . not belonging anywhere."

"Did that make much of a difference in your life?"

"Not so much as . . . Mom didn't like to live in one place more than a couple of years. We moved a lot. I changed schools a lot."

"It must have been hard to keep making friends," Marti said, thinking of how difficult it was for her children to leave Chicago to come here after Johnny died.

Sara folded her arms and looked down at the floor. "I didn't. Not really. Not until I went to college. Mom wanted me to live at home, but it was like . . . I looked around one day and thought I could be here forever. I could be like Mom. She was in a lot of movies. For her, everything was about the next shoot, the next trip for location shots. For me that meant being alone."

"Did she understand that?"

"Yes. But she hated coming home to an empty apartment."

Sara sat up, began twisting a ring she was wearing. Marti hadn't noticed it before. It was on the third finger of her left hand. Silver setting, multifaceted diamond. Or was it zirconia? Marti didn't ask.

"Is that . . ." Marti began.

"Yes. His name is Akiro Takamoto. I don't know when we'll get married."

"How did your mother feel about that?"

"She . . . wasn't happy . . . she was for me but . . . I think she thought it meant I'd leave her. Akiro is a professor of anthropology at U.C.L.A." Sara smiled for the first time. "He has so many relatives he loses track, and everyone lives in California. It isn't like we were going to move away or anything."

Marti thought the change in Sara when she spoke of her fiancé as well as what she said, and didn't say, were part of the reason she wasn't showing more emotion about her mother's death. Savannah would have realized that her daughter's small world was much bigger with Akiro in her life. That could mean big changes in Savannah's life as well. Although it didn't seem to be a source of contention between mother and daughter, Savannah seemed like a very private person. Marti could not imagine that she would be eager for a major change. She looked at Sara and wondered for a moment if she was eager to marry this Akiro, or if she was trying to escape a life where she spent much of her time at home alone.

"What do you know about your grandparents?"

"Their names. At least on my mother's side."

Marti wrote that down.

"They moved to Connecticut when Mom decided to go to New York and study acting. She told me she took me to see them when I was a baby, but I don't remember any of that. They're both dead now."

"Did you go to their funerals?"

"No, not that I can remember. I don't know when either of them died, but I think one of them must have died when I was in kindergarten. I had to stay with a neighbor for about a week, and I remember wondering what 'deceased' meant. Nobody answered when I asked."

"But you only remember this happening once."

"Yes. Just once."

"So you don't know which grandparent that would have been or when or if your other grandparents passed away?"

"No. Mom just spoke of them as if they were dead, when she mentioned them at all. So I just assumed . . . They'd be really old now. In their seventies at least."

Marti didn't smile, but she did think back to the days when she thought seventy was old, too.

"Mom has . . . there is . . . one old black-and-white photo of them but it's not very good."

"What do they look like?"

"Young, laughing, it's not a formal sitting, just a picture that was taken at a club, or a party maybe. My grandmother is wearing the jewelry."

"Did your mother tell you any stories about when she was growing up?"

"No." Sara broke off a piece of the banana bread and rolled it between her finger and thumb. "When I was in fourth grade, we had to make our family tree. There was me and Mom, and my grandparents. Mom filled in the rest of it the day before I had to turn it in, but I think she just made up the names and the dates. It was more like she didn't know much about her family, not that she wouldn't tell me."

"Can you get that photo of your grandparents for me?"

"Not unless I go back to L.A."

"Maybe she gave a friend a house key."

"No, not Mom." Sara thought for a moment. "Akiro is in Arizona, on a dig with some of his students. Mom lives . . . lived in a condo. I'll call security. Someone must have a key."

"Did your mother have . . . someone special in her life?"

"Occasionally, although they were never that special."

"Recently?"

"Not since last summer. Work was slow for a couple of months."

"Who was he?" Marti took down his name.

"He was just another wannabe film producer. Thought maybe Mom could open a couple of doors for him. After a month or so he gave up and went back to New York."

Marti made a note to check with professional organizations for his address.

"When's the last time your mother was in a serious relationship?"

"There weren't that many and they all seemed casual to me. Nothing ever lasted very long." Sara hesitated, then asked, "Are you . . . do you think you'll ever know . . . what happened . . . and why? That's what I don't understand. Why would someone do this? And here of all places? Mom lived in New York, L.A., and places where you think something like this could happen. But Lincoln Prairie? A little town midway between Chicago and Milwaukee? Why here?"

She stared down at her cup. "It's funny. When Mom told me she would be here for a few days, she talked about it being a great place to film car chase scenes. 'But,' she said, 'if anyone asks, say I'm in Chicago. I don't know anyone outside of the business who has heard of the Anstandt Expressway or Lincoln Prairie, Illinois.' "

"But *she* knew, Sara. Had she ever worked here before?"

"No."

"You're sure."

"Real sure. Until this week the closest she'd been to

Chicago was some shoot they did in Detroit, a few near or in St. Louis, and some in Tennessee."

Sara put in a call to Akiro. "They were here again . . . the detectives . . . asking a lot of questions about my family. I don't know anything about my family, Akiro. It's so embarrassing not to know anything."

"That's okay. It's like that in a lot of families. More than you'd think."

"Not in your family."

"No," Akiro agreed. "Not in my family."

"They want that picture. The one Ma had of her parents. I don't want to give it to them. I told them there was no way I could get it."

"You are afraid they will find out what you don't know."

"Yes," Sara whispered. "Yes."

Marti thought about what Sara said as she drove back to the precinct. "Why would anyone who lived here want Savannah Jones dead?"

"Just because she had never been here doesn't mean she didn't know anyone who lives here."

"Suppose someone came here to kill her?"

"Seems to me, MacAlister, that they would have tried a little harder to make it look accidental."

"Maybe they thought they did."

"If she was involved in a situation where she thought she was at risk, would she have gone to that restaurant?"

"Maybe it was someone she knew, Vik, like this guy she dated for a while last summer."

"So why did he want to meet her here? To propose? Don't forget, Marti, she met whoever it was at night in the middle of nowhere."

"She didn't ask the cabby to wait or come back, so she must have been expecting a ride back to her motel. That implies it could be someone she knew."

"Right now we know next to nothing and what little we do know could imply almost anything."

Vik was right. She was going to have to slow down, think things through. She wanted to solve this one too badly, to stay one up on the lieutenant. "Poor Sara," she said, changing the subject. "I feel bad about her not having that jewelry."

"At the rate the Des Plaines is moving, it'll end up somewhere in the Mississippi, maybe even the Gulf."

"Savannah could have become a mark," Marti persisted.

"Sure, one of the locals moseys up to the local Ritz-Carlton, otherwise known as the Log Cabin Cafe, spots the jewelry, decides it will look better on the little lady, knocks her off, has the meat-loaf special, and heads home."

"Smart mouth."

"MacAlister, Savannah Payne-Jones was a stranger in a strange town in a strange place in the middle of nowhere and she ended up dead. That's not what I'd call an unusual scenario these days."

"But she went to that parking lot to meet someone.

Does that mean it was someone she trusted or someone she feared? We've got to rule out or determine the importance of that jewelry, and we're going to have to start looking into her past." Based on what Sara had told them neither would be easy.

"You haven't heard anything from Mark Dobrzycki."

"No. but I know more now than I did when I called him. Savannah Jones had no family except for her daughter, maybe a few friends and some casual lovers. And she traveled a lot. Maybe there's something out there that we need to know. If there is, Mark can access it a lot faster than we could. I'm going to call him again."

"I can see the possibilities but I think you're overreacting. Don't let the lieutenant get to you."

This was their first difficult task force case, the first real test of their abilities as homicide cops and it was already getting publicity. "The lieutenant would love to see us blow this one."

"We won't," Vik promised. "That is not going to happen. No way."

They returned to the Anstandt Expressway, questioned Tansy Lark again, looked at the color footage that had been shot Tuesday night, arranged to have stills made of one shot that clearly showed one of the earrings and another that was a good shot of the ring. Next, they talked with everyone who had been on the set the last time Savannah Jones came to work.

It was raining again, slow but steady. The weatherman was still promising sunshine in a couple of days. Marti got on the bus. Vik followed. Inside, the bus had been gutted. Instead of two rows with two seats and an aisle between, there was one long bench the length of each side of the bus, well padded with pillows and blankets tossed here and there. Tables down the center were bolted to the floor. There was a table with a coffeepot and a refrigerator in the rear, but no restroom. The bus was empty except for a woman playing solitaire.

"Damned shame," she said, when Marti asked if she knew Savannah Jones.

The woman looked like someone Vik would refer to as a "floozy." Marti saw an aging woman still trying to look young. She was wearing vintage forties clothing, with hair dyed blond and combed in an Andrews Sisters' style, with a black net holding the back in place, just like the one Savannah was wearing. Her makeup was thick, as if there were a lot of lines and wrinkles to cover. Her eyelashes had a heavy layer of black mascara.

"Did you ever work with Savannah before?" Marti asked.

She took a drag from her cigarette and tipped the ash on the floor. "Every now and then. I'm the resident white has-been, she's the resident black has-been. No, not has-beens. 'Never was' says it better. Almost, but not quite. There are a lot more of us than big stars. Since neither of us offended anybody in our youth, they remember us when they cast these kinds of roles.

120

Anonymous, with little or nothing to say, not totally in the background, but not important either. I get to be the loser who's a hooker. Savannah's the boozer loser."

"Was she?"

"A boozer? No. A glass of wine every now and then maybe. She just loved to act, same as me. We're both suckers for 'lights, camera, action.' "

"She ever talk about herself?"

The woman shook her head. "Nobody does that in this business. Not unless they're lying or trying to impress somebody. There's nobody on these location jobs to impress."

"What did you talk about?"

"Mostly, when we were waiting in the bus or the trailer, we played poker. Savannah gave up fifty bucks Tuesday. It wasn't like her to lose. She had something else on her mind."

"What was that?"

"She didn't say, but her mind wasn't on the game, and she was humming last time I saw her."

"Like she had a date maybe?" Marti suggested.

"Nah. She wasn't one for one-night stands. Besides, it's not worth bothering with unless you're taking him home, or to a halfway decent hotel. You see that dump they put us up at?"

Marti nodded.

"Hard to play the movie star vamp role in a place like that. Good way to lose your mystique." She laughed, as if that was a joke, but the laughter didn't reach her eyes.

"Is the actress who replaced her here?"

121

"Dev? Nah. They finished her shoot about an hour ago. She said she was heading back to the motel to watch the toy boys in uniform."

"Did Savannah know her?

"I doubt it. I just met her. She's local."

They questioned five other people who had seen Savannah Jones on Tuesday without getting any additional information. It was dark and still raining when Marti and Vik returned to their cars.

Mildred met Vik at the door when he got home. She was using her walker. Their dog, Maxie, a rescued German shepherd, was right beside her. Vik had not wanted a dog, but Maxie had been trained to recognize verbal and nonverbal cues if Mildred needed her. Mildred wore an alarm device that would alert someone if she needed help. Maxie had been taught how to activate it if Mildred could not. And Maxie had become Mildred's companion, an indispensable member of the family. Now his sister-in-law, Helen, could leave the house without worrying. He could go to work without wondering if Mildred felt helpless, or lonely, or depressed. Vik gave Mildred a kiss, then reached down and rubbed Maxie's ears.

"Come and eat," Mildred said. "I helped Helen make golabki."

Vik could smell the meat-filled cabbage rolls.

"There's noodle and sauerkraut casserole, too. I'm glad you could come home so early. I was waiting supper for you."

Vik rubbed Maxie's ears again. Before Maxie came to live with them, Mildred was depressed and afraid. She seldom spoke at all. Then she began carrying on conversations with the dog. Vik was annoyed at first, but then Mildred began talking to everyone else, too. If anyone had told him that a pet with four legs and fur could make this much of a difference in their lives, he would have laughed at them, but he had seen it for himself, and, like Mildred, he wasn't depressed anymore. He wasn't afraid to leave her at home alone.

C H A P T E R

15

SUNDAY, MAY 9—LINCOLN PRAIRIE

When Marti woke up Sunday morning, the sun wasn't shining, but the rain had stopped and the sky looked as if it might be clearing. The Anstandt Expressway would be open to traffic today. The film crew packed up and left late last night. The Des Plaines River had crested two feet below predicted levels. Were it not for Savannah Jones's body, still in the morgue, and Ben's PSA test results still pending, and a skeleton they might never be able to identify, things would be returning to normal.

Loud voices followed by laughter reminded her that the boy scouts were still here, but their parents would be picking them up by noon. To Marti's surprise she realized she would miss them. Not that she wanted to be greeted by the sound of fifteen boys every morning, but this made her think of the time when her home would be quiet, her children in college or married, her weekdays and weekends undisturbed until grandchildren came along.

When Ben came in to see if she was awake, she said, "What will we do when the house is quiet most of the time?"

"Make our own music," he replied and leaned down to kiss her.

The house was quiet when the sergeant called. Tyler's mother wanted to speak to her. She said it was important. Marti took down the number and returned her call.

"C. J. was here this weekend," she said. "There's something Tyler needs to tell you."

Marti met Vik in front of Tyler's house. This time, when they went into the sunroom, there was no hot cocoa. Tyler didn't look at them. His parents, although not obviously angry, were clearly displeased.

"Here it is," Tyler said. He opened his hand. An earring just like the one Savannah Jones was wearing in her photographs was in his palm.

Marti looked at it but didn't touch it. Even in color, a photograph could not have captured the intricate design of the gold setting for the yellow stone. She took a closer look, saw the tiny rosettes among the golden swirls.

"C. J. gave it to him for safekeeping and he took it," Tyler's mother said. "Tyler was supposed to hide it for him." She looked down at the boy. "I don't know how many times I've told you that real friends do not encourage you to do things that are wrong."

Vik sat down beside Tyler. "Where did C. J. get this, son?" He spoke in a quiet, soothing voice that Marti seldom heard.

Tyler choked back a sob. "From the woman in the water."

"Did you know about this on Wednesday?"

"No. I only saw him yelling and trying to swim."

"Did he tell you how he got it?"

"Not exactly, just that he saw it first, caught on a piece of net. Then when he took it he saw her hair and her head."

"And when did he give it to you?"

"Yesterday, while we were at the movie."

"They were just here for the day," Tyler's mother explained. She still sounded upset.

"And when did you tell your parents you had this?" Vik asked.

"Not till this morning."

"And why not?" Tyler's mother demanded.

His father patted her on the shoulder. "He's just a boy, Marge. He's done the right thing. It's better that he thought about it and made a right decision than kept it to himself because he was afraid of how we would react." Tyler's mother sagged against her husband. Marti didn't need an explanation. The influence

125

other children had on your child was always a concern.

"You do the best you can," Marti told her. "It sounds to me like you're both doing the right thing." That seemed to make Tyler's mother feel better. She was warming milk for cocoa when Vik and Marti left.

They drove to C. J.'s address in Lake Forest. It was on the west side of Route 43.

"New money," Vik commented.

"Lottery money," Marti reminded him.

All of the houses were similar, multilevel gray brick with attached three-car garages. The streets were named for trees. C. J. lived on Boxwood. The pink Harley-Davidson was parked in the circular driveway alongside an identical cobalt blue motorcycle.

Vik paused to look at them. "I wonder how many suckers spent the rent money to help pay for this."

Cecil Slocum Senior admitted them to the foyer and left them standing there while he went to get Junior. Neither the marble floor nor the multitiered chandelier impressed Marti. She could hear children arguing, then a sharp slap followed by crying.

When Mr. Slocum returned, C. J. was with him. The boy with the crew cut and the ponytail gave them a belligerent stare. Marti almost expected him to stick out his tongue but he did not.

"Did you give something to Tyler yesterday for safe-keeping?" Vik asked.

"I don't know what you're talking about."

"What is this?" his father asked. "Harassment? C. J. told you everything he knew about what happened."

Vik took the earring out of his pocket.

"I never saw it before," the boy said before Vik could speak.

"Look, son," Vik said, "we're not here to get you into any trouble. It's just important that we know where this came from."

"You can't arrest me, can you?"

"We won't arrest you," Vik promised. "There's something we call a chain of evidence. That means as something goes from one person to another, we know who each of those people are. It's very important to our investigation. That's why we need your help."

The boy looked at his father. Cecil Senior gave the slightest nod.

"There was some kind of net. That was caught in it. I saw that before I saw her. I reached for it, that's when I saw her hand and her face." The boy squeezed his eyes shut as if he was trying to block out the memory.

"Thank you," Vik said. "That's all we needed to know. And you've been a really big help."

The boy seemed to be standing taller when they left, almost as if he was proud.

"Heads, she went into the river with the jewelry on," Vik said as they returned to Lincoln Prairie. "Tails, someone took it but couldn't get this earring off."

"Brooches can't unpin themselves and rings don't

just slip off your finger. This is a clip-on earring. And there's no way she would have put everything but one earring in her purse."

"There were no signs of a struggle. She must have given everything to whoever it was, or tried to."

"This earring is exquisite," Marti said. "And according to Sara, the three pieces were a matched set, but I don't think whoever killed Savannah went through all that trouble to set her up just to take some costume jewelry. They could have mugged her at that motel, broke into her room, strong-armed her maybe, taken what they wanted."

"Maybe whoever did it just didn't want any witnesses," Vik concluded. "Maybe he wondered if she would float with her head bashed in. Ask the average killer why he killed somebody and you get an answer that doesn't make any sense to sane people. Why should there be anything logical about this?"

Back in the office, Marti wondered what would happen if there was a little indirect publicity. She called Ed Gilbreth and asked if he might be able to get one of the still shots of Savannah in tomorrow's *News-Times*. A profile shot would include the earring without calling attention to it.

"She's yesterday's news," Ed told her. "If she had a recurring, nonspeaking, walk-on role in a television series, or did just one commercial, it would be different. But nobody is going to recognize her. Nobody is going to care much that she's dead. Maybe when you know who killed her and why, but you're not there yet, are you?"

Marti decided against mentioning the family jewels. "Something in the newspaper might flush them out."

"She's not a local. Something on that national television show that helps catch killers might work."

While they were on the phone, Ed asked her to agree on a time this evening when he could do a phone interview. Ben's chief and Frank Winan had okayed it. Marti teased Gilbreth about not wasting any time and consulted with Ben, who agreed to get it over with tonight. The thought of the impact an interview could have on Lieutenant Nicholson was too strong to resist, but, if she waited, Nicholson might find a way to sabotage it.

Next, Marti put in a call to John Doggett, curator of the local museum. He suggested visiting a couple of jewelers in Chicago who could tell her not just the value, but also the history of the earring. And no, he had not found any photographs of the building where the skeletal remains had been found. Nor had he had much time to look for them. He had received additional memorabilia relevant to the Geneva Theater and was busy arranging a more significant display in an upstairs hallway.

TORONTO, CANADA

Vladimir had not yet traveled outside of Romania so often that one city looked much like another. Since arriving in Canada on Wednesday, he had sung vespers in Edmonton, baptized and confirmed babies and converts in Montreal, and celebrated the liturgy today in Toronto. He had met with clergy and laity in each city and from each church represented had gained a commitment to give a monthly contribution to the Fund for the Orphans of Romania. Tonight, he, Josef, and Nicolae had checked into a Toronto hotel preparatory to leaving for the airport in the morning. They would arrive in Detroit before noon.

After they checked in, they had discovered a labyrinth of small shops beneath the street and an underground marketplace with eateries. Incognito, they bought oranges and peaches to take back to their hotel rooms, then ate a Greek salad, Italian pizza with pepperoni, and an American favorite—crispy fried chicken. Stomachs full, they followed the exit signs, emerged on a quiet street near the hotel, and walked through the downtown business district for several blocks.

"There are no children," Vladimir said. The one

thing he thought of whenever he thought of Canada was that he never saw a child alone in the streets at night, at least not in the cities he visited. "No children trying to get warm with heat from the sewer grates. No children searching through refuse for supper."

He had asked those he spoke with to be generous in giving to the children of Romania. Their faces told him how foreign the reality of so many orphans and so much need was.

"Does this do any good?" he asked aloud.

"Perhaps," Josef said.

Vladimir clapped Josef on the back. Over the years Josef had become more than his aide. Josef was his trusted friend who never lied.

"They have never gone hungry," Vladimir said. "They have never had to watch where they walk because they have no shoes. They have never stuffed newspaper under their shirt or their sweater because it was cold and they had no coat."

"Those who have much do not necessarily give much, Vladimir," Josef said. "They want to see what they give, or experience it. They want everyone to see their name on a plaque or a brick or even a program for a new play or a symphony orchestra so that everyone can see how much they gave. Money is tangible to them. They want something tangible in return."

"And all I am promising is a child's future. A child they may never see. That is not something they can see or take credit for now. They might never know the results of these gifts or be able to measure the outcomes."

"For some that will be enough," Josef said. "There are always those who listen for the voice of God and know when He speaks to their hearts."

"We will see," Vladimir said. "We will see."

Many among the laity he had met with were young. Perhaps, because much of what he told them about their homeland had happened within their lifetimes they could identify with some of it. He had suggested that if they had any relatives in Romania, they speak with them about the orphans. And many of them had children, which could make providing for poor children in a place far away seem more urgent than—he shivered—a vacation in a place where it was warmer than fifty-nine degrees in May.

"You sow, Vladimir. Others have prepared the ground, others must gather the harvest."

"And somehow, Josef, the children must eat, and be clothed, and given shelter."

"The children must have families, Vladimir. You will give those in heaven no peace until then."

"Thank you," Vladimir said. Once again Josef had brought him back to the place where there was no beginning and no end, just his God.

MONDAY, MAY 10—LINCOLN PRAIRIE

Marti and Vik left Lincoln Prairie in separate cars the next morning. Vik wanted to see Dr. Peterson at Northwestern. He was curious about the computer programs that allowed her to get information so fast and equally interested in why they were certain it was accurate.

Marti wanted to check out the earring. She took the Dan Ryan Expressway into the Loop, found a parking garage near Wabash, and walked a block and half to Jeweler's Row. The buildings were ordinary. There were no shops. John Doggett had given her several names and addresses. She had to ring a bell and identify herself to get in to see the first jeweler. He was on the second floor. The stairs creaked and the paint on the walls was peeling. She entered a small room, crowded with chests with narrow drawers and keyhole locks.

The jeweler was a skinny, elderly man with a potbelly. He wore suspenders and baggy pants. There was no jewelry on display. "Aha," he said, as soon as he took a close look at the earring. "Otto Von Weiss."

"Where can I find him?"

"Oh, he's long dead. He was German, died sometime during the Second World War. These little rosebuds within the leafy vine scrollwork are one of his signature designs, part of his earlier work, something he might have done in the thirties."

"Did he come to the United States?"

"Oh no, but it is remarkable that this did. This is only the second time I have seen his work in this country. An elderly Polish woman came in maybe thirty years ago with a ring. 'Keep it,' I told her. 'It will become more valuable with time.' But, she needed the money, so I bought a ring she was wearing. It wasn't worth what I gave her, but as much as I wanted an authentic Von Weiss, I couldn't take it from her."

Marti thought about that for a moment and wondered how Savannah Payne-Jones had managed to get a whole set of Von Weiss's work.

"You are certain that this is an original, not a copy."

"Oh yes. By nineteen-forty his work became more . . . expressive, symbolic perhaps . . . brooches with lilies and necklaces that made you think of fields of red poppies. And look." He picked up the thing he had put to his eye to look at the earring. "Here, take my loupe. Just hold it to your eye."

It magnified the jewelry.

"Now, look carefully at the back, here between this rose scroll and the place where the central jewel is set." She did. "See this mark?"

"I see a little squiggle about a quarter of an inch long."

"That's it."

Without the loupe, she might have thought it was a scratch.

"Von Weiss's family was Prussian," the jeweler explained. "They say that on an old map, this mark is part of the border between Prussia and Belgium. Although he did nothing to call attention to his ancestry it appears that he did choose to acknowledge it."

"And this mark is on every piece of jewelry that he made?"

"Yes, and he preferred to make matched sets."

"You're sure this isn't a good imitation?" Marti suggested.

"Oh no, not given the quality of the gold used in the setting or the stones."

"What are they?"

"Zirconia."

"Why that? It's not expensive, not like diamonds or emeralds."

"No, but that only means Von Weiss was specifically commissioned to make this."

"Could it have been made for an American?"

"Now that is a very good question." He considered it for a few moments. "The political climate in Eastern Europe then was . . . undergoing many changes. But, at that time, Otto Von Weiss would have been a name without meaning in this country. Germany, the surrounding eastern European countries, that is where he would have been known."

Marti realized she didn't know enough to ask any other questions about the jewelry. As for the political climate as far as she was concerned, that was then, this was now. Right now, how Savannah had come to pos-

135

sess the jewelry was not as important as finding out what had become of it. This was a homicide investigation, not a history lesson.

"What else can you tell me about this earring?"

"Oh, perhaps many things, perhaps nothing. The quickest way to find out exactly what you want to know would be to go to the library. Then, when you have more information, you are more than welcome to come back and be more specific. What I am most curious about is Von Weiss's use of zirconia."

"Why?"

"Zircon is an interesting mineral in terms of how it was formed and where it comes from. Some zircon has radioactive elements, thorium and uranium. It's the primary source of zirconium, a metal that is used in ceramics, but is also now used to make parts for nuclear reactors. This zircon was cut from a large crystal that occurs in igneous rock of volcanic origin. There must have been a special reason for putting the zirconia in this setting."

"What if he wasn't commissioned to make this?" Marti asked. "Suppose a member of his family wanted something and since he wasn't getting paid for it, he chose something inexpensive?"

"And put all of this work into the setting?"

"But it is just zirconia."

"It would not have been 'just zirconia' to Von Weiss. Not at all."

When Marti went outside the sun was finally shining,

people were out and about. There was something about walking along a crowded street in the Loop that Marti enjoyed. This was where she grew up. She seldom felt claustrophobic here. She decided to walk to the Harold Washington Library. When she got there, she was directed to a reference section on the fifth floor.

The place was deserted except for an assistant reference librarian, who pointed her in the general direction of the section where she would find something on Von Weiss. To her surprise there were two books just about him and his work.

Marti began with the thickest, two hundred and fifty pages. She assumed it would contain the most complete information. It only took half an hour to find jewelry similar to the earring. It was designed between the time of the Great Depression in America and the Second World War in Europe, a time described as Von Weiss's romantic period. Another thirty minutes or so and Marti knew that although his death was never confirmed, Von Weiss was thought to be a victim of the concentration camps, and although his work still existed, it was scarce and in considerable demand.

The sound of her cell phone ringing startled her. As she reached for it, she looked around, expecting to see some stern-faced librarian admonishing her to be quiet.

"Yes," she whispered, then a little louder, "hello."

"Detective MacAlister, this is Sara."

137

"Are you all right? Is everything okay?"

"Yes. I have not been able to get anyone to go into my mother's condo and get the picture and send it to me. They can go in, they just can't take anything out. I'm sending them a letter today authorizing them to let Akiro in to get the picture. But Akiro won't be back from Arizona for at least another week. He can get it for me then and send it overnight. I'm sorry. I don't have a key. I can't think of anything else to do. If you find her purse, her keys should be in it."

"If we find it you'll be the first to know," Marti told her. The existence of a photograph nagged at her because it remained out of reach. It could just be an unimportant piece of the puzzle. But, if the puzzle wasn't solved soon, the odds were that it would remain unsolved. "Give me a call when you get it."

Sara put in a quick call to Akiro. "I told them you wouldn't be back for another week. They should know who did it by then."

"And if they don't?"

"Then I stay. I can't leave her until I'm sure they're caught and nobody is after me."

"Sara, I don't think they would harm you."

"I'm scared. I won't go home until you're there."

"Okay. But you're sure you don't want them to try to locate or find out what they can about your family?"

"Akiro, if it wasn't something awful, Ma would have told me herself."

"Maybe she really didn't know."

"How do you not know about your parents?"

Akiro said nothing.

"Okay, okay, I don't know anything about my father either. But there has to be something Ma didn't want me to know. I've decided to respect that."

"You've decided to live in fear."

Sara had no answer for that. How could Akiro understand? Every day she asked herself what her grandparents, or one of them, had done. She imagined prison, the electric chair, suicide, an incestuous relationship. Akiro said she imagined the worst, but why would Ma withhold something good?

Marti reached for the second book on Von Weiss, a slim volume with more photographs and larger print. Although the book might not contain more information, it was better illustrated and easier to read. Von Weiss, although German, *was* known in other parts of Europe, especially those countries surrounding Germany. His work was in museums in France and England although he had never traveled that far. And there was a close-up of his mark, the mark that was etched on the earring.

She selected the pages she thought might have useful information or photos, consulted the notes she had taken, and wrote down the book titles and the Dewey decimal numbers on the spines. To that she added a list of questions.

"How did Savannah Jones get this?"

"How would it have reached this country?"

"Black market?"

"Tourists?"

"Who was it made for?"

"Why zirconia?"

That done, she checked through the index without finding any references that might answer some of her questions.

By the time she was ready to leave she was thinking of Ben. Fragmented thoughts: the high rate of prostate cancer among African-American men. Nagging thoughts. She had been in a hurry when she called him at the fire station this morning. She had forgotten to ask him if there was anything special he wanted her to buy while she was in the city. Maybe she should go to that Jewish deli in Skokie and get some "real" bagels, crusty outside, soft inside. She didn't want to worry. She didn't want to pray. What she really wanted to do was scream, "Not again, God. You can't do this to me. Not again."

When she reached the elevators, it was clear that business at the library had picked up. People were waiting to get on. She decided to walk down. She needed the exercise more than she needed the claustrophobic feeling she got in small, crowded spaces. The stairwell was empty, but she could hear the distant voices of an adult speaking and children responding. Momentarily distracted, she went down a few steps, and just as she reached for the banister, felt a pain between her shoulder blades.

• • •

Marti inhaled something that made her nose sting and opened her eyes. A paramedic was leaning over her. Her head hurt. She was lying at an uncomfortable angle, with the small of her back against the edge of a marble stair. When she tried to move the paramedic cautioned her not to.

"Just take it easy, ma'am. Do you know where you are?"

"Stairs."

"Where are the stairs?"

She had to think for a moment. "The library."

"What day is it?"

"Monday."

"What's your name?"

"MacAlister. Detective Marti MacAlister, Lincoln Prairie Police Department."

She tried to open her coat to show him her badge.

"Don't move yet."

"My wrist," she said. It hurt almost as bad as her head.

"I know. You've taken a fall. We need you to stay still while we stabilize your head and neck. Then we'll get you on a stretcher and take you to the hospital."

"My purse?"

"Ma'am, it looks like you've been mugged."

She reminded him that she was a cop.

"Oh! Your gun!"

"Shoulder holster," she said. Only an idiot would come to the city with a gun in her purse. It was

141

jammed against her ribs.

"Do you still have your weapon?"

"Yes," she said. "Earring." She tried to open her jacket enough to reach into her pants pocket.

"Earrings," the paramedic repeated. "Someone will look for them."

"No. Just my purse." She tried to sit up.

"No, no. My partner will look for it."

"Thanks." She relaxed a little, felt drowsy and somewhat disoriented, but at least she knew where she was.

Marti left the hospital with Ben and Allan a little after four o'clock, just in time for rush hour. Ben put the seat back on the passenger side and put a pillow behind her.

"Does that feel comfortable?"

"I'm fine. No, I'm not." She was approaching that ache-all-over stage of recovery from a fall. "But I'll be okay until we get home."

They dropped Allan off at the garage where she had left her car.

"I don't have time for this," she said. The doctor said she had a mild concussion and a sprained wrist. "You can wake me up every two hours," she told Ben. "But Vik will have to be in charge of me staying awake tomorrow."

"The doctor said—"

"I know, and I promise, if I get drowsy, dizzy, sick to my stomach, or have a headache I will go to the

142

emergency room immediately."

Ben sighed. "You did promise him that you would stay in bed for twelve hours."

"And I will," she agreed. "What did you tell the kids?"

"That you were in too much of a hurry to wait for the elevator and tripped rushing down the stairs."

"Good," she said, and closed her eyes.

They were about halfway to Lincoln Prairie when she woke up. The windshield wipers were on, and traffic was still heavy.

"Feeling okay?" Ben asked.

"Can I soak in the hot tub and then sleep for twelve hours?"

"What hurts?"

"What doesn't hurt?" They said they found her halfway down the flight of stairs, but she felt as if she had fallen further than that. Her purse had gone over the banister. It landed in the lobby, alerting the guard who found her. Nothing was missing. Only she knew that everything inside had been rearranged.

"So, was this a routine mugging?"

"No."

"Do you remember more about what happened than what you told the doctor and the Chicago cops?"

"No. I did feel a pain in my back. The doctor said I could have pulled a muscle."

"And? What didn't you say?"

"That somebody could have pushed me. That someone had gone through my purse."

"You will let me know if I should start worrying."

"You've got enough to worry about. We both have. That's what I was doing when this happened. From now on I'll be more attentive to what's happening, or not happening, around me."

Ben chuckled.

"What's so funny?"

"If that ever got out, your big-city, former-Chicago-cop cover would be totally blown." He reached out and touched her with one hand. It was a light touch, and fleeting. "I love you."

"I love you, too." I love you so much, she thought, too much to lose you.

"Be all right," he said, as if he could hear what she was thinking. Perhaps that was what he was thinking, too.

C   H   A   P   T   E   R

18

TUESDAY, MAY 11—LINCOLN PRAIRIE

Marti returned the earring to Evidence before going to roll call the next day. She requested several photos of it, including a close-up of Otto Von Weiss's mark. Vik raised his eyebrows when he saw the Ace bandage wrapped around her left hand and wrist. She mouthed the word "later" and he nodded.

"Wrong shoes for marble stairs," she explained when the sergeant asked her what happened. "I slipped and grabbed the railing." Her hair covered the bump on her head.

"Big Mac," Slim said as she walked into their office. He favored her with a caramel-sweet smile that showed off both of his dimples. "What's the little lady done to her hand?"

She told him the same thing she told the sergeant and didn't elaborate.

"Coffee's brewing," Cowboy said. "I'm trying something new. Tell me if you like it so I'll know not to make it again. You're all too mellow for me this morning."

Vik's wiry salt-and-pepper eyebrows almost met across the bridge of his nose.

"Watch it, Jessenovik," Slim told him. "That came damned close to a smile."

The coffee was delicious. "Yuck," Marti said as she poured her second cup.

Cowboy tipped his five-gallon hat in her direction.

"Tastes like you used sewer water," Vik agreed as he headed back to the coffeepot.

"I finally made something that even the Dyspeptic Duo doesn't like. Looks like I'll have to make it more often."

"Don't make it too often," Vik cautioned. "Three cups of this and I'll need a stomach pump."

As soon as Slim and Cowboy walked out the door,

Vik said, "So, what's this about the earring? You sounded like you were falling asleep when you called me last night. You really think someone was trying to get their hands on it?"

"Yes." She told him what happened.

"You do know it is one hell of a stretch to get from taking an earring to Jeweler's Row to being pushed down the stairs at the Harold Washington Library. Maybe, it *was* a routine mugging and nothing is missing from your purse because there wasn't anything worth taking."

"Look, I agree with you, it is a stretch . . . but . . ."

"But," Vik said. "That's not what your gut says."

"No. My gut says jewelry."

"Okay, I'll go with your gut. We focus on the earring."

Marti pulled out the copies she had made at the library. "Now," she began, "Otto Von Weiss was a jeweler. The first jeweler I went to recognized his work as soon as he looked at the earring. Then he showed me Von Weiss's mark on the back. Von Weiss was Prussian, by the way."

"Old Germany," Vik said. "Did he make this in this century?"

"Probably in the nineteen-thirties."

"In this country?" Vik asked.

"No. Von Weiss never left Eastern Europe."

"Did people from this country go to him?"

"The jeweler said he wasn't that well known outside of Eastern Europe."

"Hmm."

"Right. How did it get here? I have no idea. That's one reason why I went to the library."

Vik got them both another cup of coffee, then asked, "Did Von Weiss survive World War Two?"

"Apparently not. He disappeared in the early forties. There's no record of his death, no grave."

"Prussian." Vik tapped the eraser end of a pencil on his desk. "We could be talking Germany, Hungary, Russia, Poland. Then there's also Auschwitz, Dachau, Buchenwald . . ."

Marti shuddered.

"How old would he be now if he was alive, MacAlister?"

"One hundred and seven."

"That takes care of living somewhere under an assumed name."

"So, find out anything useful yesterday? Other than how to fall halfway down a flight of stairs without breaking anything?"

When she told him, he said, "That's it? Maybe Miss Savannah Jones knew something useful."

"Could be," Marti agreed. In their line of work it wasn't that unusual to learn more from the dead than the living.

Vik leaned back in his chair, clasped his hands behind his head, looked at her for a moment or two, and then said. "Okay. What aren't you telling me? You weren't thinking about an earring when you headed down those stairs, and you're too good a cop to let someone come up behind you and get that close."

Marti considered that. "I was thinking about Ben."

Vik didn't say anything.

She told him about the PSA test results.

"The results of the *first* test," he reminded her. "When did you find out about it?"

"Late last week."

"Why didn't you tell me, Marti?" He put his hand up, shook his head. "You don't have to explain. I've been there with Mildred. The longer you take to say it out loud, the less likely it is to become real. That doesn't make sense, but it's all you've got."

Marti picked up her mug, raised it in a small salute, and drank the cold dregs of the coffee.

C   H   A   P   T   E   R

19

Delilah Greathouse put some letters bound with a rubber band on the coffee table. She pulled down the shades in the living room as if someone would look in and see what she was reading. Then she turned on a lamp and sat on the sofa, avoiding the places where the cushions sagged. The letters had been sent to Tamar from Asher years ago. There were a lot more in the box where she stored them. Tamar received a letter almost every day for at least three or four months. Delilah had never known a man to write like that. She wondered what Asher could think up to say to do that much writing. At first Tamar wrote back almost as often, but by the time she ran away, she wasn't writing him more than once a week.

Asher's letters kept coming after Tamar went away. Delilah never did write to tell him what happened, that Tamar was gone, but Cornelius must have written him instead. The letters stopped coming and Asher never came back. Delilah clasped her hands in her lap and looked at the letters for a while. Tamar went away June 17th. She was doing day work by then and left that Friday morning the same as she always did, wearing her work clothes and carrying a bag with some clothes she could change into after work. It was payday. Tamar always went out with her girlfriends, spent $4.00 on dinner and a movie, or maybe makeup or a new dress, then came home and, except for a few dollars, gave the rest of her money to Delilah. That night she didn't come home. In the morning, when Delilah went to her room, there was a note on her bed. All it said was, "I love you too much to disappoint you, but I cannot marry Asher."

It was a long while before she read Asher's letters. Tamar's wedding day came and went, then Thanksgiving and Christmas. It was New Year's Eve when she took the box of letters off the shelf in Tamar's closet. Tamar hadn't sent so much as a postcard in all that time. Getting those letters down was like closing a book, except there was no way to do that. Tamar was her only child.

The first letter in the stack was the one she showed Cornelius.

Yes honey, I'm taking good care of myself and I'm fully trusting in my Lord and Savior for Strength, health and Joy and peace as he is the giver of all.

There were six or seven of us who took the examination for the Army but none of us made the grade. They called us in like cattle and undress all of us together then we paraded into another room and was examined all together then they looked us over and marked on a slip of paper if there were any ailments. They put on my slip intermittent heart and vericose veins in the legs. Then we had to take that slip to Lieut. Barnos and he asked if I knew what that meant. I said no. Then he said the heart skipped a beat once in a while and that the blood veins in my legs were too large. So he said I don't want to scare you but I'd see a doctor and have that corrected. Anyway now when I get some money coming in I'm going to a Dr. here and have him give me a thorough examination and if there is some ailment, then a correction can be made.

Even though Asher was Cornelius's boarder, Cornelius's wife was barren and he took to Asher like he was his own son. When Asher never returned, Cornelius decided there must have been something seriously wrong with his heart. He really did believe that Asher was dead.

The next letter was one of those she set aside because they showed her how wrong she had been to all but force Tamar into agreeing to marry Asher. She was the one who set the date, not Tamar. Long before she read these letters she knew the marriage would never happen if she waited too long.

Dearest Sweetheart,

I was glad to get your letter of the 4th yesterday morning so I was so glad to hear from you. I am more than please to hear that you got to bed real early on Monday, that's a good, good, girl.

I haven't as yet received any mail from you my sweetheart today yet but maybe I'll get one this afternoon. If I don't I'll be patient until tomorrow and then I'm sure I'll have some more.

Glad to hear the Services are good and that the Lord is present Glad to hear souls are won and that they have Victory in Him. Glad to hear Joe Edwards was present. May we trust the Lord also for his conviction and repentance?

And Tobias feels a little timid. Well poor fellow. God has good use for a Soul that feels unworthy, and if the controls are turned over to the Lord.

So Miss Rand isn't satisfied with the compleckson the Lord gave her. What a woman won't do sometimes in order to make herself attractive to others.

Yes Honey, I'm taking good care of myself, and I'm fully trusting in my Lord and Savior for

Strength, health and joy and peace as he is the Giver of All.

Well Dearie when I think about that I'm all alone I just get sick at heart but I'll soon be with you forever. I don't like to be alone like this. It's just like nothing to live for. I understand now why the Lord gave us women He knew we need a Pal here on earth. And I am so glad He has given Me a Dear Pal and that's only you. You're the only one who can satisfy the lonesomeness in my heart. Well dear I'll close for this time. May the lord bless you and be with you. Take good care of yourself sweetheart.

Delilah knew as soon as she read that letter how wrong she had been about Tamar and Asher. Tamar was not a churchgoing young woman. She went more frequently when Asher was courting her, but she hardly went at all once he left. Tamar liked honky-tonk music and those Delta blues. She could dance for hours without once sitting down. Tamar was not a fast woman. But she enjoyed life, and life, for her, would never be lived in the church.

Delilah also knew why Cornelius, the son of a preacher, wanted so badly to be the father of a preacher as well, if not by birth, then by some kind of adoption. Cornelius had looked at Asher and saw the son he never had, and looked at Tamar and saw the daughter he thought she could become.

As for her, she had married the old man her mother

chose for her, birthed Tamar, and buried him. All what she had left was their girl child, Tamar, so alive, so full of joy, so full of life. And she had feared for Tamar. She was too outspoken, didn't know her place in the white folks world. She was always getting into trouble in school for saying what she couldn't, asking questions what she shouldn't. She did bite her tongue working for that woman who called her "you" and ordered her around like slavery hadn't been abolished, but she got paid for doing that. A little money can seem like a lot when you're young. Tamar had a spirit that had to be stilled before it really got her into trouble. Asher had been the balm she thought would calm the wildness in Tamar's soul. But these letters only proved to Tamar how much he would have bound her soul and so she left.

In her own youth, Delilah had always been an obedient child. She did not understand Tamar's need, not to be bound but to be free. Had they lived in the South she would have feared for Tamar's life. Safer here, she only wanted to protect her from herself until age and wisdom tamed her.

Asher wanted a woman Tamar could never be. It would have been better had she given in to that longing to love Tamar as she was, a filly running free in a pasture without fences. Better for all of them if she had just left well enough alone. Now Delilah would never know the woman Tamar became or what had happened to her as she grew into her grown-up self. Now she had nothing at all.

20

Marti and Vik went to a Dairy Queen drive-through for a late lunch, then met with John Doggett at the museum. The elegant Victorian house dated back to the turn of the century. Marti hadn't been there since John became curator and she was surprised by the changes.

"The last time I was here, everything just kind of filled up the rooms," she said. "Now you've got it so organized that I almost expect the lady of the house to show me into the parlor and ask the maid to serve tea."

John laughed. He was a big man, and moved slowly. His love for things old, his perception of their historical significance showed in the gleam of the furniture and even the way the extra-long drapes were hung so that they pooled on the carpet.

After John showed them around, with obvious pride, he led them to a small kitchen in the rear of the first floor where there was a coffeepot, microwave, and small refrigerator.

"Tea or coffee?"

Something about the place suggested tea and digestive biscuits, but Vik and Marti chose coffee.

"I've found a few pictures and postcards." They were arranged in plastic protectors. "No need to wear gloves when you look at them."

John gave her three postcards first. They were long panoramic shots of the whole block, including the old Geneva. Vik was wrong. They had not made that many changes when it was renovated. Marti could also see the building where the skeleton had been found. There were windows on the second floor. The postcards were postmarked August 1942 and April 1943. In the third postcard, flag-bearing sailors were marching down Geneva Street and the windows were gone. It was postmarked July 1945.

There were five photographs. They were not pictures taken of the building, but you could see at least part of it. A woman was waving from the second floor window in one of them. It was dated July 12, 1943. When Marti asked John if she could borrow it, they compromised. He would have it enlarged if it became necessary. In one photo she could make out the printing on a window that was closed: "Dr. Levine, Dentist." There were four windows in all. In another picture they were gone. The back of that photo was inscribed "D-Day, 1944."

As Marti drove them back to the precinct, Vik said, "Big deal. Now we know the windows were bricked up sometime between July 12, 1943, and June 6, 1944. Now we just have to find out who was renting the place back then. Considering we haven't been able to find anyone as far back as the sixties . . ."

"Not yet," Marti reminded him. "That does not

mean we can't find someone in nineteen-forty-three or forty-four."

At her insistence they stopped at the Lake County Planning Department. Dennis Moisio introduced himself as a third-generation Lincoln Prairie resident. He and Vik swapped stories about when they had Little Fort Days and complained about how much the annual Scoop the Loop had changed. That done, Marti got down to business.

"Let me look through some records for you," Dennis said. "I think we can find that out for you easily enough. It might take a few days, but I'll get on it right away."

Dennis spent another twenty minutes showing them old city maps that were hung in the conference room along with framed photos from the 1890s that hadn't made it to the museum. Vik lingered over one of the city police department, circa 1899, while Marti thanked Dennis for his willingness to assist them.

Lupe and Holmberg were at their desks when Marti and Vik returned to their office. Both were in uniform and looking from their notebooks to their monitors and then keying data into the computers. Holmberg looked up, then doled out a stack of faxes. Otherwise, both uniforms ignored them. Marti checked her watch. They were late getting off shift and had to be catching up on their own paperwork. She looked at the stack of faxes and sat down.

"Copies of the rental contracts from the great-

156

grandson, who sold that building," she told Vik.

"About time," he complained. "He was supposed to send them last Friday."

The documents were in chronological order, beginning with the most recent contract between owner and Realtor for renting the building. Marti flipped through them without enthusiasm. Seven Realtors had handled the rental of the property. They had the information from the most recent. She wrote down the names of the next six. The dates went back to September 1, 1945.

Everything relating to the car hitting the building in 1978 was at the bottom. There was no mention of a second level in any of those reports. She picked up the phone.

The great-grandson's wife answered her call and yelled to him to pick up the phone. Marti identified herself and thanked him for sending the faxes.

"This is everything you have?" she asked.

"That's all of it."

Marti thought for a moment.

"According to our records, your great-grandparents bought the building in nineteen-twenty."

"They didn't trust the stock market. They were getting old, wanted to leave something to my grandfather and invested in that property instead."

"Do you know where your grandfather was between July of nineteen-forty-three and June of nineteen-forty-four?"

"Dead," he replied. "Both he and my grandmother were dead by then."

"And they willed the house to their two daughters. Which one was your mother?"

"Rosie."

"Where were your aunt Rachel and your mother between those dates?"

He laughed. "Right here. I was born here April Fool's Day, nineteen-forty-three."

"Can you check with your Aunt Rachel just to be sure?"

"I'm afraid not. She's still with us, but in spirit only. Alzheimer's. She's the reason I sold the house. Aunt Rachel is healthy as a horse, but she doesn't even know who she is, let alone anyone else. Her doctor says she could last another five or ten years. Selling that building provided me with enough money to make sure she's well taken care of."

Marti thought of the photograph dated July 12, 1943. "Would you happen to have any photos of your mother and your aunt taken in nineteen-forty-three?"

"Sure. I can have my son scan them into the computer if you give me your e-mail address."

She gave him her e-mail address at the precinct and asked him to send them as soon as possible. He assured her that would be tonight. After she called John Doggett and asked him to have his photograph enlarged, she passed the faxes to Vik.

"If Lupe and Holmberg don't get a match on those photos," he said, "we'll be right back to square one."

Lupe swiveled around in her chair until she was facing them. "Anything new on the drowning victim?"

Marti let Vik fill them in on that.

"An eastern European jeweler in the nineteen thir-ties who disappeared in the early nineteen forties," Holmberg said. "There was a lot going on in that part of the world back then."

Vik snapped a pencil in half. "There still is. What else is new?"

"I know, but it was different then. The Nazis were obsessed with art."

"This is jewelry," Vik pointed out. "Looks like something you'd buy at Woolworth's."

Holmberg and Lupe looked puzzled. Marti decided not to date Vik by telling them it was a place also known as the "five-and-dime," a precursor to Target and Kmart.

"When's the last time you went to the Art Institute?" Holmberg asked. "The Nazis had their own ideas as to what was valuable art and what was degenerate art, so they didn't just confiscate personal property. They pil-laged churches, museums, people's homes, you name it, and they decided what they would keep, sell, or destroy."

Vik leaned back, locked his fingers at the back of his neck. Marti could tell he was ready to have a little fun with Holmberg. "That doesn't sound like such a bad thing," he said. "You take those sculptures in Chicago, that bird-looking thing that looks like some nutcase had a bad day. Or that red thing. You get a little steel, bend it a few times, slap on a coat of paint, and call it something weird like 'Oblivious Angles'; somebody decides that it's art and you pick up half a mill, go home and make another piece of crap. People don't know what the hell they're looking at, and spend another fortune trying not to look stupid."

"Vik, Hitler didn't like guys like Monet and Picasso."

"He didn't like Picasso? The guy who thought part of a face upside down, a third of a triangle, and three blobs of paint was art?"

"Luckily, we think Hitler sold most if not all of his work, so not much was destroyed."

"Damn, what a missed opportunity."

"Jessenovik!" Holmberg was becoming annoyed.

Vik came close to smiling.

Marti decided it was time to intervene. "What could have happened to this jewelry?" she asked. "How could it have gotten here, Holmberg?"

"Someone could have bought it here. Or, they could have stolen it."

"Immigrants?"

"Depends. People who were allowed to leave Eastern Europe in those days had to sell or give away everything they had. They literally left with the clothes on their backs and a one-way ticket."

"A ticket to the United States?"

"No. France or possibly England. Someone who was already here would have to sponsor them in order for them to get into the States."

"Could someone have taken this jewelry with them to France, then brought it here?"

"Not likely. Before they were allowed to cross the

borders of their country they would have to have a total body search."

"Suppose some woman just wore it?"

"It would have been taken from her. This was wartime. And from what you've told me, Otto Von Weiss never left Eastern Europe. At least not that we know of. Anyone from that part of the world would have a hell of time getting out, or worse, be considered inferior."

"But it did get here, Holmberg."

"It sure did. Think about it."

She did. "Americans?"

"Soldiers probably," he agreed.

"Captains, generals?"

"There was this group . . . run by the Allies—British and American—" Holmberg thought for a few moments. "I can't remember what they called them. They were supposed to help recover the art that had been stolen. I'm sure there were ways they could pass it along to friends and families. This is all guesswork, but if this Von Weiss never left Eastern Europe, there might be a dozen ways it could have got here. But if it came here between the mid- to late thirties and forties, this is the best I can come up with."

Vik took out a permanent marker, made one black dot on his mug, and said, "If these windows opened, I could toss this out as far as I could throw it, and we could find this piece before we could find a World War Two vet who would admit stealing anything and bringing it into this country."

Holmberg said, "You asked."

"Well, you could have come up with a better answer."

"Can't handle reality, Jessenovik?"

For Marti, this reality meant that if the jewelry played into the death of Savannah Jones, they sure were going to have one hell of a time finding her killer by focusing on it.

"Square one," Vik said.

Marti pulled out the file with everything she had on the Jones case. It was a thin file. "You've got it," she agreed. It was much too thin.

"Now that we've covered the Jones case," Lupe said, "have you got anything for us on the skeletal remains?"

Marti brought them current on their trip to the museum and their visit with Dennis Moisio at the planning department, then they quit for the night.

Marti made it home in time to spend some time with the boys. They were busy with homework, but let her watch as they went on the Internet for information. She always managed to learn something new about computers from them. Tonight it was "bookmarks."

"See, Ma," Theo said. "There are fifty-seven pages of stuff about Brown vs the Board of Education of Topeka, Kansas. I think I might need stuff from about ten pages, so if I bookmark them, I'll be able to go back and get those ten pages."

Marti watched the process and made a few notes, just in case it was something she could use.

"We're reenacting the trial, kind of," Mike explained, "But we have to find out things that could have caused the decision to go the other way and what made it come out the way it did."

Marti thought that was a rather sophisticated project until she recalled that last year in public school the boys were taught there were four parts to the cell and not twenty-eight, or was it twenty-nine?

"I'm doing the closing arguments," Theo explained.

"And I've got the opening arguments," Mike said. "School is fun."

"What makes it so much fun?" Marti asked, remembering when Mike was in elementary school and the class clown.

"We have to think about stuff, not just do it," he explained. "I like having to figure things out."

"School was more fun when it was easy," Theo disagreed. "I didn't have to pay attention all the time."

That was fine for Theo, Marti thought. He was curious about everything. He came home and studied things like the cell on his own. Mike and Joanna were much less ambitious and much more willing to let the teacher determine the requirements. They would meet them, whether high or low, but the notion of independent study was seldom one of their priorities.

Satisfied that everything was okay with the boys, Marti ambled down to the den. Ben was on duty, but they had been spending long, late nights together this week: talking, making love, or just holding each other.

Marti heard the music before she reached the door to the den. Then she noticed the lights were off. She flipped the switch to the ceiling light and stepped into the room. Joanna and Tony sprang apart. Their clothing was not disheveled. Marti considered that a plus. They both looked embarrassed, but like Momma, Marti had no tolerance for that "Ma, you embarrassed me in front of my friends" foolishness.

Marti sat in her recline. She did not lean back. "Nice music," she said. It was something slow. She was sure she didn't want to pay any attention to the lyrics, but the melody was okay. She didn't waste any more time on polite conversation.

"If you two want to be left alone together in this house you will both have to behave responsibly. Joanna, if you don't want to be grounded after school, and would like to be able to stay out until curfew, you will have to behave responsibly. Furthermore, few things in life are accidents. Certain kinds of nonaccidents are less likely to happen with the lights on. If you two are not able to find acceptable things to do together, that probably means you don't have much more than this in common and your time would be more profitably spent making new friends."

She got up, turned off the CD player, turned on both lamps and the television, said, "Joanna, we can discuss this tomorrow," and left.

Momma was upstairs in the kitchen. Marti didn't tell

her what Joanna had been up to. She would take care of that with Joanna when she got home tomorrow. Instead, she made a cup of herbal tea and sat at the table. "What are you getting ready to cook?" she asked.

"I'm making a few changes to that oven-baked French toast recipe I made last week."

"Changes? It was great."

"Well, I thought some pecans with butter and brown sugar on the bottom of the pan might add something to it."

"How early will this be ready in the morning?" It had to be refrigerated overnight.

"How early are you getting up?"

"Crack of dawn, as usual."

"Then there will be some down here waiting for you, child."

Momma made a cup of tea, too, and sat across from Marti at the table. "Ben told me about the results of his test," she said. "He's worried about you."

Tears sprang to Marti's eyes. She didn't speak.

"I don't believe in my heart that anything bad is going to happen to him."

Marti wiped at her eyes. "Did you hold him?"

With certain people Momma had the gift of touch. She could feel sickness and wellness and healing. For as long as Marti could remember, Momma had always been right.

"What did you feel?"

When Momma didn't answer right away, she said, "It is bad, isn't it?"

165

"He's going to be all right, child."

"But something's wrong now."

When Momma didn't say anything, Marti wiped at her eyes and got up and poured more hot water into her cup. "You better tell me," she said when she returned to the table.

"I can feel sickness," Momma admitted. "But I can't feel—"

"Death," Marti said for her.

"It isn't a bad sickness, but he's just not well right now."

Then maybe it was an infection. "Momma, I can't lose him. I can't lose anybody else. These children can't either."

"Oh, baby," Momma said. "You think the Lord don't know that?"

"It's not what He knows, Momma. It's what He allows to happen."

"Then we've got to do some serious talking with Him about this now, don't we."

Momma was silent for a few minutes, then said, "You know, child, twenty-seven men took that test, and eight of them have to be tested again. Ben's the youngest; oldest one isn't but fifty-two. Maybe God is already telling us something. That black men don't have to die young from this, that they got to take better care of themselves like other folk do. Sometimes you can look right at a blessing and not recognize it. I think that's what this is."

"I can't lose him," Marti said again. "I can't."

"Everything happens for a reason, child. We've just got to wait a bit, see what happens and try to figure out why if we can."

Usually, what Momma said was comforting. Tonight Marti just felt afraid and alone.

C   H   A   P   T   E   R

21

WEDNESDAY, MAY 12—LINCOLN PRAIRIE

When Marti walked into the office, Geronimo, her favorite pit bull, rushed over to greet her, tail wagging. Marti wasn't sure if Geronimo was white with brown markings or vice versa. One brown section of fur was shaped like the continent of South America; other parts looked like big paw prints.

"Hi, boy," she said. As soon as she spoke he sat, even though she hadn't told him to.

Vik came in right behind her. To her surprise he squatted down beside the dog and began rubbing and patting him. Not that Vik didn't like dogs, but she could see the effect that Maxie, Mildred's German shepherd, was having on him.

"Good boy. It's good to see you again." Vik held out his hand, said, "Paw," and they shook. Then he looked up at Cowboy. "How come he's here?"

"Vet visit at nine."

"Is he okay? You're not having him neutered, are you?"

"Geronimo had a vasectomy," Cowboy informed them. "Expensive, but he got to keep all of his parts. He has an ear infection now."

Geronimo shook his head with unusual vigor as if to confirm that.

The scent of Obsession for Men announced Slim's arrival. "Where's the coffee?" he wanted to know. Then he, too, bent to pet the dog. "Coming in to work today, huh, Geronimo. Not that I don't see enough of you as it is."

"Did you sweet-talk Lieutenant Lemonface, Slim?" Cowboy asked.

Slim gave him that slow Cupid's-bow smile that revealed double dimples. "I almost charmed the pants off her." It was general knowledge that Lieutenant Nicholson could be charmed by Slim and at least one other attractive detective who served under her command. "She agreed that there is no reason why you shouldn't be here, didn't she, boy?" Geronimo wagged his tail. "After all, we've got canine units, and now we've even got the cavalry."

"Two horses," Cowboy reminded him. "I'd be riding one of those big boys if there was any way those little ladies of the night could live without me and their clients didn't hate my guts."

"Has Geronimo had breakfast?" Slim asked. "They've got doughnuts down in Traffic."

"Been there, tried them," Cowboy told him.

"They're a day old and stale."

"So where's Fred?" Marti asked.

"He hasn't up and got married, has he?" Vik wanted to know.

"He's painting two apartments for me today. I don't know what I'm going to do when he completes those veterinarian assistant courses."

Geronimo, tired out by all the attention, stood up, stretched, shook his head again, and ambled over to the far side of Marti's desk where he could sleep undisturbed.

When Marti checked her e-mail she found the picture of the two sisters, Rosie and Rachel. She was surprised by the clarity. It was black and white. Both women, although not beauties, were attractive. You could see their resemblance to each other immediately. Marti printed off a copy for Lupe and Holmberg, made a notation reminding them who the two women were, and sent the grandson a thank-you note. Five minutes later Marti got a call from Frank Winan. He wanted to meet with them at two o'clock to discuss the Payne-Jones case. Marti agreed, but admitted they didn't have much.

Vik hefted the thin file in his hand. "Damned little here," he grumbled.

"I told Frank that."

They reported to Frank on a periodic basis when they were working one of his cases. It was a lot easier than reporting to the lieutenant. Frank was a real cop.

He hadn't spent sixteen years sitting behind a desk. He had worked the streets, come up through the ranks, unlike Nicholson, whose first three-month patrol assignment lasted six weeks and was her last. Nobody seemed to know why.

When a call came in from Frank Phillips, Marti was so intent on the Jones case notes she had to stop and think for a minute before she remembered the friendly, gray-haired, restaurant owner with the red, white, and blue checked bib apron.

"Old Cal is sitting right here, having lunch," Phillips said. "He might have some information for you. When folks came in last night I made it a point to ask them if they saw anyone or anything in the parking lot last Tuesday night. Everyone who comes in here is a regular," he reminded her. "Cal doesn't seem to know much, but I told him to sit a while just in case there were some questions you wanted to ask him."

Marti thanked him and reached for her jacket. The odds seemed slim, but maybe they would have something for Frank this afternoon. When she and Vik arrived at the restaurant, a dozen pickup trucks were parked outside. Inside, most of the customers were grizzled old men sitting on stools at the counter, smoking and eating. The special of the day was pork butt, boiled potatoes, and cabbage, but they had all opted for burgers with fries piled high and soaked in ketchup.

Marti looked toward the tables in the nonsmoking

section. Four little old ladies with stiffly curled, blue-tinted hair were sitting at the same table they had been sitting at when she came here last week. To Marti's surprise, the jukebox was playing "Don't Be Cruel," and a group of men who looked to be under fifty, wearing business suits, were sitting together in a far corner, plates piled high with fruit and salads.

Frank Phillips, wearing his usual patriotic bib apron, smiled and held up one finger. He pointed to a booth at the far side of the room. Marti and Vik slid into the booth and watched as Phillips ladled soup into bowls, put them on a tray with a basket of rolls, and served the elderly women. On his way back, he gave one of the men sitting at the counter a tap on the shoulder. The man got off the stool. He was wearing faded jeans and a plaid flannel shirt. None of the other men seemed to be paying any attention as he walked toward them.

"These are the folks I wanted you to talk with," Phillips explained. "This is Detective MacAlister and her partner, Detective Jessenovik."

Cal turned back to the bar, picked up his glass of dark pop, came back and slid into the seat across from them.

"I didn't see much," he said. "But I did go over to her and ask if she needed any assistance. When she said no, and just kind of stood there, I figured she was waiting for somebody. So I suggested she come inside out of the rain and watch from the window. She declined, said she wouldn't be outside that long."

"Was she?" Vik asked.

"Outside long?"

Vik nodded.

"I was kind of worried about her being out there by herself like that, so I kept an eye on her. Maybe five minutes after I came inside, a car pulled up."

"What kind of car?" Marti asked.

"One of them little gangster-looking cars that make you think back to the days of bootleg liquor and Al Capone."

"A PT Cruiser," Vik said.

"That sounds right. Silly-looking, if you ask me. I'm not sure if these geniuses go back to old things because they think we'll feel nostalgic or if they just run out of new ideas."

"What color was it?"

"Something dark. I didn't pay much attention after that. I just wanted to be sure the lady was okay. It seemed like she was, since her ride came."

"Did the car have any detailing on it?" Vik asked.

"Nothing that I could see."

"How did she enter the car?" Marti asked.

That stopped him for a moment. His expression suggested that he considered it a dumb question, but was willing to answer it if he could remember. "Well, she just grabbed the handle on the passenger side, opened the door, and got in."

"Nobody got out and assisted her?"

"No. Couldn't tell you who else was inside either. They turned off the headlights soon as they pulled in off the highway. Good way to have an accident, but folks don't think these days. Seems like it would occur to somebody that as fast as other folks drive nowadays, in good weather or bad, they ought to use a little common sense themselves. A lot of stupid accidents happen out there." He nodded toward the window even though there was no view of Route 41 where they were sitting. "No need for them to happen at all if folks would use their heads."

"What time do you think it was?" Marti asked.

"Nine-oh-seven," Cal said.

She didn't bother to ask him why he was so certain of that.

"I checked the clock when I came in," he volunteered. "There were still so many kids here scoffing up spaghetti that I thought my watch must be off. Looked at it a couple more times because I didn't want her to be standing out there alone for too long. Thought she might get stood up and need to call a cab or something."

"Did you get a look at the license plates?"

"Never thought to look. It's one of them things you think about after something happens."

"Not a total waste of time," Vik said as Marti turned the key in the ignition. "A PT Cruiser is a little more noticeable and memorable than a Saturn. Too bad we couldn't get anything on the license plate."

Back at the precinct, they checked through their notes.

"About the only thing I can come up with," Marti said, "is that we put out a bulletin asking if any of the police or fire personnel working in the vicinity of that bridge and that forest preserve noticed a PT Cruiser."

"Unlikely," Vik said.

They kept reading, seeking something they had missed or overlooked.

"The only witnesses we have are the cab driver and Cal," Marti commented. "And the only physical evidence we have is that piece of hairnet found at the bridge and one earring." Once again, she went through the Xerox copies of what she had on Von Weiss. "Simplest scenario: a soldier brought this back when he came home from the war."

"Why not," Vik agreed. "They brought home German Lugers, live grenades, and venereal disease. The problem with that, Marti, is that we don't know enough about Jones's background to begin looking for a soldier, not to mention the fact that survivors from that war are becoming scarce. If one of them did bring this back, the odds are good that he's dead by now. Sara's grandparents are dead."

"I can't see any way to trace it back that far," Marti agreed.

Marti let Vik drive to their meeting with Frank. She got out her cell phone and punched in Mark Dobrzycki's private number.

"Savannah Payne-Jones is clean," he told her. "But she was an actress. However unimportant she may seem, sometimes those are just the people you're looking for. They can be couriers, carriers, mules, whatever. So I've got a list of all the movies she appeared in, however briefly, and a list of everyone else involved in each film, from actors to producers to lighting and sound technicians, repairmen, hairdressers, wardrobe, you name it. Luckily she did most of her later work on location. At least I think it might be a bit of luck. Authenticity and accuracy aren't at the top of the list of most B movies. They shoot most of their stuff on a set. We're running all of the names we've come up with through our systems. We'll get some hits and we'll follow up on them, see if and how Jones's name pops up and check that out first."

"You're actually going to investigate this?"

"Sure. Even if Jones comes up clean, it's like trawling the bottom of a cesspool. You never know what you might catch. And, what makes it even better, if we do come up with anything, no matter how remotely it's connected to Jones, we've got a valid reason for looking."

"Do you know something I don't?" Marti asked.

"Not yet. Filmdom is just one of those industries where all things are possible, and you've presented us with something we can use to justify a routine dredging operation."

"Sounds like a lot of work."

"No, it's just a matter of someone who knows his way around a few computer programs working with someone who knows what he's looking for when he reads the data. Piece of cake. Might take a day or two, though. This lady was in a lot of films to remain so unremarkable. Her parts were so ordinary she might as well have been invisible. That in itself makes her a perfect choice for certain types of covert criminal activity."

"Well," Vik said, after Marti hung up and repeated Mark's side of the conversation. "Maybe this will turn out to be one of those cases that makes national head-lines," he mused. " 'Obscure actress unmasked as Mafia boss of major international drug cartel.' And, when you think about it, the way Lieutenant Lemon-puss went off over a picture of you and Ben on the first page of Section Two of the local newspaper, something like that could push her right over the edge."

"Or push me right out of a job."

"Not with that kind of publicity."

"Not to worry, Jessenovik, nothing like that is going to happen."

What Marti was thinking about as she said that was how women, particularly those with rank, were still viewed within the department. She didn't have any sympathy for Nicholson, but if she were a male, there wouldn't be any sexual innuendos or comments about her ability to manage stress, no "Lemon" nicknames, not to mention the humor associated with under-mining or circumventing her authority.

Not that Lieutenant Nicholson bothered to do any-thing to improve those perceptions. Marti had worked hard and long to earn the nickname Big Mac. When someone called her that, it wasn't sarcasm, it was a compliment. She had gotten past the "that time of the month" comments, the question of whether or not she was capable of handling the job. She had made it easier for a woman to be accepted as a cop, and without saying much of anything. Now along comes Nicholson tearing that down, making it that much harder for another female to get rank or command.

Marti didn't want to be a lieutenant, because she didn't want a desk job. She wanted to be what she was, a homicide detective. As difficult as her current major cases seemed to be, there was a lot of truth to be found in the "thrill of the chase." She couldn't imagine anything else giving her the high she got from actively investigating someone's death, as morbid as that might sound. Nicholson had no way of knowing that, but even so, she had no business acting this way. It was like Momma said—"Someone has to make the footprints so others can walk in them." Marti didn't think any female officer would be given what Nicholson had been handed. Not anytime soon. As it was they had brought her in and not promoted from within.

The Regional Task Force offices were located in a two-story building. It sat alone, a conspicuous red brick on what was otherwise rural and still underdeveloped land in the northwest quadrant of Lake County. A dozen cars were parked behind it. Vik pulled up alongside the red BMW Frank drove when his wife let him and he wasn't trying to remain anonymous in a gray Honda.

The building still smelled of fresh paint. Marti and Vik had an office, but since Frank still wasn't sure if this would be a permanent or temporary location, the only thing they had done besides having computers installed was hang a calendar.

"Coffee?" Frank asked when they walked into his office. He had a great view of a large field slowly changing from black loam to green sprouts. Some farmer had planted something neither Marti nor Vik could yet identify.

"Black with a spoonful of sugar," Vik said when the secretary came in, speaking for both of them. Frank had explained that his first criteria for hiring a secretary was that she could think on her own and the second that she could make decent coffee. This lady's coffee was almost as good as Cowboy's.

Marti and Vik had several cups while they brought Frank current. As promised, there wasn't much to tell. Cal's observations and Mark's did beef things up a bit, but it wasn't that helpful at this point.

Frank stroked his graying handlebar mustache for a minute, looked over their reports, then said, "Well, I don't think you're standing still on this one. You've found out quite a bit about the woman, which includes not knowing a hell of a lot more because there's not much more that's easily accessible." He thought again, this time stroking gray hair back from a receding hairline. "Sounds like a quick trip to L.A. could be in order."

"Who's going?" Vik asked.

Winan leaned back and chuckled. "Who do you think?" He opened a drawer and pulled out two folders and handed one to each of them. "Now, here's airline confirmations, itinerary, hotel reservations, and your task forces credit cards, charges on which you are strictly accountable for." He pointed toward the wall. "She's not an accountant, but she believes the IRS lurks everywhere.

"Now, your flight leaves O'Hare at seven tonight and you arrive a few minutes past ten Pacific time. An L.A. lieutenant, Julie Webber, will meet you at LAX and see that you get into the condo. This schedule assumes that you'll search the place and catch some shut-eye. If you find anything, you might want to sleep on it. The lieutenant will see to it that you do whatever you have to. If you can't make that noon flight back, just reschedule."

Marti went through the contents of her travel folder. This was the first time she had ever been sent halfway across the country to work on a case. Vik just sat there. Finally he cleared his throat. "Sir, Lieutenant Nicholson . . ."

"Right," Frank said. He looked up at the wall clock. "You've got just about enough time to go straight home, spend a little time with the family, and pack. Don't worry about Lemonpuss or Lemonface or whatever they're calling her now. I'll give her a call as soon as you leave. If you need anything from the office, have Lupe Torres or Brian Holmberg pick it up and bring it to you."

As soon as they were heading for the front door, Vik said, "Jeez, he even knows her nickname."

Marti smiled. She'd seen enough political games to know this trip might be a necessity, but a nice side benefit was that it would let Nicholson know who was in charge.

Dinner was almost ready when Marti got home. She told Momma about the trip, called Ben at the fire station, then explained to Mike, Joanna, and Theo. Momma speeded up dinnertime by making biscuits instead of waiting for the yeast rolls to rise. Marti would have just enough time to talk with Joanna and get ready to leave.

It was Theo's turn to say the blessing. Marti reached for the biscuits and insisted on butter, not liquid margarine. Joanna had made what Marti thought was a vegetable casserole that she had eaten a few times before and didn't like. Usually Joanna's recipes did improve over time, but tonight this one didn't even smell good. Marti tried not to frown when she tasted it. Without looking too closely, she identified chopped broccoli, sliced carrots, and spaghetti squash, which would have been bad enough. A lack of seasoning made it even worse.

"Do we have to eat this?" Theo asked.

"Do we?" Mike echoed.

"No," Marti decided.

Momma nodded agreement.

Marti got them busy dishing up the tossed salad and found a package of frozen hamburgers in the freezer.

After dinner, Marti followed Joanna to her room. She pushed aside the clothes piled on her unmade bed and sat down. "Now," she said, "I don't have much time before my flight leaves, and this can't wait, so let's talk. That is the first thing you have ever cooked that I absolutely could not wrap my tongue around without throwing up."

Joanna sat on the floor near the closet, which was as far away from Marti as she could get. "I think I forgot to put in a few things."

"That's not like you either, nor is what was going on last night."

Joanna looked down at her sock-covered feet and watched her toes wriggle. Marti could see that something was troubling her so she waited.

After almost a minute of silence, Joanna said, "I know about Ben. He has cancer."

"He doesn't know what he has. The doctor doesn't know. I don't know. So how do you know?"

"Someone told me. She knows someone who saw the test results for the prostate cancer test."

Marti knew that "someone who knows someone" meant that one of Joanna's church friends knew someone involved with the testing who either had a big mouth or was careless about what she left lying around. She went over and sat down beside Joanna. After a few moments, tears began streaming down Joanna's face.

"We lost Daddy," she said after a few minutes of silent crying.

"I know," Marti answered. She took Joanna into her arms and rocked her. "I know, baby. I know."

"What do we do? And don't say 'pray' like Momma would."

"We wait," Marti said. She explained about the second test.

"And if his count is still up when he takes the second test?"

"We wait again."

"And if he's going to die?"

Leave it to Joanna to ask aloud the question she couldn't even bring herself to think about. "I don't know."

Joanna pulled away from her. "You have to know. You have to. If you don't, what will the rest of us do?"

"We will be a family, Joanna. We will lean on each other, cry on each other's shoulders, we will not be afraid to smile or laugh, or live. We will shed many tears and continue to make memories we can all hold on to. Remember how Johnny used to dance with you?"

Joanna smiled through her tears. "He would bow and take my hand and we would waltz."

"Yes. Even when you can't touch someone, you can see and hear and remember him. You will not run to the arms of a boy who cannot feel as you feel, or love who you love, who cannot give you the comfort that we will give each other as a family."

Joanna sniffled, picked a T-shirt from the pile of clothes on the floor, and used it to blow her nose. She sat very still her with head on Marti's shoulder. Eventually she said, "Did Momma touch him?"

"She feels something," Marti admitted. "But she doesn't feel death or dying. Sickness maybe, and maybe for just a while. That wasn't of any comfort to me, so it might not comfort you. But I believe Momma does have the gift of touch with some people and I believe in what she feels when she touches them. And I trust her to tell me the truth. And so do you."

"Everybody thought Mother Loomis was going to die," Joanna said. "Momma put her arms around her and said she felt healing."

"And that was almost six years ago," Marti added. "Mother Loomis is ninety-two years old now and still sound of mind and body."

She stroked Joanna's hair, held her close, and marveled that this child in search of peace and hope could give those gifts to her.

22

Marti loved to fly at night. Being in an airplane gliding through the darkness was almost like turning the world upside down and looking down at the stars instead of up. It was only the alignment of streetlights when they were above traffic that made the difference. She liked the real sky better, with an order that wasn't as obvious, but she looked down until the city was behind them. The last thing she remembered was the darkness surrounding them and a few wispy clouds.

Vik shook her awake. "Los Angeles," he said. She had fallen asleep without unfastening her seat belt.

Lieutenant Julie Webber was a tall woman, heading toward plump but not there yet. She wore her hair in a short, easily managed cut, dark brown with natural gray highlights. She smiled and held out her hand as she came toward them.

"Welcome to Los Angeles. How's Frank?"

"Just fine," Marti said, and added, "A good man to work for."

"That he is," Webber agreed. "I worked under him for twelve years before I moved out here to help take care of my parents." She guided them along the concourse as she spoke. "He spoiled me for any other boss, but he also taught me what a good boss was, and how to put up with the . . . you know."

"We sure do," Vik and Marti agreed.

The condo Savannah Payne-Jones lived in wasn't more than a fifteen-minute ride from the airport. It was unlike anything Marti had seen before and Julie Webber had to explain the layout.

From the outside it looked like it was built atop a hill, but when Julie keyed in the password and the gate swung open, they rode to the top of the hill, drove around to a unit in the back, and entered through the kitchen. Vik scooped up the mail that was scattered on the floor, and put it into a plastic evidence bag.

Stairs led down to the living room, with a cathedral ceiling, two long windows with small balconies overlooking the street and the city. Everything, walls, furniture, carpet, was white. They went down another flight of stairs and found a small hallway with a bedroom and a large bath. There were no windows.

"Basically we're more or less underground now," Julie explained. "Think of a hill, cut it in half and haul away the dirt. Build two stories at the top and put two stories along the side and you've got it." Half a level further down there was a washer and dryer. There was a master bedroom with a huge walk-in closet and a bath at the bottom level. Marti thought of the side of the hill they were facing and felt claustrophobic.

"What if there's an earthquake?" she asked. Suddenly all of the news footage of mudslides carrying houses along for miles came to mind.

"We try not to think too much about things like that."

"The builders sure as hell don't give it any thought," Vik commented. "And the buyers have a death wish."

They decided to begin the search here.

"I'll just relax," Julie said. "If you two don't know just what you're looking for now, you will if you find it."

Marti shot half a role of color film and one in black and white before she and Vik began a methodical search. Jones was an orderly person. Her clothes and shoes were separated and hung by type and color. Marti turned out all of the pockets, kept the matchbooks, and put the Kleenex in a plastic evidence bag in case someone decided later that they should check for DNA. Even the lingerie and underwear were sorted that way when Marti went through the drawers.

Prescriptions for an antidepressant and antianxiety medication were in the medicine chest. Marti took all soiled undergarments out of the hamper and put those in another plastic bag. She found several boxes of condoms in the nightstand by the bed. Marti saved the jewelry box for last. Jones had some very nice modern, expensive pieces. Marti identified a ring with a well-cut diamond solitaire and matching earrings, a genuine pearl necklace, a real emerald pendant, and a collection of crystal jewelry, some of which looked antique, all of which she was certain were made by identifiable craftsmen.

"Whatever the value of the Von Weiss pieces," she commented, "Jones has stuff in here worth a lot more."

"Sentimental value," Julie murmured.

Vik came over to where they stood. He had a bag filled with his personal, favorite source of information, Jones's papers.

Marti listed and bagged all of the jewelry and they began the journey upstairs. Uphill, Marti thought, and shivered in spite of herself at the thought of all that dirt collapsing before they reached the kitchen.

The washer and dryer were empty.

"Well, well," Vik said when he opened the top drawer of one of two dressers. He called Marti over to snap a few photos, then took out and bagged an old sepia photograph in a pewter or silver frame. That was the only item they found in the room. The bed was made, two lamps turned off, one with no lightbulbs, the closets and bureau drawers were empty. Marti continued to photograph everything.

When they reached the living room she felt an overwhelming sense of relief. Then she went to one of the windows, looked down the hill at the steady flow of traffic and thought about the possibility of the earth shifting beneath them. Her stomach felt queasy. That hamburger for supper, she decided, but she knew it wasn't that.

Julie Webber took them to a restaurant that served seafood. Marti had lost her appetite at home hours earlier but enjoyed a bread bowl filled with clam chowder. Vik, who hadn't been exposed to Joanna's questionable cuisine and didn't seem affected by the possibility of an earthquake or mudslide, ordered the surf and turf and ate with gusto.

When she was alone in her motel room, which was not only on the first floor, but built on level ground that was nowhere near any huge earth mounds, Marti took out the framed photograph. The frame was pewter, heavy. The dull finish complemented the muted gray, black and white of the photograph. The man was standing, but leaning toward the woman. He wore a wide-brimmed fedora that created shadows along the hollows of his face. Both were light-skinned enough to pass for white.

Marti wished she could tell the color of the woman's eyes. They were light, but were they that shade of brown that Sara and Savannah Jones shared? The woman sat with her hands clasped in her lap. Her face was more animated than his was. Her mouth was compressed as if she wanted to burst out laughing. Marti caught a hint of mischief in her eyes. Her dress was modest, almost. The bodice was tight and there was just a glimpse of her breasts where it buttoned down the front. There was just the slightest tilt of her chin. Posed together as they were, leaning toward each other, looking intently at each other, but not touching. There was something about the photo that, to Marti's eye, exuded a subtle but distinct sexuality.

The back of the photo slid right off; beneath was the usual piece of cardboard. When Marti pulled that out she found a letter. The paper was unlined with many creases and brown with age. It was written in black ink, the handwriting slanting downward and easy to read. When she unfolded the paper she could see that someone had balled it up, then smoothed it out, causing most of the creases. Curious, she read:

My Dearest Sweetheart,

Your letter of Sunday was received this after-noon. I am glad to hear you are well and taken care of, but I don't know if I like so much that you keep such late hours. And your mother and aunt are worse aren't they. You all have gotten quite bad since I left, haven't you. Haven't you a guilty conscience tho? I'll bet you have. Maybe when I come to Lincoln Prairie again you will look so tired and played out that I'll be disappointed in you or will I find my darling girl and just as pretty as a daisy? Well we'll see.

It certainly is drawing nigh unto the time when our Lord will come to call his own, as everywhere there seems to be such strife and discontentment. Of course the harvest is plentiful for all His chil-dren to work hard but it seems that so many of His children are hanging on the hoe handle, so to speak, and only waiting for their time to receive their pay. It must Grieve our Lord to see so many that are careless and wandering. I trust dear hear that both of us may be so in love with our Lord that we may ever be ready to go where He Wants us to go and . . .

Both sides of the paper were covered. Page two stopped here. Marti read it again. There was no date on the letter or the photograph. When she was finished reading she wasn't sure who the letter was written to, but she was certain that if it was the woman in the snapshot, the man standing beside her was not the man who had written it.

C H A P T E R

23

PITTSBURGH, PENNSYLVANIA

There was something about cities in the Untied States at night that Vladimir liked. Perhaps it was just that he didn't know enough about the places he visited and his stay was too short to recognize the underbelly that came with darkness. In Bucharest, he knew there were adults as well as children who scavenged and stole, committed all manner of crime. He knew that happened here as well. But he didn't know Pittsburgh as intimately, as personally as he knew Bucharest. Further, he could do nothing about anything that happened here. He often could not do much more in Bucharest, but he did not have the same sense of failure or feel the same responsibility for it here as he did there.

Again Vladimir walked with Josef and Nicolae.

"Ce mai facet?" Nicolae asked.

"I am fine," Vladimir answered. "All is well."

The streets were well lit, just as in Toronto, and this was also the business district. But, here the streets were littered and the poor and the homeless, the drug addicts and alcoholics, did not scurry into the alleys and out of the way places. They loitered in plain sight along the sidewalk and in doorways.

Nicolae was fearful in these streets and kept close. Josef, like Vladimir, felt that God protected and God permitted and would do both now, just as He did every other moment of their lives. Vladimir thought they must look like foreigners to the vagrant population, for nobody approached them. They made their way without being accosted to the street where the bridges began. Three of them, all crossing one of the rivers that surrounded Pittsburgh on three sides.

"There is something about this country, these cities, that I like," Vladimir admitted. He could not identify what it was. The open face of poverty perhaps. The lack of perfection, perceived or real. "There is something normal about this place. Not right, but normal."

"Perhaps this is the human condition that we speak of so often," Josef mused. "Perhaps it does not put on faces, pretending to be what it is not. It seems certain that those who want to help these chosen poor of God know their limitations and do not rail against what

191

they cannot do, but persist in doing the good that they can."

"And equally certain that those who chose blindness remain blind," Vladimir said.

"Those you have spoken to at the churches so far have not given us promises, Vladimir. They have given us specific pledge amounts. They have given us checks."

"Because they can feel the hunger, Josef. The cold. Because these people are here on the street day and night where they can see them. The poor we have with us always. Here, you can see the poor all around you, and smell them and even avoid them, but there is no way you cannot see them if you come into the city. If you work for the corporation or the bank or the restaurant or clean at the hotels, you see them always. And, there are those who know that they could become like those they see."

"They try to keep us from seeing this side of the city, Vladimir. But there is no way to do that, is there? They take us to the homes surrounded by grass and sheltered by trees, where all is clean and well kept. And still we come here and we see. Is poverty worse here than it is in Romania? We are a poor country. We think of the United States as a rich country. Yet we see this. Is that why the people we visit, who do not live near this, call the places where they live gated communities?"

"If so, Josef, that is good in its way. But only if there is someone who calls their attention to what the gates

192

close off. I think there are many who live in these gated places, yet must come into the city and see these people who live on the street. I believe there are those who see and care and do what they can."

"And woe to those who do not," Josef said. "Although we would be stoned and cast out if we told them that."

"I trust more in the pledges and promises of those who can see poverty than those who look away," Vladimir admitted. "The sharing will be greater here than in those places where there is no want."

"Strange, isn't it," Josef replied, "that we expect a greater harvest from those who are poor themselves than from those who have much."

They walked halfway across the bridge. Vladimir looked back where they had come from, Pittsburgh, a city he had a walking acquaintance with, then to the city at the far side of the bridge. A city whose name he did not know. A city he had not and might not ever visit. A city whose streets he most likely would never walk at night. Unlike Bucharest, it was also a city that did not need his reminders of poverty or charity. For a moment he felt that weariness that comes not with physical effort but with this thing he prayed about daily, but could share with few.

He was glad that it was Josef who weighed and made such decisions as to where they must go. There was little good he could do in the world save by his presence and his encouragement and supplication—begging, as Josef often rightly called it. Even that responsibility often seemed more like a burden than a gift. It would be worse if he had to decide where to beg.

Vladimir put his arm around Josef's shoulders, then around Nicolae's. "Do not be afraid," he said to Nicolae. "Despite our best intentions and worst efforts, time goes on, life goes on, the world suffers and rejoices and goes on."

Smiling, he turned toward Pittsburgh. The land of the free, he thought. Then what is freedom?

C H A P T E R

24

THURSDAY, MAY 13—LINCOLN PRAIRIE

It was one twenty-three Chicago time when the Boeing 737 Marti and Vik were napping in touched down. They picked up Vik's car and drove directly to the precinct. As soon as Marti dropped off the evidence bags she brought back from Los Angeles, Lieutenant Nicholson's secretary was right at her elbow.

"She wants to see both of you right away."

This time there was no three-minute wait. The lieutenant was standing by the window with her back to them. She turned, arms folded. "You are both on report for an unauthorized absence and leaving this jurisdiction without the knowledge or consent of your immediate superior."

"We were working the task force case," Vik volunteered.

Marti said nothing. Behind her back, her hands were clenched into fists.

"Let's get this straight right now," the lieutenant said. "We play by my rules. Nothing, I repeat, nothing happens around here without my knowledge and my consent."

"Frank Winan . . ." Vik began.

"Frank Winan be damned. You two are suspended from duty until further notice and that includes all Lincoln Prairie and all task force responsibilities."

"Oh no," Marti said. "We are not going there today. We do not owe you anything but courtesy when we're working a task force case. And since you don't have enough home training to show me any respect, I don't feel obligated to tell you shit, nor do I intend to." Marti took a step toward the lieutenant, and Nicholson stepped back. "You're afraid of me," Marti said. "I scare the hell out of you, don't I? You've sat behind a desk your entire career while I was out there working the street." She took another step forward.

Nicholson took another step back and then she was against the window and could go no further. "Why . . . why . . . you . . . you—"

"Back against the wall, Lieutenant? Cornered? Don't know how to get out? That's what we're here for. *To save your sorry ass.*" Marti punctuated each word by jabbing her finger into Nicholson's chest. "Remember that when you're writing us up."

With that Marti turned on her heel and walked out. Vik was right behind her.

"She *was* scared," Vik said, when he caught up with her. "She's a cop and she was backed into a corner and didn't know how to get out." He sounded incredulous.

"That's because she's never been in one before," Marti said. "It's called on-the-job experience."

As they passed the secretary's desk, she gave them a thumbs-up.

The sergeant waved them over. "Looking good, Big Mac," he said. "Looking good." He gave her a copy of the *News-Times*. There were pictures of her and Ben in uniform on either side of the headline. She couldn't remember Ed's exact questions or how they answered them, but the interview was about the two of them as a husband-and-wife team. They spoke of their family life, but didn't allow any photos. Their jobs were peripheral.

"Thanks," Marti said. "I appreciate this." Her hand was steady as she accepted the newspaper, but she was still mad as hell.

"We appreciate you," the sergeant said. "Both of you. And you earned this one, Big Mac." He tapped the edge of the *News-Times* with his fingertip.

The office was empty when they opened the door. Marti felt as if she had been away for a week instead of one day. There was no coffee aroma. Her in-basket was overflowing. She put down her briefcase, gave the spider plant the last of what was in the coffeepot, spread the newspaper on her desk, and checked the date.

"Hot off the press," Vik said. He put the bag filled with Jones's mail and papers on his desk, then looked over her shoulder. "No wonder the lieutenant had her shorts in a bunch."

The article was on the third page of the weekly family section. Between the formal photos of her and Ben in uniform, Marti read, "Not your Typical Couple, Not Your Typical Blended Family." A brief recap of how they became widow and widower concluded with "their initial professional respect, although not love at first sight, became a lifetime commitment to each other and their children."

Then there were the typical questions. She worked long hours, and sometimes seven-day weeks. Ben worked in shifts, forty-eight hours on, forty-eight hours off. How did the family handle that? "My mother," Marti had responded. "She's always there for all of us. And friends, church members, sometimes someone we work with. And, we get a lot of support from both departments, and especially our partners."

Ben added, "Communication. That and making sure we are participating in our children's lives and activities. One way or another, they always have a parent or adult available for school, church, sports, and recreational activities."

Ed Gilbreth added brief comments from Vik: "She's my partner. We're cops. We're always there for each other." Ben's partner, Allan: "We're all family. We take care of each other." Deputy Chief Dirkowitz, formerly their lieutenant: "MacAlister is an outstanding member of this department. When you work this closely together and so much depends on your partner and any other officers involved in a given situation, the closeness, the concern, the respect, the dependability have to be there." Ben's fire chief: "In both the fire and the police department, one person's life can depend on someone else at any time. They always have our complete support." And their pastor: "As a church, as a community, we have to respond to the challenge of being the village that raises the child."

"Not bad," Marti admitted, pleased and also noting that there was no comment from Nicholson. She called Ben. "Seen the newspaper?"

He laughed. "Seen it—I've got twenty-five copies of it and one of them is framed and ready for hanging."

They talked for a few minutes, and Ben suggested that she and Vik meet him at a local restaurant for before-dinner drinks. "I got that promotion."

"Yes!"

"And I feel like celebrating," he explained.

Marti thought about the second PSA test come Monday, and the possible results. "Sounds like the best offer I've had all day."

"And be sure to bring Vik along."

"Don't worry, he's already nodding his head and he doesn't even know what we're talking about."

Vik took the newspaper from her before she could

fold it. "Belongs someplace else," he told her. He found some scissors and cut out the article; then he fastened it to the wall. "This must not have made the lieutenant too happy either." He was silent for a moment, then said, "Looks like we declared war."

"I did."

"No, *we* did. As much as you want to take her on alone and as much as I'd like to watch, we are partners."

Marti gave him a big hug. "Thanks. I know you're always there for me. It's just that I'm the one she has it in for, not you."

"She isn't going to let go of this one, Marti. And win, lose, or draw that will not make her any easier to live with."

"Maybe she will," Marti said. They both knew the scent of fear, but Vik had not been standing close enough to Nicholson to smell it.

Vik rubbed his hands together, opened the evidence bag, dumped everything on his desk, and settled in to begin sorting through the Jones papers.

Marti took everything out of her in-basket. Vik had the largest pile. There were no forensic reports. She did have six "while you were out" messages with names and phone numbers written on yellow paper, but no messages. She sighed as she picked up the phone. She'd had a hard time getting to sleep in L.A., strange bed, and strange room. The adrenaline high from dealing with the lieutenant was wearing off and she was beginning to feel exhausted.

Mark Dobrzycki had called at nine fifteen this morning. Damn. She meant to call him from LAX.

She punched in his private number.

"Yeah, Dobrzycki."

"Yeah, MacAlister."

"Did you find anything useful in L.A.?"

"Just an old photograph I was looking for."

"We didn't find anything useful."

"Oh." She didn't bother to ask why he hadn't told her the FBI had already tossed the place. "When did you go in?"

"Before you did."

"What did you take out?"

"Nothing. We have this little camera that takes pictures of documents. That photo was the only thing we found that could be of interest."

Marti didn't ask about that either. "Find out anything I should know about?"

"Not yet."

"Mark, you will let me know if you do."

"Of course," Mark told her.

Sure, Marti thought, just like you let me know you tossed the place before we did.

As soon as Marti hung up, she said, "Maybe bringing Mark in on this wasn't such a good idea. If he does find out who did it, he's not going to give him up unless and until the Bureau gives the okay." She had been hoping Mark would make it easier to find some peripheral person with a grudge or an ordinary motive. Mark was thinking Mafia, drug cartel, and other major crimes. "If he does catch our subject, I think he'll at least let us know that much. If it's a small catch, he might even let us have him. In fact, if they need to talk to whoever did this, letting us arrest him for the homicide would open the door for them to question him without creating any suspicion."

"Ever work with him before?" Vik asked.

"Yeah."

"What's the score so far?"

"Three out of four."

"That's not bad when you're dealing with the Feds."

"I had to wait until the third one walked out of a federal prison before I could arrest him."

"Better to wait for a sure thing than be where we are now."

Marti stood up and stretched. "Is it your turn to make coffee or mine?"

"I've got it." Vik was out of his chair and heading for the coffeepot before she could fake a protest.

Sara Jones had called. Marti hesitated, decided not to mention their trip to L.A., and picked up the phone. She apologized for not calling sooner.

"Have you found out anything about why my mother died?"

"We're working on it."

"Can I take her home soon?"

Marti shuffled some papers and pulled out the coroner's jury schedule. "It goes before the coroner's jury next Tuesday. You should be notified as to date, time, and place. I'll see what we can do about it then. Can you stay here that long?"

"I'm not going anywhere without my mother."

"And otherwise everything is okay?"

"Yes."

"Is there anything else I can do?"

"Just find out why she died. Please." Sara sounded like she was crying.

Vik turned on his computer and checked his e-mail. "Not a word from Lieutenant Lemonpuss," he said. "I'm going to go ahead and send her today's reports. I think you should, too."

Marti thought about that for a few minutes. Then she turned on her computer. There was nothing from the lieutenant for her either. "Why bother," she said.

"You're right," Vik agreed. "I'll just type something up and send it to her twice, one from each of us."

"Sounds good to me." Even as she spoke, Marti realized she really didn't care.

C H A P T E R

25

Sara began crying as soon as Akiro walked into the pastor's living room and the pastor's wife left, closing the door behind her. He held her, rocking back and forth. "I am here. I am here," he whispered, smoothing her hair.

When she felt calmer she said, "Do you think they know? Could they have found out?"

"I think someone would have been arrested or something would have happened by now if they did."

"I can't go back until I know. What if they come after me?"

"Sara, Sara, we are talking about a gambling debt. The worse that could happen is that they could make *you* give them the money."

"If they killed her, Akiro, they have to think I know who it was."

"Why don't you just tell the police? Then they can catch them."

"Akiro, do you know how often my mother gambled? She gambled everywhere she went, even if it was just a poker game with the people she worked with. She won big. She lost big. I have no idea of where she lost this money, when, or who she owes."

"Then how do you know she owed someone money?"

"Because I know my mother."

"What makes you think they would kill her over the money? That doesn't make sense to me." Sara shook her head.

"I don't know. Why else would she be dead? It wasn't an accident."

"Think, Sara, think. Dead people can't pay gambling debts. You said she won and she lost. If she was a habitual loser and ran up huge debts that she couldn't pay off, killing her might make some sense. But she also won and paid off her losses. Killing her because of a gambling debt does not make sense." He held her away from him. "Please, Sara, tell the police. You are safe here. Stay until they find out who these people are and talk to them. Please."

"Maybe. We'll see. Let me think."

"What do they know so far?"

"That she had that sentimental jewelry she always insisted on wearing for luck. It's missing, except for one earring. And there was no way she would part with it voluntarily. She believed it was what brought her luck."

"And?"

"They still want a picture of my grandparents that's in her condo. Akiro, she didn't even look at it. It's in a drawer in my room." She began crying again. As soon as she moved into her own place Ma had stripped that room bare. It was as if she had never lived there.

"I didn't mean to hurt her, Akiro. But I had to have a life of my own."

Ma became so remote after that. As if they were casual friends. As if she was like her parents, her grandparents, gone. What had they done to make her feel that way? What had happened all those years ago?

"Did she ever really love me, Akiro, or was it just that I was hers, almost a mirror image of herself? Did she see *me?* Or was it like looking in a mirror and seeing herself when she was younger?"

"I think—" Akiro began. He hesitated for a moment, then rushed on. "I think she was afraid to love anyone too much, even you, maybe especially you. I don't think she was mean-spirited or even angry. I think that was how she protected herself. I think when you left the only way she could deal with it was to make it look like you had never lived there. I don't think she knew what else to do."

"You are kind to her, even in death."

"My family is large, and always as happy as they seem to be. There is much that goes on between and among them that I don't hear about until months later. Then I can look back. See how they spoke and talked to one another, see how they changed, see how they realized once again that family is family no matter what. You just do not have that perspective. Think what could happen if we could choose in advance whom we would love. Not once have I ever heard you say your mother didn't love you. That is because in your heart you know she always did."

Sara held on to him. "Keep telling me that."

"For as long as you need to hear it."

"I must seem strange to you, a person with no family, no history."

Akiro smiled. "Only until I listen to or think about the sound of a dozen women talking all at once, and in Japanese. I have heard so much about my ancestors I could write a book. I can remember my grandmothers putting me on their laps and telling me stories about dragons and bravery. When it was time to leave, they would place their hands on my head. I thought it was some kind of blessing."

"I love you," Sara said. She felt complete with him.

So much of her life seemed to be missing. Akiro's parents accepted her, included her in everything. His sister was her best friend. They were so much a part of his life. It made her realize how small her world had been without him, and gave her a sense of what family was that she had never understood until now.

"I love you," she said.

Akiro kissed her forehead, then her mouth. Then he smiled. His smile made her think of the sun rising.

"Ma drowned," Sara said. "In a river near here that's flooding. Someone hit her on the head. She fell or was pushed in." She thought saying that would chase away the happy memories of time spent with Akiro's family, but realized that because Akiro was here with her, it could not.

C   H   A   P   T   E   R

26

Marti picked up a yellow memo on her desk. A call had come in from the county planning office. Dennis Moisio had information on one of the Realtors who had handled the rental of the building where the skeletal remains were found.

"There were two Realtors in town in the forties," he explained. "This one listed the place from the time the sisters left town in March nineteen-forty-three until mid-nineteen-forty-nine."

"Are you sure of when the sisters left?" Marti asked

"Well, the place was vacant as of March fifteenth."

Marti took down a name and address. When she told Vik, he said, "This guy was the rental agent for the place in 1949 and he's still living?"

"Moisio wasn't sure about that. He didn't think he should call them and ask any questions."

"A civilian did something right? Moisio must have gone through that citizen's academy program *and* paid attention. Maybe there is some hope of solving this one."

This case, Marti thought. The lieutenant's case. For a moment she hoped it would never be solved. No. She was angry with the lieutenant, not the deceased. He had a right to his identity.

Marti got out the file and pulled the photo of the two sisters taken in 1943 by the great-grandson as well as the photo of the woman in the window taken in July 1943. She and Vik arrived at the Montgomery address unannounced. It was in a quiet neighborhood with big old houses. Genteel, some might say.

"Mrs. Montgomery?"

"Miss," the woman at the door corrected. She looked to be in her early forties. Her hair was blond and worn long and straight. She was wearing jeans and an oversized T-shirt and had a large metal spoon in her hand that looked like it had been dipped in spaghetti sauce. She looked at them expectantly.

Marti and Vik showed her their I.D.s. "We were hoping a John Montgomery lived here."

Dimples flashed as she smiled. "My father. He did.

He passed away ten years ago. Now I live here. I'm Ellen Montgomery. Is there some way I can help you? Why don't you come in."

As she led them into the living room, Marti glanced across the hall and got a glimpse of a formal dining room. China settings and crystal goblets indicated guests were expected.

The room they entered was small with flocked wall-paper in different shades of a mossy green. Marti sat on a dainty sofa. Vik looked down at the matching chairs and remained standing. Ellen Montgomery sat beside Marti on the edge of the sofa. Marti showed her the two photos without comment.

"Where did you get this?" Miss Montgomery asked. She held up the shot of the woman waving from the window.

"It's a copy of one they have at the Lincoln Prairie Museum," Marti explained.

"Oh-h-h." It came out like a sigh. "This is my mother. But I don't remember ever seeing it. It must have been tucked in with Dad's memorabilia. I didn't think anyone would ever actually look at that stuff. But it was a part of Dad's life. I didn't want it to just sit here. My grandfather got into the real estate busi-ness first. I'm a Realtor now. I thought that even if the pictures and such were not worth displaying they should at least be accessible for their historic value."

"Yes, ma'am," Marti said. "And we're very glad that you did. Do you know the two women in the other pic-ture?"

208

"No, I'm sorry. I don't recall them at all. They aren't relatives. That's all I can tell you with any certainty. Where was this taken?" she asked, indicating the picture of her mother.

"That's the building near the Geneva Theater that they're renovating. Your father was the rental agent when this was taken."

"The place where the skeleton was found?"

"Yes, ma'am. Do you recall any work being done on the building at that time?"

"I, well, I wasn't born yet."

"Do you have a sister or brother or even aunt or uncle who might remember?"

She thought for a moment. "It depends on when you're talking about. When this picture of my mother was taken she must have been pregnant with Bill; Gerry would have been three. Benny was born in forty-seven; I came along eight years later. As for other relatives, my uncle Bernie had a heart attack in seventy-six and my Aunt Beth passed away in ninety-two. There isn't anyone else. I'm afraid there's just me, and I didn't even know Dad rented out the place until now."

"This is a process of elimination," Marti reminded Vik and herself as they returned to the car.

It was a little after six when Marti and Vik left the precinct.

"Step on it!" Marti called as Vik got into his car. "We're already ten minutes late." He was waiting for her when she arrived at Flaherty's to meet Ben and the group for dinner.

The waiter led them to a table where Ben, his partner, Allan, and Allan's wife, Susan, and Mildred were waiting. Vik stopped a few feet from Mildred and just looked down at her. Marti thought she saw a glistening in his eyes that could be tears.

"Moje cerce," he whispered. My heart, Marti translated. He stepped closer, touched her face, kissed her cheek, and sat down.

Later, at home, Marti sat up in bed. Beside her, Ben had his head on the pillow. Reaching down, she traced the curves and features of his face. She caressed his cheek, felt the rough stubble of his beard, leaned down, and inhaled the citrus aroma of his cologne. She thought of Johnny for a moment. Remembered the long days when she longed for just one more look at him and knew she would never see him again. She closed her eyes, her fingers touching Ben's face, feeling the smoothness of his eyebrows, the tiny scar near his left ear, the bridge of his nose, the curve of his lips; seeing him with her mind's eye, memorizing his face.

"Momma gave me a big hug today," he whispered. "Then she laughed. She said she was so glad I wouldn't be leaving anytime soon. I know she has the gift of touch, but I'm not sure what she meant."

"I think she feels something is there."

"Me too." He was quiet for a few moments, then said, "But she laughed. I've been feeling better about this test ever since." He was silent again. "That's why I thought we should have dinner tonight with our partners, without the rest of the family, to kind of . . . keep in touch with all of the good things, the good people in our lives, to not take them for granted. It's different with our families. We know what it's like to kiss somebody one morning and never see them again. I was looking at Vik and Mildred. They don't know that yet. And who knows, maybe something might happen to Susan or Allan. I wanted us to have one good memory of being together. The time might come when we have to be there for them."

He pulled her down and she snuggled against him.

"I'll be sure to have a little talk with Tony about Joanna tomorrow. Kids. They don't know the half of it." He kissed her. "This is only the beginning. There is so much more to love than this."

"Umm-humm," Marti agreed. "This is the fun part though." But part of this did last forever, the hunger to be touched.

C   H   A   P   T   E   R

27

FRIDAY, MAY 14—LINCOLN PRAIRIE

arti overslept and missed roll call Friday morning. Slim, Cowboy, Lupe, and Holmberg were all in the office when she arrived.

Vik arrived a few minutes after she did. The coffee smelled exotic and Mildred had baked a coffee cake. Slim sauntered over to Marti, a smile spreading across his face.

"I take it you've seen the write-up in the newspaper about me and Ben."

"That we did," Slim admitted. "And while we are all here to congratulate you, that is not the sole purpose of this conclave."

"Word is," Cowboy added, "that Lieutenant Nicholson is more than a little put out about that newspaper article, and the Dyspeptic Duo's trip to Los Angeles put her right over the edge."

"So far over the edge," Lupe went on, "that Holmberg and I have been ordered not to assist you in any way with any current investigations."

"Which means," Holmberg concluded, "whatever you need, you've got."

"From all four of us," Slim added.

Marti felt a familiar acid churning in her stomach. She took a couple of deep breaths.

"We also hear," Slim went on, "that said Dyspeptic Duo were not in the mood to take stuff and that said lieutenant was so advised."

"And?" Marti said.

"We don't take kindly to outsiders coming in and taking over," Cowboy said. "Not unless they show us some respect."

"Right," Slim agreed. "We take orders. We don't take shit."

"And furthermore," Cowboy added, "we don't like it when someone disrespects one of our own."

"Therefore," Slim said, "please be advised that ninety-seven percent of the members of the Lincoln Prairie Police Department have personally requested that we take whatever action is necessary to aid and abet our fellow officers, the Dyspeptic Duo, in any or all of their endeavors."

"The other three percent allows for suck-ups," Cowboy explained. "That said, me and Slim are going to amble on over to the courthouse and see if we can bring a few johns to justice, or at least embarrass them. Just remember"—he cocked his middle finger and pointed with his index finger—"we've got your backs."

Marti sat for a few minutes, thinking that through, then looked at Lupe, then Holmberg. "I don't have that much to lose in this situation. Neither does Vik. You do, especially you, Holmberg. You're a first-year man. You've got the right people's attention and you're well respected."

"Not for being a suck-up," Holmberg said.

"Agreed, but you don't have a history yet."

"I'll take my chances."

"Okay," Vik said. "Marti and I are going to go over the latest on the skeletal remains case and the Savannah Jones case. All who care to may listen in. Those who have work to do or find it boring are free to leave."

"Well," Marti began. She told them about the call

213

from Dennis Moisio and their visit to Miss Montgomery.

"So, we do know who the rental agent was during the time the place was renovated," Holmberg said.

"Unfortunately, the only people who might be able to tell us more about that are either dead or demented," Vik added.

"And so far," Holmberg went on, "we have no evidence to support the possibility that the sisters, Rosie and Rachel, were in the area after mid-March nineteen-forty-three."

"But we've narrowed the time range when the second floor must have been sealed off to April of forty-two through June of forty-four," Lupe added.

When they got to the update on the Jones case, Holmberg said, "I can start playing around on the Internet tonight. I'll see what I can find out about Von Weiss in particular and zirconia in general, and pick up a few historic facts about Eastern Europe in the thirties and forties. I might even get into gemology."

"As for me," Lupe added, "I think I'll just see what I can pick up about that building where the bones were found while I'm cruising the 'hood. Get a feel for the times maybe. Who knows? It was renovated sixty-odd years ago. There are a few folks who lived here back then who aren't dead yet. Or demented."

Marti wanted to hug them both. "Be careful," she warned.

"Not to worry," Lupe assured her. "Lieutenant

Lemon's got a few brownnosers, but they know they are significantly outnumbered. Holmberg and I can handle ourselves. Just do what you've got to do. One monkey don't stop no show."

Marti laughed until her sides hurt. Even though that wasn't that funny, it was something she had heard Momma say ever since she could remember.

Dennis Moisio called again a little after ten. "Any luck?" he asked.

"Nothing that tells us when the false ceiling was put in or who did it," Marti told him.

"Oh, you need to know that, too?"

"Yes. We thought that if we could find the person who rented the place out, they would know, but Mr. Montgomery is deceased and the only relative who was alive back then has advanced Alzheimer's."

"Let me see what I can find out," Dennis offered. "We have access to those kinds of records, too. I'll call if I find out anything."

Marti thanked him and hung up.

Holmberg was on the computer and printing something. "This Dennis Moisio is doing okay." He brought over several sheets of paper. "I'm on a search engine checking out Von Weiss. I'm going to look for a few other things, too. I'm not sure of exactly what you'll find useful, so I'm narrowing the search to expanding on what we know. If something else comes to you, just tell me."

Marti scanned the printout. "If we could find out

why he used zirconia, and maybe any other gems that seem unusual, we might be able to get a better handle on whether someone specifically wanted Jones's jewelry, or if they just wanted unusual, and therefore valuable, work by Von Weiss."

"We might be looking for the proverbial needle in a haystack," Holmberg said. "The Nazis took everything from the Jews that looked like it might be of value, even furniture. Not only that, they looted just about every eastern European museum and church. Nobody was exempt from the looting or the oven. They marched through Europe, looting as they went, and sent everything to Germany. Then the Soviet army did the same thing when they marched through Germany. It's all part of the war game. There's no way of telling what was lost, stolen, destroyed, or is in someone's private collection."

"So you don't think we're going to be able to narrow this down?"

"Well, this Von Weiss was no Fabergé. There aren't many people who would look at that earring and say, 'Oh, a Von Weiss.' But I think you've done a good job of narrowing the parameters."

"Do you really believe there were American soldiers involved in any of this?"

"Sure there were." He thought for a few moments. "When the Allied troops went into Germany there was this group of English and Americans; they called them monument officers. They were supposed to find the artworks, take care of them. But it was so chaotic over there as the war ended. . . ." He shrugged.

"Then one other thing we might want to find out is the names of local World War Two veterans from Lake County and try to find out if any of them were involved with these monument officers. That's the most obvious way that the jewelry made it to Lincoln Prairie. Can you do that?"

"You're going to end up with a lot of names."

"Yes, but hopefully by then I'll have a short list to compare them with."

Holmberg gave her a thumbs-up and began tapping on the keyboard.

Marti filled her mug with coffee and returned to her desk. Instead of reaching for the case files, she leaned back, inhaling the aroma of Cowboy's "Arabic blend." The most thought she had given to any war was Johnny's war—Vietnam. Now she realized how limited her perspective was. Guns, grenades, explosives. Those who died, those who survived, those who learned how to enjoy life again, those who found isolated places within where they remembered what they could not talk about or forget. She felt depressed.

"Who do you know who came here from Europe during World War Two, Jessenovik?"

"I wasn't even born then."

"But you're Polish. Eastern European. What was it like for Von Weiss?"

"I don't think we need to know that."

"Me neither, but Holmberg has got me thinking."

"Then think about what's in those files."

A half hour later, Vik slammed a folder, gave it a push that sent it to the edge of his desk, and said, "Old Mrs. Stoker."

"What about her?" Marti asked.

"I think she might be Hungarian."

He leaned back, arms folded, eyebrows almost meeting in a scowl, and gave a deep sigh. "Oh what the hell. We're not getting anywhere here." He looked at Holmberg. "What's taking so long?"

"I've been printing, I'm printing now. I'll have something for you real soon."

Vik picked up the phone. When he hung up he said. "Let's go. She's hard of hearing and still speaks with an accent, but her daughter can communicate with her in Hungarian."

The house they went to was a small traditional Tudor that sat back on a large, tree-filled lot. It made Marti think of a castle. As they went up a cobblestone walk, Vik said, "She's eighty-seven, tends to fall asleep without warning. The daughter said we'd get more out of her in Hungarian. She's going to interpret for us."

"How long have you known her?"

"I don't know her. She and Mildred's sister Helen belong to the Lincoln Prairie Woman's Club."

"Didn't we talk to them once?"

"We were the reassurance committee when they were having those break-ins around here, tagged along with Officer Friendly, met at the library. Helen says Stoker's the one who was snoring."

A woman who looked to be about fifty opened the door. She was wearing a dress and an apron. "Vik, so nice to see you. And you're Marti. I remember. You spoke to our women's group five years ago. I came right home and called a locksmith. We had dead bolts installed two days later. Mother is right here in the dayroom. Just follow me."

The dayroom was a corner room with windows framed with lace curtains along the two outer walls. Outside, the sky was overcast, but the room was painted a cheerful pastel yellow. Daffodils bloomed in clay pots arranged on a bookcase and there was a vase with an arrangement of cut flowers on the table in the center of the room. Classical music played in the background. Marti recognized the melody, but couldn't name the composer.

Mrs. Stoker was dozing in a reclining chair placed where she could see out of the windows. Her face was scored with fine wrinkles. She was wearing a sweat suit and socks. An afghan had slipped to the floor.

"Just pull those two chairs over by Mother, Vik, and I'll make tea. We'll just let her sleep for a few more minutes."

She set up a couple of tray tables and returned with a tray of individual teapots and matching cups. "Mother enjoys having company."

When Mrs. Stoker was fully awake and had enjoyed one cup of tea and requested another, her daughter turned to Vik. "What would you like to know?"

"How she got here during the war."

After her daughter asked the question, the old woman spoke slowly but in a surprisingly strong voice, "It wasn't the soldiers," the daughter translated. "It was the government, the laws. For everything we did, there was a law or rule to be broken. Careful, you always had to be so careful. Where we lived, it was two little rooms and there were eight of us. We only went out to get food. They let us buy whatever was left over from what was sent to Germany. We were their allies then, part of the Axis. That was how they treated their friends.

"You could see the change, that they did not trust us. My aunt came to this country, then my uncle, and another uncle. Then there were whispers that we would be occupied. We were afraid of the camps, even though we were not Jews. You did not have to be a Jew to go there, just an enemy. We were becoming the enemy. The soldiers became meaner. We were afraid. Fear was like air, everywhere. Even when they were nicer to us, we knew what was happening other places. Always we got up in the morning and thought today I might be arrested and sent to the camps. Always we thought we would die.

"Our uncle sent money so that we could leave. Small amounts that they might not take from us. When our papers came, we sold everything we could and gave the rest away. Even until we left we feared we would not be allowed to go. The day that we left we were searched before we got on the train. We even had to take off our underwear. We could take nothing with us. I had a stuffed dog, Fritz. He was made from scraps of fabric that matched one of my dresses. My mother would not let me wear the dress that matched Fritz because she was afraid they would think we were rich or Jews. They took Fritz. He was all I had brought with me and they took him. Mama squeezed my hand very tight. I knew I must not cry.

"The train was very crowded, but no one spoke. All you could hear was the train whistle, the wheels on the tracks. Everyone had their hand in their pocket. That was where their papers were, the papers that said they could leave. There was a man who had a cold. He stuffed his glove into his mouth so they would not hear him cough and decide he was not fit to leave and send him instead to the camps. At the border they searched us again. There were three of them. They made me turn around, lift my arms, bend over. No man had ever seen my body until then. Later I told Mama that no man ever would again."

The old woman laughed. "Even after I was married, I never let your poppy see me without my nightgown on. And always the lights went out before I would get into the bed."

She sighed, turned her face toward the window, and dozed off again.

"Is she all right?" Marti asked. "Have we tired her out?" The old woman had talked much longer than she expected before taking a nap.

"No. She's fine. I could tell you what she told you

myself, but she insisted. I have heard it many times and would not care if I never heard it again. But the telling makes her feel strong, resilient. As strange as it may seem, I think that talking about surviving those days makes her even more determined to live a long life. You should have known her when she was younger. She was always happy, always laughing. There was always joy in our house, and always too much food."

"How did she reach America?" Vik asked.

"They stayed in France with friends of my uncle for several months because the scarcity of food in Hungary and what was available to eat was very hard on my grandmother. She needed time to regain her strength in order to survive the sea crossing." As she spoke, she gathered the teapots and teacups and stacked them on the tray. "She is very proud, you know. Proud that she did not cry when they took Fritz. Proud that she did not let them see her shame when she had to undress. And . . ." she went to the door, "Fritz, here Fritz."

A medium-sized mixed-breed dog skidded on the hardwood floor as he ran into the room. "We have always had a real dog named Fritz."

Neither of them spoke as Marti drove back to the precinct. There was an inch-thick stack of printouts on her desk. Holmberg was gone. Marti thought about food. They had skipped lunch, but she didn't feel hungry. War. Damn. She knew the Holocaust was unlike any other recent war experience, and that wars of extinction occurred before Christ. The concept of the Holocaust wasn't what made it different. It was the method, the arrogance of superiority, and the intensity of hatred. Jew and Holocaust had become synonymous; so had Cambodia and Vietnam.

The camps, Mrs. Stoker had said again and again. The fear. Until today, Marti had taken it for granted that the Jews were the only ones targeted. Now she realized that the scope of the crime was much wider than that. Anyone could be the enemy. Non-Jews were gassed, too. Even now, after listening to Mrs. Stoker's story, the magnitude of the atrocities of war was beyond her comprehension. "You had to be there," Johnny told her once when she had awakened him from yet another nightmare. "You had to be there."

She shook her head as if that would clear the word pictures from her mind and began reading the computer printouts Holmberg had left for her. The first half-dozen pages were all about zirconia; where it could be found in measurable quantities, mined, and sold. Romania was the only significant European country. There was no indication that due to scarcity zirconia was ever a popular gem of choice.

The next half-dozen pages could have been called "The Known Travels of Von Weiss." The man moved around a lot, but he seemed to travel in circles. Marti wondered if he could have left, just as Mrs. Stoker did, or if he was prevented from leaving. Other artists had made it to France; poets and playwrights, architects.

Why did Von Weiss stay? And why did he use zirconia crystals?

"Find anything?" Vik asked.

"Lots."

"Anything useful?"

"Not so far as I can tell." That earring was still all they had. The rest of the pieces Jones had were missing. "It's a start," she said. "What have you got?"

"Less than you."

She put the Von Weiss papers aside. Holmberg had actually found a list of World War Two veterans from northern Illinois. It wasn't in alpha order, but taken from newspaper articles. Obituaries memorialized those who hadn't come back. Holmberg had aster-isked the names of those still living.

The phone rang while she was reading.

"Is this Detective MacAlister?"

"Speaking."

"This is the jeweler you brought the Von Weiss to on Monday."

"Has someone else brought something in?"

He laughed. "Von Weiss has become quiet popular it seems, but they did not come to me. I was attending a monthly meeting we have. Dinner, a little wine, a few informal transactions, and unofficial conversations, things all businessmen do."

"And?" Marti urged when he paused.

"It seems that two other people came to Chicago this week to have a Von Weiss appraised."

"Two? Who were the jewelers? Give me their names."

"Oh, but I cannot do that. And you wouldn't want me to. I would never be privy to information from any of my counterparts again."

Marti decided not to argue the point. "What can you tell me?"

"A woman with a bad dye job—red hair—had a pair of garnet cuff links. A black woman with braids and dark glasses had a brooch with a peridot crystal in a silver setting."

"Peridot, what's that?"

"Well, it's somewhat rare, and perhaps more commonly called olivine. My guess is that it came from Norway. This brooch was quite valuable, a beautiful golden-green crystal, surrounded by smaller, deep green crystals. The garnet is a more common gem. We refer to it as a demantoid, which is not important to you, but these particular gems were absolutely exquisite, green like emeralds, very rare, very beautiful, worth a lot of money. My friend said that based on the quality, plus the fact that it was definitely a Von Weiss, it must have been mined in the Ural Mountains in Russia. The best demantoid in the world comes from there."

"Could your friends tell when Von Weiss made them?"

"We can date his work by the settings. The cuff links were made during Von Weiss's minimalist period, early forties. The setting is very simple, a series of curves. The brooch had intertwining lilies and would have been made after the earring you showed me, late thirties."

"And these women did not give their names or any-thing?" Marti asked.

"No, no. And, the name Von Weiss meant nothing to them. And they just wanted an estimate of their value."

"Does that suggest anything to you?"

"Unfortunately, yes. I suspect . . . I strongly suspect that they are going to sell them to a private collector and we'll lose them forever. We will never know the scope of Von Weiss's work. All these pieces belong in a museum."

"Then I hope we can find them."

"Please let me know if you do. What work we have seen of his, and most of what is in museums or other known collections, has more familiar, more popular gems, diamonds and the like. These gems are a glimpse of his work that we have not seen before. I think there is a special reason why these gems were used." He hesitated. "Perhaps I can explain it this way. My oldest daughter has some shards of glass that my grandmother salvaged after Kristallnacht—what you call in this country Crystal Night. They are to be given to the oldest daughter in each generation. A remem-brance, perhaps. Maybe a warning. Or maybe just hope that it will never happen again. My grandmother never explained. But sometimes she would take out these pieces of broken glass and laugh. Other times she looked at them for a very long time and wept."

"Thank you," Marti said. "Thank you for the time you've taken to tell me all of this. Please thank your friends."

"We are all hoping that you will somehow be able to recover at least some of this. If I hear anything else I will call you."

After he hung up Marti thought, a black woman. Where would a black woman have got something like that in the forties? It wasn't likely that there were any African-American monument officers. Blacks had enough trouble getting the Tuskegee pilot's trained and airborne. The armed forces were segregated then.

Vik didn't say anything for a few minutes when she told him what the jeweler had said. He sat with his head in his hands. Eventually, he said, "Damn. We've got one hell of a nightmare of a case here. The more we find out the less sense it all makes." A few moments later, he added, "I suppose we've had worse."

"Not that I can remember," Marti said. For the first time in recent memory, she could not find a significant correlation with any of the information they had so far. It was like having a limited number of puzzle pieces, none of which fit together, and no picture of the entire puzzle. She wanted to check in with Mark Dobryzcki. She was hoping Dennis Moisio would call back. And finally, she was hungry.

"Why don't I order a pizza?" she suggested. She didn't think they would be leaving on time tonight.

"Fine by me."

"Ground beef, Italian sausage, and extra cheese?"

"Sounds good. And onions, bell peppers, and olives."

"Green or black olives?"

"Black."

Marti wasn't sure her stomach could handle that many toppings. "How about pineapple while you're at it? Or eggplant." Joanna had made a pizza once topped with eggplant and squash.

Vik scowled at her.

C H A P T E R

28

When neither Mark nor Dennis had called by four thirty, Marti reached for the phone. She called Dennis first. She didn't have his home or cell phone number and he was a salaried county employee. When he picked up, she was surprised that he hadn't already left for the weekend.

"Oh, hi," he said. "Look, I usually leave at four on Friday, but I think I'm on to something. Can you stick around a while longer?"

Marti smiled. "Don't worry. I won't be going home anytime soon."

When Mark answered, he said, "I'm right in the middle of something, Marti. I'll call you as soon as I can," and clicked off.

Marti settled back to wait for the pizza to be delivered and the phone to ring. While she was waiting, she went through Holmberg's printouts again. She got a phone book and wrote the phone number for every veteran's name she could match with those on his list. There weren't many, and just because the name matched didn't mean it was the same person or even a member of his family. It was too late to check with any veterans' organization, so she picked up the phone. One hour and one pizza later, she and Vik had made it through the names with phone numbers and talked with fourteen vets. Two were women, four were sailors, and one was a pilot; the rest were Army, what Vik referred to as "grunts." Everyone she spoke to was reluctant to talk about the war. None of them knew what she was talking about when she asked about monument officers.

She was going to have to begin contacting veterans' organizations first thing Monday morning. She wanted to believe she wouldn't need to by then, but the way things were going, or not going, that seemed unlikely. She checked her e-mail. There was nothing from Lieutenant Nicholson. Vik was submitting daily reports for both of them, but Marti wondered if her lack of communication meant that she was still deciding how to retaliate.

"Vik, did you ever ask Stephen about why the old brick and the new brick matched?"

He gave her a blank look.

"The building where we found the skeletal remains," she reminded him. "The bricked-up windows."

"Oh, that. I didn't say anything because he didn't know. The only things he could come up with was that it could have been salvaged from another building that went up at about the same time and was being torn down. Or, and he thought this was a very remote possibility, the same brick was made or kept in stock for an extended period of time because of the availability of the materials used, or its popularity. But I cannot think of one other building on or near Geneva Street made with that brick."

When Mark returned her call, he said, "Savannah Payne-Jones was quite a gambler, loved card games, preferably blackjack and poker. She had two outstanding gambling debts when she died. She was into a Nevada casino for forty grand and a private dealer for another thirty-five grand. These guys are being very cooperative and we're still talking with them. What we're trying to find out now is how long she'd been at it, how often she got into the hole, how she got out, how reliable she was about paying her debts. This is small change to the casino, but big bucks to the dealer."

"Would he have killed her because of it?" Marti asked. "Would he take her jewelry to recoup some of his losses?"

"That's what we're looking at. We're holding him. At worst the casino probably would have barred her from playing. This dealer is new to the game. If he's got a lot of debt, and she was the best-known debtor, he's a possibility."

"How likely is that?"

"This guy is young and just starting out. Gambling is like any other business. People have misconceptions, watch too much TV. They make mistakes when they don't have the experience to handle something."

"You will let me know if you've got anything else?" Marti pressed.

"As soon as I can."

That was an ambiguous answer, but honest, which was more than she had expected.

Marti shared Mark's side of the conversation with Vik. He was shaking his head before she finished.

"Too much of a long shot," he concluded. "Even if he gives up this new dealer, I wouldn't buy into it without a confession and some corroborating evidence."

"Why would she voluntarily meet this guy, or his messenger?" Marti agreed. "And why here? It's not even getting local coverage, let alone national coverage. That's no way to build a reputation for being a bad guy."

"Unless she was his best-known customer," Vik said. "Which isn't saying much,"

"Whoever killed her has to have the jewelry," Marti said. "The question is, was the jewelry the mark, or was she? If it was the jewelry, if it was to pay off a gambling debt, the killer had to be smart enough to know it was worth something. Otherwise the jewelry was taken because it had some intrinsic value to whoever killed her. The question then becomes, who knew Jones would be here, and who did Jones know well

231

enough to get into a car with without being under duress? If on the other hand, Jones was the mark and the jewelry incidental, then why was I pushed down the stairs at the library?"

"We're stretching that one, too, Marti. If it was deliberate, someone had to know you were going to Jeweler's Row and then follow you to the library."

"Following me wouldn't have been that difficult. I enjoyed that walk through the city. Stopped and got a Chicago-style hotdog. Relaxed." As far-fetched as it seemed, she still wasn't ready to concede that she was a random mark. "The jewelry," she repeated. "That is the only thing that sets Jones apart." Like it or not, getting pushed down those stairs and having her purse rifled convinced her of that. "A lot of people gamble. And a lot of people go into debt doing it. Some of them kill to get the money to pay, but killing someone over thirty-five or forty thousand dollars doesn't make a lot of sense."

"Unless it was the inexperienced dealer." Vik ran his fingers through his hair. "But what is it about the damned jewelry that makes it that important?"

"Hell if I know," Marti admitted. "The larger question is, how did an African-American woman come into possession of a Von Weiss brooch? How did Jones?"

"Which brings us back to why would someone commission a set of jewelry that was zirconia set in gold?" Vik ran his fingers through his hair again. "Every potential lead brings a dozen more questions."

232

Marti looked at Holmberg's printouts again, checked the notes she made while she was talking with the jeweler and made a list:

Zirconium—Romania
Garnet—Russia
Peridot—West Germany

She showed the list to Vik. "Von Weiss visited all three countries."

"So how would jewelry made in three different countries all end up in Illinois?"

Marti had no answer. She got a cup of coffee that had been made this morning and kept hot. Then she began looking for the blank spaces, the questions she hadn't thought to ask yet. Once again, her mind settled on a black woman with many braids and an emerald brooch. If that woman was somehow involved in Jones's death, did that mean she came here from someplace else and gained Jones's trust because she was black, was she someone Jones knew? Did she live in Chicago, or here in Lincoln Prairie?

Marti found Tansy Lark's business card and called the cell phone number scrawled on the back. After she identified herself, she asked, "Was there any publicity given to local media here about the shoot?"

"Of course not. Word gets out, but if we officially release information we'd have so many gapers we'd need extra security personnel. It would be a royal nightmare. We wait until the film comes out to do that.

233

We want them to go to the theaters, not the film site."

"We have an African-American newspaper in Chicago. Did any of their reporters make any inquiries about Jones?"

"Officer, let's get real. Nobody, black or white, has ever called and asked about Jones anywhere or at any time that I was working with her. We are not talking Oscar-winning performances here. We are not talking Oscar-nominated films. Savannah Payne-Jones doesn't . . . didn't . . . have a name in this business. She was the woman behind the wheel of a car, the woman who walked through the revolving door, or sat at a table in a restaurant, cleaned up, or served food. That's it."

Marti thanked her. Then she called the Chicago newspaper anyway. The man she spoke with did check their recent archives, but it was too vague a search. Then she thought of Elroy Reed, editor of *The People's Voice*. It was a free, local, multiethnic newspaper, published monthly. Momma always got a copy because it carried a lot of news about the African-American community that wasn't printed in the dailies. She got Elroy's answering machine and left a message.

"Jones did get the jewelry from her mother, who got it from Jones's grandmother. That could have happened during or not long after the war. I'm certain there were no black monument officers, but anyone—a cook, steward, valet, whatever—might have been able to get their hands on it."

"That only solves the question about Jones," Vik said. "What about the other two women?"

Marti turned on her computer and phoned home. Theo and Mike had been working on their family trees for almost a year. She explained that she needed to know how to find someone's parents. Theo suggested the Social Security Death Index database and Mike added that once she knew when and where they died she could look at local newspapers for the obituary. Marti could not believe they were so matter-of-fact about it. She couldn't believe they had actually visited those sites, but they must have.

Tears came to her eyes and she put her head in her hands. What if they had to tell the boys that Ben had prostate cancer? Should they? Maybe they should tell them slowly. Daddy needs an operation, then wait and see what the prognosis was before they took it any further. Yes, she decided. She would talk it over with Ben tonight. His first wife and Johnny had both died suddenly and unexpectedly. There would be time to help the children to adjust to whatever was going to happen. And as Momma had reminded her several times, black men also survived prostate cancer, many people survived cancer if it was detected early enough.

When Dennis called back, Marti realized she had forgotten he had said he was going to.

"Sorry this took me so long," he said. She looked at her watch, six forty-five.

"The secretaries were gone and I had to go through their files myself. And trust me, I take my life in my hands when I do that. If one file is out of order I am in deep trouble."

"I appreciate your doing this. You must be long overdue at home."

"No problem. You got my curiosity up, I would have gone nuts this weekend if I didn't at least try to find something out."

"Did you?"

"Well, what I've got is the name of the contractor who did the brickwork and put in the false ceiling."

Marti grabbed a pencil.

"Warren Newsome Senior."

"Newsome," Marti repeated. "I've seen that name around town on construction projects."

"He sold the company years ago, not long after his oldest son died in the war. But the business was established in 1885, so they kept the name."

"Thanks," Marti said. "I really appreciate this and I owe you big-time. If there's anything I can do for you, just let me know."

She knew that those could be dangerous words for a cop to say, but the stories she had heard today, the things she had learned, had put her in a peculiar mood. Not sad exactly, more like melancholy. She read the names of the Web sites again, then told Vik about Newsome.

"It's a little after seven. Do you want to see him tonight?"

"This has been one hell of a long day, Marti. What I really want to do is go home to Mildred and Maxie, have a little real food, put my feet up, and watch an old movie."

"I'm with you," Marti agreed.

"This Newsome family. I think there's just some old guy left. Unless he dies in his sleep tonight, he's not going anywhere."

"With our luck . . ." Marti began.

"With our luck we'll get to hear another sob story tomorrow. I've heard enough for one day. Turn off the computer. Let's go." She turned it off, reached for her jacket, and thought of spending a few hours with the kids and the rest of the night with Ben.

C H A P T E R

29

Thomas Newsome put his dinner tray on the table. Harriet could cook and she loved to indulge herself. Tonight it had been prime rib, twice-baked potatoes, and a lobster salad with artichokes and avocado. He leaned back and closed his eyes, still savoring his dinner. Edmund, his youngest brother, had always loved lobster. Gentle Edmund. One day he saw Cook throwing them alive into a pot of boiling water and never ate one again.

After Warren Junior was killed in France, it did not surprise him when Edmund came to him one night and said, "Dad wants me to enlist, take Warren's place on the front line, but I can't."

Whenever Warren wrote, Dad read the letters to them, so they knew what it was like.

"Warren shot children, Thomas. I could never kill a child, not even if he, too, had a gun and would kill me if I did not fire first. I would rather be dead than do the things Warren Junior did. I will not go to war. I will not. I don't care that Dad believes that's unpatriotic and calls me a coward. I cannot kill."

As bravely as Edmund spoke, Thomas knew that Edmund wanted just one person to support him, to stand up to their father with him. Mother was too passive, used to Dad having not just the last, but the only word, to say anything. She was overwhelmed by Warren's death. There was nobody but him to speak up for Edmund, and he did not.

Two days later they got up and came down to breakfast and Edmund was not there. There was a sealed envelope at his place at the table. Dad tore up the note without telling them what was in it. Whatever Edmund said, he didn't need the note, or any other reminders. They never heard from Edmund again. He would never escape the knowledge that it was his voice that was never raised in defense of his brother. He would never forgive himself for that silence.

He was equally responsible for his father's death. He would never know what made Dad stop the car, get out, and step on the downed line. He would never forget he was the cause of Dad leaving the house during that storm. It was a minor accounting error that could have waited, but just once, he wanted to be as important to his father as Thomas Warren Junior had been—and still was, even in death. He had insisted that Dad had to come to the office immediately, told him that the problem could not wait.

Thomas stood. His joints were stiff from sitting so long. He went to the cabinet and took out the carved chest. The patriarch would be in Skokie on Sunday. Harriet was driving him there for the Liturgy. He would bring this, and after the Liturgy, he would give this and half his fortune to the Church. Harriet would be furious if she knew, but there would be enough money left to keep them in caviar for the rest of their lives.

He opened the chest, took out the sheaf of paper, and looked at the jewelry. He would have to make his confession when he returned them. Dad came home from work with packages from Warren until just before Warren died. All Dad ever said was that they were originally from Romania, where his parents had been born. He knew Warren Junior could not have come into possession of them by any legitimate means. He knew Dad was proud of Warren's ingenuity, not ashamed of his pilfering. He didn't think any of it had any monetary value. He just knew that it wasn't theirs to keep. It did not belong to Dad or to him. Warren Junior's medals and commendations were displayed downstairs. His room was just as it had been the day he went off to war. Dad had found solace in that. Somewhere, perhaps in Romania, there might be someone who would be equally comforted by what was in the chest.

He stared at the Theotokos—the Bearer of Christ—the Mother. Why was she sent here? She did not accuse him. She did not judge him. Why did she look inconsolable in her sorrow? Did the contents of the box belong to someone especially dear to her? They said a mother's love was unconditional, but his mother had not been strong of heart. The pain caused by Warren's death caused hers. She could not bear the weight of it. This mother had born the weight of much pain.

"I see forever." She always said that to him, or at least that was what he heard in his mind. "I see forever." He was beginning to understand what that meant. The pain of forever *was* unbearable. The pain he had caused Edmund seemed small in comparison to her pain, but loving Mother that she was, she understood that it was almost more than he could bear. He touched the chipped, discolored wood. He touched her face, yellow-brown with age. He would be alone without her. He wished he did not have to give her back.

SATURDAY, MAY 15—LINCOLN PRAIRIE

Marti and Vik met for breakfast at the Peacock Restaurant on Bellgrande Street. They lingered over coffee because they didn't want to arrive at the Newsomes' home until nine.

Vik put four packets of sugar into his cup after the waitress refilled it. "I asked Helen about the Newsomes. She has a tendency to remember things it wouldn't occur to anyone else to even notice. According to Helen, Harriet Jennings was a graduating class behind Helen and they got partnered for some junior-senior service project. Warren Newsome Senior had three boys. Harriet married his middle son, Thomas. Following family tradition, Thomas's only child, a boy, was named Thomas Newsome Junior. When Tom Junior preceded his father in death, Thomas Senior became the last of the line."

"What about his two brothers?"

"Nobody knows what happened to the youngest, Edmund, and guess what? Thomas's oldest brother, Warren Junior, was an officer in World War Two. He went in as a private and got half a dozen medals and a couple of promotions for bravery. Got blown away in France."

"Then he didn't have the opportunity to bring back any Von Weiss jewelry."

"Unfortunately no."

"Suppose he mailed it?" Marti said.

"To who? And how would we find out?"

That was the most frustrating thing about his case, the lack of connections. What did Jones, a redhead, and a black woman with a weave have in common other than the jewelry? At this rate, she would never find out.

"Maybe, when we do close the Jones case, Vik, and we will, Sara will be willing to donate the earring we do have to some museum or something, so that more people know that Von Weiss existed and did make an important artistic contribution in his lifetime." It seemed such a waste somehow, that he wasn't better known, that what the jewelers had found out by looking at his work this week might never be documented or proved, perhaps never even mentioned again.

"Listening to that Mrs. Stoker's story does make you stop and think, doesn't it? Stephen was there when I told Mildred and Helen about it last night. I think he's going to get in touch with Theo and Mike to find out how to go about starting a genealogical search. God only knows what he'll find out about our family. I'm not sure I want to know."

Thomas Newsome lived in an older part of town near the lake. There was no formal name for the subdivi-

242

sion. It was known as Hidden Glen because Glen Street was the only way to enter from Sherman Avenue, and there was nothing but trees the first quarter of a mile in. Some old-timers still called it Gold Mine Village, because the homes were custom-built in the early 1900s when few could afford to build there.

The Newsome house was a two-story gray brick built on a half acre of land. There was a clear view of the lake to the east. The western boundary was marked with birch trees and red maples. Bulbs were blooming in the formal gardens. Robins in search of worms paid little attention as Marti parked and walked with Vik to the house. Sparrows squabbled in a low hedge beneath the first floor leaded-glass windows.

A woman Marti assumed was a housekeeper or cleaning woman answered the bell. She was wearing jeans and a man's long-sleeved shirt. An oversized triangular scarf tied at the back of her neck protected her hair.

When they introduced themselves and showed her their I.D.s, she seemed surprised. "Oh, Dad's upstairs. He doesn't come down anymore; the stairs are too much for him." She spoke as if he was expecting them. "Come on in and I'll take you up to see him."

Inside, the house was more functional than ornate. There were no glass chandeliers or marble floors. On the other hand, everything Marti could see looked as pristine as it must have been when it was brought here and set into place.

Upstairs, it was a bit different, looked more like a

place people lived in than a museum. Magazines were scattered on a table in the hall. A fat orange-and-white cat swished its tail as they walked by. The woman led them into a room without knocking. It looked like a sitting room, with a desk, sideboard, and bookcases. An elderly man with wire-rimmed glasses looked up from a book he was reading. He was sitting by the window in an oversized, thickly padded chair with a table and a lamp beside it.

"Company, Dad," the woman said.

Thomas Newsome was dressed in brown corduroy pants and a beige cable knit sweater. He didn't seem surprised to see them, but from the look he gave the woman, Marti got the impression that he was annoyed.

"Thank you, Harriet," he said in what once must have been a stern voice. "Do you suppose you could find them a couple of chairs?"

"Let me help," Vik suggested and followed the woman out of the room.

"I know this is an intrusion and we're disturbing you," Marti said. Newsome looked sturdy and in good health, but she got the impression that he was frail.

"No matter," he said. "I'm sure something of importance brings you here."

Vik and Harriet returned with armless, straight-backed chairs. Vik put Marti's chair closest to the old man and sat down further away.

"Oh, Dad," Harriet said. "You've got this old thing out again." She picked up a carved, ornate chest made of mahogany. "I'll just put it away."

The old man did not object.

"Mr. Newsome," Marti began. "Your father, or per-haps your grandfather, did some work that we would like to ask you about." She took out some photos she had taken of the house. "This is a building on Geneva, not far from the theater."

He looked at the photos, then at her. "I don't recognize it, but I assume you're correct."

"It was built near the turn of the century. Sometime between April of nineteen-forty-three and June of nineteen-forty-four, windows, which were here"—she pointed—"were bricked up. A staircase was taken out and a false ceiling put in. We just found out from the County Planning office that Newsome Construction did the work." She showed him a before-work photo when the windows were there. "Can you tell me any-thing about it?"

The old man looked at the photos a few more times. "I would have been eighteen, nineteen when the changes were made." He rubbed his chin, then leaned forward. "I don't remember this in particular, but based on the quality of the work, I would definitely agree that we did it."

"The work was done at least forty years after it was built, but the brick matches perfectly."

"Yes. It would if there were any way to get the same bricks. We might have done a tear-down. If you tell me exactly what it is that you need to know I can call the owner of the company. We kept meticulous records and I'm certain he can find out whatever it is."

"We have an approximate date when the work was authorized, but we also have a photo showing that the work wasn't done that summer. What I would like to know is exactly or as close to that date as possible when the actual work was done and by whom."

"I'll put in a call first thing Monday morning. I'm sure we can provide you with that information. Those kinds of details have been archived, not just for historical reasons but to document that we did not contribute to any of the environmental problems that the city is currently experiencing. May I ask why you want to know?"

"Someone recently purchased the building and discovered the second floor while he was renovating. Skeletal remains were found in a closet. We're trying to identify who it was. If we can pinpoint the date the work was done it might make it easier to identify the victim."

The old man clenched one hand into a fist as he looked away. "A body," he said. He spoke as if he was out of breath. A few moments later he added, "I wish we had known at the time. It's bad enough not to be able to have a loved one brought home and interred in the family plot. It must be terrible to have someone go missing and not even be certain they are dead."

Marti was about to stand up when she thought of the box Harriet had put away. "That box, it's beautiful," she said. "Is it handmade? It looked really old."

The old man unclenched his hand and smiled. "Tomorrow the patriarch comes all the way from

Bucharest. It is a gift for him. He will be surprised." He looked toward the cabinet where Harriet had put it. "I shall miss her," he said. "I shall miss her terribly, but it's only right that she goes home. And soon perhaps, I will see her again."

Marti thought it odd that he referred to the box as "her." She didn't ask why.

The old man pushed a button when they stood and thanked him. "Don't mention anything about the box or the patriarch to Harriet," he cautioned. "She's going to be very angry with me when she finds out what I'm going to do, so I don't intend to tell her until we're ready to go to the Liturgy."

A moment or two later Harriet bustled into the room. The button must have triggered a buzzer or a bell.

"Mrs. Newsome," Vik said. "I'm sure you don't remember this, but my sister-in-law, Helen Jablonski, partnered with you in high school on a senior-junior service project."

Harriet gave them a wide smile. "Of course I remember," she said. "Helen and I worked together at Victory Hospital bringing newspapers and books and magazines to the patients. You must be that shy young man who married Helen's younger sister, Mildred."

She scratched at the scarf that covered her head. "Bad perm," she said. "Wrong shade and my scalp is sore. If Helen or Mildred go to Sophia's beauty shop, tell them not to let the new girl anywhere near them. Her name is Peggy Jeanne."

Outside Marti said, "You were shy?"

Vik scowled and said nothing.

Thomas Newsome felt a sharp pain in his chest as soon as the detectives mentioned finding a skeleton. He had tablets for the pain and he only experienced it when something stressful or unexpected happened. It didn't happen often, but the older he got the more he worried that he might be having a heart attack. If Harriet didn't keep after him so much to have a check-up, he probably would see the doctor.

He did remember when those windows were bricked up. He didn't know about the stairs to the second floor being removed. Dad got up one Saturday morning, called some of the workmen, and told him to meet him at the rental property on Geneva. He didn't know if the owner or the renter or the Realtor had asked Dad to do it, but the job was completed in three days because that was when the new renter was scheduled to move in. They had to work that Sunday, something his father had never previously allowed.

He had no idea whose remains they could be. His first thought was that Warren Junior couldn't have done anything to whomever it was because he was overseas. Now that he was aware of it, he wanted to know what had happened as much as the police did. He didn't believe Dad had anything to do with it, but it was strange that the second floor wasn't thoroughly checked before being sealed off. It wasn't like him to be so much in a hurry to get the job done that he didn't inspect the quality of the workmanship.

31

Vik didn't say anything until they were back on Sherman Avenue and Marti asked him what he was thinking about.

"What was in that chest?" he said. "And who is 'she'?"

"Whatever it is, 'the patriarch' will have it tomorrow. Is he talking about that Serbian church and monastery in Libertyville?"

"I don't think so. Did he say Budapest or Bucharest?"

"Bucharest, why?"

"That's in Romania. It would have to be a Romanian Orthodox church. It must be somewhere in Chicago."

Holmberg was there when they got to the office. Marti was glad to see him, but there was no welcoming coffee aroma.

"I don't smell any coffee brewing."

He looked at her and smiled. "Yes, ma'am. I'll get right on it."

When the coffee was perking he asked, "Got any real work for me to do?"

"Do I ever. Find out everything you can about the Newsomes and the Joneses. Go as far back as you can, hopefully that will be as far as World War Two."

"You've got it."

"Lord, I hope so."

Marti had just settled in for another morning of going through her mail and reading Holmberg's computer printouts when the sergeant called to say that Sara Jones and Akiro Takamoto were there to see her.

Sara was radiant. "This is my fiancée, Akiro Takamoto."

At five feet three, she was shorter than her fiancé, a very attractive Japanese man who was about three inches taller. For some reason, when Sara had mentioned him, Marti had gotten an impression of an older man. Perhaps because he was a college professor. She was pleased to see that Takamoto didn't look more than a few years older than Sara's twenty-three. Marti motioned to them to sit down and offered them coffee. They declined.

"There is something I should have told you," Sara said. "Ma gambled. She always was either loaded with money or in debt to someone she gambled with. That's the only reason I can think of that would make someone want to hurt her."

"Was she ever hurt or threatened because of her gambling debts?"

Sara shook her head. "Not that I know of. But now you read so many things in the newspaper. People are killed every day for much less."

"But she did not receive any threats that you're aware of?"

"No. She was always on good terms with those she gambled with. She always had a lucky streak and paid off her debts. That's how she got the money for the condo. A three-day poker tournament in Vegas."

"Sara, we are aware of the gambling and also that she owed about seventy-five thousand dollars. Was that a lot of money for her?"

Sara shook her head. "She was lucky. Until now. She owed a casino twice that amount a couple of years ago. She won it all back and then some. The gambling is why I know she was wearing the jewelry, and that someone must have taken it. The only time she didn't wear it was when she went to bed. Otherwise she always had it on. She thought it brought her luck. She would never be without it. She might have put the brooch in her purse. But not the ring or the earrings."

"What do you think happened to her?" Marti asked. "We know where she went, that she met someone. Why would she do that? And here of all places."

"A private gambling party?" Sara said. "Or someone she met who was going to a casino, if there is one within a hundred and fifty miles."

"Did you talk to her while she was here?"

"Just once. She always called when she got where she was going and again when she left to come home or got to the next location."

"Did she mention anything about gambling while she was here, either before she left L.A. or when she called?"

"Just that she heard there was a riverboat somewhere, but didn't know if it was anywhere near Lincoln Prairie."

"Would she have gone if she could?"

"Oh yes. She was addicted. Lucky for her she won more than she lost."

"You're sure she wasn't planning to meet someone when she got here? That she didn't know anyone here?"

"She complained that all the action she had found out about in Lincoln Prairie was offtrack betting. For her it was strictly cards. She wouldn't go near anything else. Didn't trust her luck. She said the jewelry didn't work for her when it came to the lottery, horses, or greyhounds. She said she had a feel for the cards and she could read people. Said she couldn't do that with animals and she wouldn't bet against the odds with the lottery, not even for fun."

"Would she have called you if she did go to a game and win big?"

"No. She would surprise me when she got home."

Marti gave her a stern look. "You withheld information, Miss Jones. That's never a good idea, and especially not in this kind of investigation. Are you sure there isn't anything else I should know?"

"Tell her," Akiro Takamoto urged.

"I'm afraid," Sara said. "I'm afraid to leave here without knowing what happened. If it has something to do with her gambling, I could be next."

"Do you feel safe staying with the pastor's family?" Marti asked.

"Yes."

"Has anyone called or tried to contact you?"

Sara shook her head.

"Do not lie to me about that," Marti said. "This is an open investigation. We can protect you if necessary."

"No. And I didn't lie."

"Withholding information amounts to the same thing."

Sara's chin jutted out. "I will tell you if anyone contacts me."

"If you cannot reach me, dial nine-one-one, tell them who you are, and that I told you to call. Someone will be there immediately."

"Yes, ma'am. But I do feel safe there. I have no reason to leave the house; someone is almost always at home, and Akiro will be with me all day for another week. This should be over by then."

"I will also have all the patrol units assigned to that area do an hourly drive-by. They won't stop or come in, but they will be watching for anything unusual."

Sara smiled. "Thank you."

She and Akiro left as they had arrived, holding hands.

"So," Vik said when they were gone. "Jones could have met someone who said they knew where there was a private game or even to go to one of the casinos."

Marti could not let go of the jewelry theory. "It had to have something to do with that jewelry," she insisted. "Sara just said she would not go anywhere without wearing at least the ring and earrings. If she was going someplace to gamble, she certainly would have had them on."

"So someone knows she likes to gamble and wants the jewelry."

"But we're talking about zirconia, Vik. The jewelry that was appraised by the jewelers this week was valuable. Nobody who knew anything about gems would have mistaken that zirconia for anything but what it was, or thought it was worth that much. If it did play into what happened, that jewelry had to have some intrinsic value. And whoever has it only has one earring. I have the other one and I had it with me when I went to the library."

A call came in. It was Frank Phillips, the restaurant owner. "I've got a lady here who says she was in the parking lot when the car arrived that the Jones woman left in."

It took Marti and Vik less than ten minutes to get to the restaurant. Traffic was so light for a Saturday that she didn't even have to use the siren until she came to a red light.

When they went into the restaurant, Marti looked for the ladies with the blue hair, but they weren't at their usual table. The old geezers were there, though. The woman who saw the car was having lunch with two little girls with long dark hair, who looked old enough to be in first and second grade.

"I can't tell you much," she said. "I'm not sure I

would have paid any attention at all if they were regulars."

"Just tell us what you saw, ma'am," Vik said.

"Well, it was one of those cars that they're making now that make you think of speakeasies and flappers."

Marti wrote that down verbatim, but put in parenthesis "PT Cruiser."

"It was dark blue."

"You're sure of the color?"

"Oh yes. It was the same color as my husband's car. The woman behind the wheel was black, but I couldn't tell you much else. It was raining and she had on a rain scarf. I remember her leaning over to open the door on the passenger side, but that's about it."

"What about the woman standing in the parking lot?"

"She walked toward the car when it pulled into the driveway. She got right in."

"Was anyone else in the car?"

"I only saw the two of them."

"You didn't by any chance notice the license plate? Even one letter or number could help."

The woman shook her head. "Sorry. I didn't pay any attention to that at all."

"What year did your husband buy his car?" Marti asked. She hoped they wouldn't be reduced to checking out paint samples.

"It's a 2001 Impala."

They hadn't had lunch. Vik ordered three burgers with fries to go and had to insist on paying for it.

"Wait," the woman said as they were leaving. "When the car door opened, and the interior light came on, I saw the back of the driver's head. There were braids, lots of braids that the rain scarf didn't cover."

"A black woman with braids," Marti mused. She kept pretty much to the speed limit as they drove back to the precinct.

"And that description, such as it is, matches that of the black woman who went to the jeweler."

"And that woman had a Von Weiss brooch."

"I hate it when more information is almost as bad as no information," Vik complained. "We're still going in circles."

"Not quite," Marti said. "We've made a connection between the two women. And now we can be reasonably certain that the jewelry is involved, not the gambling debts."

Holmberg was waiting when they got back. While they ate, they discussed what he had, or rather had not, found out about the Jones family.

"Jones's parents did live in Connecticut, in a small town near Hartford," Holmberg began. "They died in a car crash. Sara and Savannah are listed in the obituary, but no parents, siblings, or other relatives or friends. I went through back copies of the newspaper. Nothing but a one-paragraph article about the car crash. Hit and run. I couldn't find anything to indicate they found the other driver. There is no mention in the obituary about any organizations they belonged to, where they attended church, what kind of work they did, nothing, just the essentials."

He paused and took a couple of bites from the burger. "Umm, lots of onions. Good. Now, there was a private graveside service. The article about the car did say they lived in an apartment complex and that the accident happened close to home. I called, spoke with the manager. He's got twelve units. Nobody's lived there longer than six years. I called the newspaper; the guy who wrote the article is deceased also. I made copies of the obituaries. I think it's a total dead end. Pun intended."

"Why am I not surprised," Vik complained.

"Anything on the Newsomes yet?" Marti asked.

"Lots." Holmberg munched on some fries. "Check the printouts on your desk. They go way back. The obituaries on the grandparents, the parents, and the war hero son are over half a column long. And there are also articles on the grandparents coming here from Romania and founding the company; Warren Senior—he died when he touched a live wire on Yorkshire Road during a thunderstorm; and the death of Thomas Newsome's son—heart attack."

"And," he added, reaching for a packet of ketchup. "There was some speculation as to why Warren Senior got out of his car that night. A wounded deer was found nearby. But there was no damage to his car. There was some speculation that he might have seen the deer at the edge of the road and got out to see how badly it was hurt. The coroner's jury ruled it accidental."

He polished off the rest of the burger and then went on. "There are at least two dozen articles on the son, Warren Junior: medals he was awarded for heroism, field promotions. Some went back to high school, mostly sports. He would have been quite a local hero if he made it home. Thomas Senior, the guy you talked with, sold the company in the mid-eighties when his son died. There was nobody left to inherit but Thomas Junior's wife, Harriet."

"What else do you know about Warren Junior?" Vik wanted to know.

"He was the one who was outstanding in the field, whatever field he chose, football, golf, tennis, the military."

"Does he sound like the type who would ship stolen goods home?"

Holmberg considered that for a minute while he polished off the fries. "Let's say there is no mention of him ever doing anything that was less than exemplary."

"But you don't buy it?" Marti said.

"Would you? Nobody's perfect."

"What about the youngest son?" Vik asked. "Edmund."

"He's interesting, too, but more for what we don't know about him, like where he is—or was. He was mentioned in his mother's obituary, but there was no mention of him in his father's. I've looked everywhere I can think of and haven't found a trace of him. Even if he's dead now, he must have done something back then to change his identity. Some people can just disappear, but not usually from a family as prominent as his. There's nothing in the Social Security death database, so either he never got a Social Security number or he used a different name when he did. As for newspaper articles, neither Edmund nor Thomas ever made it, other than being mentioned in the obituaries. Warren Junior was king of the hill."

The telephone interrupted them. It was Elroy Reed.

"Elroy!"

"Marti! Does a call from our local homicide cop mean I'm a suspect or are you calling to say you enjoyed the latest edition of the *The People's Voice*?"

Marti laughed. "Neither. Did you run an article or make any mention of a bit-part actress named Savannah Payne-Jones?"

"I sure did, in the issue that ran right before she was killed. She was here filming car chases for *Deadly Deceptions*. Drowned, didn't she?"

"Yes. Did you interview her?"

"No, we requested a PR packet from her agent."

"Did you publish a picture of her by any chance?"

"Of course. Do you know her story? She had surgery for thyroid cancer and they damaged her vocal cords. Even though she couldn't speak much above a whisper, she managed to keep on doing what she loved, acting."

"Yes. I am aware of that. Could you get a copy of that article to me real quick?"

"Sure thing. Give me your e-mail address."

While they waited, Marti updated Holmberg on their activities involving the Jones case.

"Finally, a corroborative witness," he said. "And her hairstyle matches that of the mystery woman in Chicago. It looks like you're closing in."

"Right," Vik said, scowling.

"This is my first experience with a case as complex as this," Holmberg admitted. "The way you follow up on every little detail, it must feel great when all the time you put in pays off. I can see why you have such a high closure rate."

Marti looked at him for a minute, then burst out laughing.

"What's so funny?" Holmberg asked.

"You mean that, don't you?" she said.

He looked indignant.

"No, no," she said. "I know you mean it. It was just so . . . the lieutenant," she admitted. "Looks like I've gotten too used to being criticized."

"We're a team," Holmberg said. "Even if Lupe and I only help out as needed."

When Marti checked her e-mail a few minutes later, Elroy had sent the article about Savannah. She was most interested in the photograph. It was in color and Jones was wearing the earrings. Her hand was posed so that the ring showed. The photograph even captured the lightness of her eyes. She showed it to Vik. "Someone either recognized the jewelry, or recognized her."

"Or both," Vik said. "And at this point, that could be damned near anybody."

"But most likely someone with a lot of braids and a dark blue PT Cruiser."

"Jeez, MacAlister. That really narrows it down."

"Time out," Marti said. "Think you can come up with another pot of coffee that's just a little bit stronger than the last one, Holmberg?"

Vik leaned back with his mug cupped in both hands and put his feet up on his desk. "What was the name of that beauty shop Harriet Newsome mentioned?"

"Sophia's."

"It sure would be interesting, wouldn't it, if that bad hair job involved red dye."

"You can't get that box out of your mind either, can you?"

Vik shook his head.

Marti got the number to the beauty shop from Information. When she hung up she said, "Harriet said russet and Peggy Jeanne thought she said rust. Apparently there is a significant difference. Russet is a brown dye with reddish highlights. Rust leans more toward bright red with orange highlights."

"Aha," Holmberg said. "Could Harriet Newsome be our lady with the red hair and the green garnet cuff links?"

"If she is," Vik said, "I wonder what's in that box that Newsome doesn't want her to know he is giving to the patriarch tomorrow."

"What patriarch?" Holmberg asked.

"Hell if I know," Vik admitted.

"Tomorrow?" When Vik confirmed that, Holmberg got on the computer. Five minutes later he said, "This has to be it: 'His Beatitude, Vladimir, patriarch of all Romania, metropolitan of Ungro-Wallachia, archbishop of Bucharest will be celebrating the Liturgy at the Romanian Orthodox Church in Skokie, Illinois, on Sunday, May sixteenth at eleven A.M. Reception Sunday evening after vespers.' There's even a picture of him. He wears white, just like the pope."

"Would you print that out?" Vik asked. "And get the address and directions to the church?"

A few minutes later, Holmberg handed him a couple of printouts.

"How would you two like to go to church with me tomorrow morning?"

"Sounds good to me," Holmberg said.

"Is this like going to Mass?" Marti asked. She had attended funerals at Catholic churches.

"No," Vik said. "Well, up to a point. They chant or sing everything. There's no organ or anything. And whatever His Beatitude does is done behind a screen. Actually it's more like a bunch of doors with spaces in between. The congregation has to peek between the cracks to see what's going on at the altar."

"And it begins at eleven o'clock," Marti said.

Vik consulted the printouts. "Right. Suppose we arrive late, say eleven thirty, and stay in the back? We don't want to be conspicuous."

Marti looked at him to see if he was joking, but he was serious. "If *we* want to be inconspicuous, we better just wait outside until the people come out after the service. His Beatitude will have the box by then and we can just identify ourselves and ask to see what's inside."

"Sounds like a plan," Holmberg agreed.

"Let's get there by ten thirty then," Vik said. "Make sure Newsome and Harriet show up. We can see His Greatness . . ."

"His Beatitude," Marti said as she nodded in reluctant agreement. Ben would repeat the PSA test on Monday. She had wanted to go to church with her family in the morning and spend the rest of the day with them.

"Yeah. His Beatitude or whatever," Vik said. "If we time it right we'll catch the three of them together. I'm betting there's some jewelry in that box, compliments of Warren Junior. One of them should be able to tell us how it got there."

"Maybe even where some of it went."

"And maybe, MacAlister, if we get very lucky, they will also know or know of someone who drives a PT Cruiser, has a lot of braids, and is in possession of a pair of Von Weiss cuff links."

Marti reached for the phone. "The car and the hair are pushing it."

Ben answered her call and she explained what she had to do tomorrow. "Maybe we can all go out for pizza and a movie tonight."

"Is Momma allowed to watch movies that are rated PG-13?" Ben asked.

"No sex, no profanity. She doesn't like violence either."

"So much for that idea."

"I just want us to have time with the family and maybe a little fun before Monday."

"Gotcha," Ben said. "Me and the kids will plan a surprise."

That done, Marti read through Holmberg's most current printouts, which included a picture of and the history of the church in Skokie, as well as the patriarch's photo. He was wearing white, but he looked young; mid-sixties was Marti's guess. Instead of a miter, he wore what looked like half a box covered with white fabric that also hung to his shoulders like a short veil.

CHAPTER 32

SUNDAY, MAY 16—SKOKIE, ILLINOIS

Marti and Vik watched as Thomas Newsome and Harriet Newsome walked from the parking lot to the church. Holmberg was in a separate vehicle, watching the rear entrance.

"They're in," Vik told Homberg. "Newsome is carrying a briefcase. The box must be inside."

"How long does the service last?" Marti asked.

"Hard to say, not more than an hour if it's anything like Mass."

They settled back with some MacDonald's breakfast sandwiches and coffee.

When the Liturgy was over, Vladimir went into the vestry and bowed before the icon of the Theotokos. The service had been long and he was tired. He was about to remove his vestments when he heard a voice behind him.

"Your Beatitude?"

He turned. An elderly man was standing there. "I'm Thomas Newsome," he said. "I've brought something that you must take back to Romania." He took an ornately carved chest out of his briefcase.

A woman burst into the room. "Oh no, you don't!" Her voice was low, but shook with anger. Her hair was an odd fiery red. "That's mine!"

She looks like a wraith, Vladimir thought. What family dispute am I caught in?

"Please," he said. "Sit down." He indicated some chairs arranged in a circle.

"Give it to me," the woman demanded. She pulled out a gun.

The man, Thomas, stared at the gun, said, "Dear Lord, where did that come from?" He clutched at his chest. "Harriet, put that gun away!"

The church service lasted over two hours. Marti and Vik waited until people stopped coming out of the church.

"They're still inside," Vik told Holmberg. "We're going in. Keep the rear door covered."

The interior of the church was unlike any church Marti had ever seen before. There were no statues, just the most beautiful paintings she had ever seen.

"Icons," Vik mumbled.

The screens that separated the altar from the congregation were gold and depicted the four evangelists, Matthew, Mark, Luke, and John; Mary with the Child Jesus; and at the top, the risen Christ, with an angel kneeling on either side.

"Awesome," she whispered.

Vik walked past the gold panels and down a short hall. Marti followed.

They heard a man's voice, speaking softly, and stopped.

"Harriet, you don't need a gun," Vladimir said.

Marti and Vik unholstered their weapons. As she did so, Marti hoped they would not have to fire them in this beautiful church.

Silently, Vladimir repeated the Jesus prayer. Aloud he said, "Surely we can resolve this." He took a step toward her. When she didn't warn him away, he took another step. "I am a man of God, Harriet. I mean you no harm. Nor do I intend to take anything that is rightfully yours." When he was close enough, he took her by the arm and guided her to a chair. "Come. Sit. Let's talk about this. I don't even know what is inside." He indicated the box.

When she was seated he said, "Maybe you should put down the gun. I know nothing about them, but it doesn't seem safe. I know you mean me no harm." She hesitated. "Why don't you just give it to me?" Slowly she did. He had never handled a gun before and was surprised by how heavy it was.

"Now. Let's talk about this. May I open the box?" He touched the ornate carving. It depicted the screens that shielded the altar. "Beautiful," he murmured.

Harriet sat stiff and still in the chair beside him. Thomas Newsome was still standing. "Please sit, Thomas," Vladimir suggested. The man looked at him for a moment, as if he was speaking a language he didn't understand, then he took the chair the farthest from where Harriet sat.

Vladimir opened the box. There was an envelope on top. He opened it. Inside was a cashier's check for a sum large enough to take care of many orphans. He looked at Thomas, who nodded. He took out the sheaf of papers, scanned them, and realized it was some sort of manuscript. Then he saw the jewelry. "Why does this belong in Romania, Thomas?" he asked.

"Because that's where it came from," Thomas explained. "I don't know for certain how the jewelry got here, but my brother was in Europe during World War Two. I think he must have got his hands on it somehow and sent it to my father. That's all I can tell you. I am an old man. I cannot die with this in my possession. And I need to make my confession."

"May I call in one of my aides first?" Vladimir asked.

Thomas nodded.

Vladimir decided to take the gun with him. When Vladimir opened the door that led to the church proper, he saw a man and a woman. They, too, were holding guns. The man put his finger to his lips. The woman pulled out a wallet with a photo on one side and a badge on the other. She mouthed the word "police." The man pulled out his identification also.

Vladimir nodded, made a note of the names on their I.D. cards, and said nothing. He handed the woman, Marti, the gun. "Josef," he called to a man stripping the linen from the altar. "Could you come look at this, please?"

The male officer, Jessenovik, put his finger to his lips as Josef approached.

"There is someone here I would like you to meet, Josef, and something they brought me that I would like you to see." Vladimir led the way into the vestry. "This is Harriet, and this is Thomas."

Josef nodded toward them, sat near Vladimir, and opened the box. He looked in the envelope first. His eyes widened, but he said nothing. Then he looked carefully at the papers. "Eugène Ionesco," he said. "He was born in Romania, but lived in France. This looks like part of an original manuscript. It's written in Romanian, not French." He read a few paragraphs aloud. "I think it might be a rough draft of a scene from *The Bald Soprano*." He weighed it in his hand. "That could mean he began writing much earlier than anyone was aware of."

Josef looked at the jewelry. He turned it over, checking the back. "There is a jeweler's mark," he said. "But I don't recognize it. I can find out easily enough."

"Thank you, Josef," Vladimir said. "I need to speak with Thomas alone. Harriet might like a tour of the church."

Harriet took a long look at the contents of the chest, then let Josef take her arm and lead her out.

Marti followed them into the church. There were no pews, just a couple of benches along the side. The congregation must stand for the service. The benches were probably for the elderly and disabled.

Harriet looked around. She seemed exhausted.

"Could you stay with her for a few minutes?" Marti asked Josef.

"Certainly. We're going to take a look at the icons."

Vik stayed inside while she went out and found Holmberg standing at the rear entrance. "I need you to take Harriet Newsome back to the precinct. She had a gun. Cuff her and put her in the backseat. Stay parked out back until Vik and I leave with Newsome. We'll take him in."

When Marti went back inside, Vik waved her away

from the door to the vestry. "He's making his confession," he told her.

Vladimir bowed his head as he listened to Thomas's confession. When Thomas was silent he said, "You have done your penance already, years of penance, my son. How can I help you find peace?"

Thomas took the Theotokos out of his jacket pocket. He had wrapped the Mother in velvet. "This, too, must go back," he said.

Vladimir unwrapped the small icon. He touched the aged wood. Tears were streaming down Thomas's face.

"We have many icons," Vladimir said. "And there is no way to find out who this might have belonged to fifty or sixty years ago." He thought of the icon in his bedroom, and the one in his vestry. He prayed before them every day when he was in Bucharest. He traveled with one a little smaller than this. He could not imagine being without them.

Vladimir blessed the icon and gave it back to Thomas. "I think this belongs to you. She will bring you much comfort if you let her. Go now in peace. God forgives your sins. Forgive yourself."

"Now," Vladimir said as he took the envelope out of the box. "Can you afford to give this to the Church? It is a great amount. God does not require such a gift from you. He is always there to forgive."

"I have given you half of my wealth."

"Then this is a donation for the orphans of Romania."

He took Thomas by the arm and they went into the church proper together.

Vladimir gave the envelope to Josef. "This is a donation," he told Marti, "not a written confession." Then Vladimir held out the box. "You will need this, I think."

"Yes," Marti agreed, "but perhaps not for long. You're going to sit with me while I write two lists of what's inside. I'll need your signature on both. I'll sign also. We'll return everything as soon as we can."

"And I will speak with Harriet, please, before she leaves," Vladimir told Marti. "I am certain she meant me no harm. Often people are not as they seem." He looked at Marti for a few moments, and felt a sudden sadness. "You are troubled," he said.

"My husband might have cancer."

He nodded. "Suffering is difficult to understand and even harder to accept. I have found that anticipating it is the worst of all. In there, just now, I said what we call the Jesus prayer. It is very simple. 'Lord Jesus Christ, have mercy on me.' As often as I have said it, I am still often amazed at the many different ways He chooses to answer."

"Thank you," Marti said.

"May I give you my blessing?"

When she nodded, he placed his hand on her head and prayed.

Vladimir got into the backseat of the car beside Harriet. "Did you come here today to harm me?"

271

"No. I just wanted to make you give me back the box."

"I would have done that if you asked. I would not have kept the box while you were at odds about what to do with it. Can you tell me why you felt you must have it?"

"He's seventy-nine. He'll die one day. I'll have nothing and I'll be alone."

"You are Orthodox?"

"No. Presbyterian."

"You go to your church?"

"No."

"Go," he said. "Find peace."

He got out of the car and walked up to Marti. "I don't know how you handle things like this, but she meant me no harm. She just wanted the contents of the box. This is not something she will do again. I will not be involved if she is charged with anything."

"Will you be leaving soon?" Marti asked.

He smiled. "The day after tomorrow. Soon I will be back home in Bucharest." Josef and Nicolae's efforts had gone well. And he thought of the cashier's check; his prayers for the orphans had been heard. Josef would ascertain that Mr. Newsome could indeed afford to give it to them, and make sure Harriet would be provided for. Then, God willing, he would truly be able to help some of his children find homes.

33

LINCOLN PRAIRIE

Marti was concerned about questioning Thomas Newsome. He was elderly. He looked pale. They didn't handcuff him. Twice on the ride back to Lincoln Prairie he clutched at his chest.

"Who is your family doctor, Mr. Newsome?"

He told them.

"We're going to take you to Lincoln Prairie Memorial Hospital. Can he see you there?"

"Yes."

"Good. They'll check you out. I'll call ahead and I'll make sure your doctor knows you are coming."

Marti also called Holmberg and told him to meet them at the hospital after he took Harriet in.

"There's no gold-and-zirconia jewelry in the box," Marti said as they left the hospital. "But there is a pair of cuff links with green stones. I'll have to confirm it, but they must be the ones the woman with the red hair showed the jeweler. But those two haven't killed anyone."

"She did pull a gun on His Gracefulness."

This time, Marti didn't bother to correct him. "Just wait until you see it," she said.

When Marti got into the car she unlocked the glove compartment and took out the evidence bag with the gun.

"It is an old one," Vik admitted. "We'll see what Forensics can tell us about the last time it was fired."

Harriet was locked in the interrogation room, sitting at a table with a bench on either side. Everything was bolted to the floor. She looked terrified. That red hair was frizzy and seemed to exaggerate her fear.

"Am I under arrest?" she asked.

"Not yet." Marti waited until Vik and another officer who would be recording their interview came in. Then she read Harriet her rights, made sure she understood them, and asked if she wanted an attorney present. Harriet shook her head.

"Please give verbal answers, ma'am," the recording officer said.

"No, I do not want my lawyer. What is it you want to know?"

"Where did you get the gun?" Vik asked. His voice was gentle, as if he was speaking to a child.

"It's just an old gun that's been in a trunk in the basement for years."

"Who does it belong to?"

"Us, I guess, me and Dad. It was there when I moved in with Tom, my husband."

"Have you ever fired that weapon?"

"No."

"Do you know of anyone who has?"

"No."

"Why did you take the gun to church today?"

"I just wanted the box. When Dad said he was bringing it to the patriarch and I couldn't talk him out of it, I thought I could use the gun to make the patriarch give it back."

Vik rubbed his chin. The ideas people came up with. Marti agreed, touching her lower lip.

"You didn't think you could just ask him to return it?" Vik asked. "He seemed like a very nice man."

"Everything is valuable, even the papers. All of it is worth a lot. Everything I have and will ever have depends on Dad. And I never gave him a grandchild. He will never forgive me for that. I just wanted something of my own when he died. Just in case."

"Do you know where the things in the box came from?"

"Originally from Romania. I don't know how they got here. I suppose Warren Junior had something to do with that. He was the only one of us who ever went to Europe."

"Is all of the jewelry in the box?" Vik prodded. "Did you keep any of it? Maybe for a rainy day?"

"No. I just wanted to sell some of it. It's old and clunky. It looks like something Greta Garbo might have worn. I can't imagine why it's worth so much."

Vik was quiet for a minute. Finally, Harriet asked, "Now am I under arrest?"

"Not yet," Vik told her.

She began to cry.

When Vik looked at Marti, she was ready with some Kleenex.

"Now," he said. "We took your father-in-law to the hospital and . . ."

"Dad? What's wrong?"

"Nothing as far as we know. We just thought they ought to have a look at him, given his age and what happened today. I'm going to call and see how he is. I'll be right back."

When Vik returned, he said, "He's fine but your family physician wants him to stay in the hospital overnight for observation and he's ordered more tests in the morning."

"Overnight? But I have to cook dinner for him."

"I'm sure they'll see to it that he eats."

"Hospital food? Dad?"

"Would you like to see him?"

"Oh, yes. Poor Dad. He's only been in the hospital once since I married Tom."

Marti noticed the way Harriet spoke of Tom as if he was still alive. She had done the same thing when Johnny died, but not for long. What was worse was thinking of something that she wanted to tell him and catching herself before she called out to him or reached for the phone. If Ben . . . no . . . Ben would be fine.

"We're going to have someone take you to the hospital . . ." Vik began.

"Not in a police car!"

"No, ma'am, but your car isn't here yet. Will you need a ride home?"

"Home? I can go home?"

"I talked to the deputy chief. He said we could release you on your own recognizance."

"What does that mean?"

"You sign some papers, agree not to leave town. Do you have a passport?"

"No."

"Good. Your car will be returned to you tomorrow. How will you get home from the hospital?"

"I'll probably stay the night. If not, I'll just take a cab."

"Is there someone we can call?"

"I'm going to call the housekeeper. She'll spend the night at the house in case I need her."

When Vik had assured himself that Harriet would be okay, he took her to the sergeant's desk. Holmberg was there, waiting to take her to the hospital.

They turned over the gun to Forensics, signed in the box at Evidence and went up to their office. Vik sat without speaking. Marti brought him some coffee.

"You feel sorry for her," she said.

He picked up the cup, looked down at it. "I gave Mildred money," he said. "I gave her all the money we received as gifts for our wedding. My father told me to. He said a woman needed to feel independent. So Mildred has always had her own bank account. I just make the deposits. I don't ask what she does with it."

Marti smiled. "It sounds like Mildred's doing okay now."

"She's doing fine. And it's been six months since she had a relapse. The doctor has her on some new medication."

"That's good," Marti said.

"MacAlister . . ."

"Yes?"

"About Ben. Everything will turn out okay. History won't repeat itself. He'll be fine."

"Thanks, partner." She hoped he was right.

Marti met Ben at Staben House. He wanted to spend some time with Lynn Ella.

"Hi, Aunt Marti," she said, keeping her distance. She was still shy and quiet with everyone except Ben. She gave Ben a big hug. "Guess who's here?"

He laughed. "Who?"

"Rucha. She's my tutor, come on." She took Ben's hand and he let her pull him into the kitchen. Curious, Marti followed.

"Rucha's family came here from India. If I had a map I could show you where it is. I can spell it too, I-N-D-I-A."

Marti thought Rucha was beautiful. Dark hair, her unblemished olive complexion and dark eyes spoke of her ancestry. She looked to be twelve or thirteen.

"Today we're doing math," Lynn Ella said. "See! I got them all right except this one." Ignoring Marti, she showed Ben the paper. "Iris says I'll be ready to go to school by August." She still would not verbally acknowledge Iris as her mother.

Marti felt depressed when they left. But Ben seemed to be in a good mood.

"Momma's fixing something special for supper," he told her. "From the aromas coming from the kitchen I'd guess there will be cake for dessert. Yellow with chocolate icing." His favorite.

The kid's surprise last night was home videos, followed by *Jumping Jack Flash* and *Ghost*. Her favorite movies. While they were watching they had popcorn and root-beer floats. Everyone's favorite snack.

Now Ben walked her to her car. "I'll follow you home." He looked down at her. "Everything is going to be all right," he said.

Like a child, she wanted to say, "Promise?"

C　　H　　A　　P　　T　　E　　R

34

MONDAY, MAY 17——LINCOLN PRAIRIE

It was almost eight o'clock in the morning when Delilah heard the knock on the door. That Cornelius. They did have a key for each other's house. He was coming for breakfast and she hadn't even put the oatmeal on yet. She sat and looked out the front window when she got up. The sun was shining and the daffodils and tulips planted years ago were still coming up.

She opened the door without putting the chain on

first. "Why, Officer Torres. I thought you were Cornelius."

"Check first anyway," Officer Torres cautioned.

"What in the world . . ."

Officer Torres was carrying three plastic grocery bags in one hand and a gallon of milk in the other.

"I thought if I came early enough you might not have started breakfast and you'd make me some of your blueberry pancakes."

"Well, just come right on into the kitchen."

Officer Torres put the bags on the table. "I wasn't sure what to bring," she said. "At my house we have scrambled eggs with cactus and chorizo wrapped in a tortilla."

She took three packages of fresh blueberries out of the bag, then five-pound bags of sugar and flour, a box of pancake mix, two dozen eggs, and three pounds of sausage, along with molasses, maple syrup, orange juice, and cranberry juice, and a three-pound can of Folgers coffee. That would be a treat. Delilah always bought a pound of house brand.

"Good grief, child. You've got enough here to feed an army."

"Did I bring what you need?"

"Oh, yes. I'll get a nice batch whipped up for us. My, won't Cornelius be surprised." She reached for the box of pancake mix. "Anything interesting going on in Bullfrog Bog? It hasn't gotten warm enough yet to sit on the porch. We ain't had much excitement here no way since you've been around."

"You want some excitement?" Lupe teased.

"No, not really."

"How about a neighborhood cookout for the Fourth of July?"

"You serious?"

"Me and the other guys who work this beat have been talking about it."

"That really would be somethin'."

Delilah was cracking eggs in the bowl with the pancake mix when Cornelius came in. "You got your hearing aid turned on, Cornelius? We got us some company. And we got blueberry pancakes and link sausages for breakfast, thanks to Officer Torres here."

Cornelius adjusted his hearing aid while she was talking. "Good to see you again," he said.

"I've had a real taste for Miss Delilah's cooking for a while now."

Cornelius grinned. "She don't do too bad for an old woman."

"Cornelius Jefferson!"

"Township folk been coming out just like you said," he went on. "They plowed out the snow for us this winter and they say they'll be coming to cut the grass this summer."

Delilah added more milk to the batter, then carefully folded in the blueberries so the batter wouldn't turn blue. She knew that Officer Torres had come here for a reason, and it wasn't just to have pancakes. She never came empty-handed, though, and even better,

Bullfrog Bog was a different place since she'd been around.

The whole neighborhood was safer with Officer Torres around. No more teenagers hanging out on the streets. She helped catch the kids who were doing the break-ins last year. Delilah even went back to sitting on the front porch with Cornelius most summer evenings. Besides that, Officer Torres visited all of the old people around who lived here regularly, had the fire department put in smoke alarms and the township office install dead-bolt locks. She made sure they was checked on if it got real hot or real cold. They even had a way to let her know if something was wrong in their homes.

Delilah put some of the sausages in a skillet and began making the pancakes. Time the food was on the table; Officer Torres was showing Cornelius a newspaper article.

"Is this that actress what got drowned when we was having them floods?" Cornelius asked.

"Does she look familiar?"

Cornelius hesitated. "No, too young. How would I know a young pretty actress like that? Says here she comes from . . ." He pulled his glasses down his nose a bit for better focus. "Los Angeles."

Delilah put a plate stacked with pancakes on the table. Then she looked over Officer Torres's shoulder and stared at the picture of the woman. "What you say her name was?" she asked.

"Savannah Payne-Jones."

"Never heard of nobody named that," Delilah said, but she sure enough recognized that jewelry and those eyes. "She got any children?"

"A daughter, Sara. She's twenty-three, teaches math and science."

Delilah blinked a few times. She couldn't cry. "And this Savannah came here from Los Angeles. Was she a big star?"

"No, just bit parts, but lots of them. Actually, she was born in Medford, some town near Boston."

"That's in Massachusetts somewhere, ain't it?" Delilah asked. What in the world would have made Tamar think to go there?

"Yes. We haven't been able to find out anything about her parents, though. It's as if they just showed up one day fully grown and got married. We got a copy of their marriage license and all of the information on it is false."

"False how?" Delilah asked.

"Parents' names. Where they were living before they married. Where they were born."

"Can't you just ask them, being as you know who they are. They must want to come claim their daughter."

"They died," Lupe said. "Car accident nineteen years ago."

"Where were they buried?"

"In Connecticut. We've got a picture of them though. I'll bring it over if you'd like to see it."

"Might be interesting to see it," Delilah said. There

283

was no need to speak up until she was absolutely sure. Behind her, the sausages were sizzling. Delilah rushed to the stove, and put them on a plate. They had browned nicely. "Juice or coffee," she asked.

"Coffee," Officer Torres and Cornelius said almost at the same time.

Delilah brought two steaming cups to the table, poured some of the sugar into a sugar bowl and found a pitcher for milk. Good thing Officer Torres had brought that; she was out of it for the rest of the month. She poured some cranberry juice for herself.

She had to make herself eat. It felt as if there was some huge lump in her throat. The actress in that picture had to be Tamar's child. She didn't know of anyone else but her husband, Tamar's daddy, and Tamar who had those light-colored eyes. As for the jewelry, nobody but Tamar could have given it to her.

Officer Torres apologized for not being able to stay. She left the newspaper article on the table. When Cornelius started to say something, Delilah gave him a look and he shut up.

"What's wrong, Lila?" Cornelius asked as soon as Officer Torres left.

"Take another look at that picture Cornelius. A good long look."

"I saw the jewelry," he said. "Knew right away who it belonged to and who gave it to her."

"Take another look at Savannah."

He pulled his spectacles halfway down his nose and

held the paper closer to his face.

"This can't be Tamar," he said.

"No, but it's got to be her child. Asher gave Tamar that jewelry," she told him. "You might of made like wasn't nothin' going on, but Asher got them packages from Mr. Newsome's son, who was off in the war. Asher wasn't nothin' but their handyman, Cornelius. There's no way that rascal Warren Newsome Junior would send anything to Asher lessin' it was something his father shouldn't be getting in the mail himself. That Warren Junior—town hero, my behind. Nobody put it in the paper when he beat that boy near half to death, nor when he assaulted that teacher. Then there was that car he wrecked while he was drinking and driving. None of that ever got told."

"Lila, I know this here actress looks just like Tamar, and there might not be too many people with that color eyes, but we don't know nothin' more than what Officer Torres told us, and she sure didn't tell us much."

"She told us much as she wanted us to know. You remember them cuff links Asher was sportin' and showin' off before he left? Them ones that looked like junk with them big green stones? I bet he took them from those boxes what came those first few weeks after Warren Junior died. I bet Mr. Newsome didn't see any of what was inside. I bet that jewelry he gave Tamar, what Savannah's wearing in that picture, come out of one of them packages, too."

Sara. She had a great-granddaughter named Sara.

"Think about it, Cornelius! That's probably why Asher went to Michigan all of a sudden without ever even talkin' about goin' anywhere. . . . And him always talkin' like he was such a good Christian man. He did that 'cause of you, Cornelius. Knowed you were a preacher's son and wanted to stay on your good side. I never did believe it myself."

She hadn't showed him but that one letter Asher sent Tamar, the one where he talked about that trouble with his heart. And that was just to spare Cornelius more grief. But it was time now that he knew. Somehow she had to look after her great-granddaughter, make sure nothin' happened to her.

Cornelius got up and poured himself another cup of coffee. He looked hurt, but in his heart he had to know that what she said was the truth.

Delilah felt too agitated to put the food away and wash the dishes. She forced herself to do it anyway, and as she worked, she began to feel calmer.

Cornelius waited until she had cleaned up and was sitting down.

"So, why didn't you tell Officer Torres nothin'? She been good to us, Lila. We should be helping her."

"Someone else we got to talk to first," Lila said. "That woman what come visitin' Asher Hunt, that one what called herself Laura Hunt."

"She was his cousin, Lila."

"That's what they said. She come back six months after he was gone askin' for whatever he left here, wanting that watch he gave you. You never ought to have gave that to her, Cornelius."

"Might have been what he woulda wanted, her bein' kinfolk and all."

"Maybe," Delilah insisted. "Wherever Asher went, you can bet she knows. And now my granddaughter's picture is in that newspaper wearing the jewelry Asher gavé Tamar. She comes here and all of a sudden she's dead."

"You sure shoulda told that to Officer Torres."

"Cornelius! Use your head! I got me a great-granddaughter, Sara." She said it again, "Sara." Her great-granddaughter, a gift from Tamar. "I can't have her mixed up in nothing that's to do with the police that has to do with her mother, or Tamar and that fool Asher Hunt, lessin' I know what it is for sure. Now you get yourself over to Sadie's house, Cornelius. Remember how that Laura was writing to her, trying to get information about us, and askin' if anyone heard from Asher and if he come back? Sadie might be almost as addle-brained as you sometimes, Cornelius, but she don't never throw nothin' away. You see where them letters come from and use Sadie's phone to call that Laura and tell her she got to come talk to us now!"

Cornelius scratched his head. "Seems to me like the police ought to be talkin' to Miss Sadie, and Laura," he said. "Not us."

It wasn't easy, but Delilah managed to shed a few tears. "We talkin' 'bout my kinfolk, Cornelius, only kin I got. My Sara! My great-granddaughter! You heard Officer Torres. Tamar and whoever she married is dead. Now my granddaughter is dead, too. I ain't never goin' to get to know her, and her bein' an actress and all. Ain't nobody left but my great-grandchild. I got to be sure how Asher got that jewelry 'fore I can talk with anybody. Tamar's dead, Cornelius. She's dead." This time the tears came easy. "Ain't nothin' I can do for her now except to make sure nothin' bad is said about her. Least not in public. And protect her grandchild, my Sara."

"Asher's cousin Laura did came around one time just before he left for Michigan," Cornelius admitted.

"You didn't tell me that, Cornelius Jefferson."

"You was upset enough that she was comin' around at all. Worried for Tamar as well. They talked for a long time. He must have told her something. That's why I ain't never quite believed he was dead. They planned something. He might even be with her now. We got to tell Officer Torres all of this," Cornelius insisted.

"What if Tamar or Asher did something that we don't want the police to know?"

"Ain't no more need for secrets."

"Says you, who kept one from me all these years! Sara, my great-granddaughter is twenty-three. She's just a child. I got to do this for her. You want it to come out if Asher was a thief? And worse, have him arrested if he still is alive?"

Cornelius bowed his head at that, studied the red-and-white squares on the plastic tablecloth for a few minutes. Then he got up. He reached for his hat and shuffled on down the hall and out the door. For the first time, as Delilah watched from the window as he walked down the street, he looked old.

Alone, she looked at the picture again. Savannah. Her granddaughter. Someone she would never know. Never. But she would know Savannah's child. She would meet Sara. But first she had to protect her somehow and that meant finding out what Asher did, and if Tamar left because she was involved in whatever it was. Officer Torres would help her keep it out of the news if it was something bad. Officer Torres would handle whatever it was in a way so that nobody ever had to know.

C H A P T E R

35

Marti and Vik went to Lincoln Prairie Memorial Hospital right after roll call. Mr. Newsome was sitting up in bed reading the *Chicago Tribune*. He was hooked up to an IV, but looked much better than he did when they brought him here yesterday. A picture painted on wood, something Marti now knew was an icon, was on the table by his bed. It wasn't more than five by seven, but the paint had faded with age. Mary looked desolate, no smiling Child, no dead Jesus, nothing. Just her. She seemed to be looking at something that brought her an inconsolable sorrow.

Marti thought of Ben and looked away.

"How's Harriet?" Newsome asked. "She could never harm anyone, and she doesn't give a whit for what's in that box. Security is such an odd thing for her to be concerned about. We've always taken care of her. I didn't want to send her home, but she was getting herself all worked up unnecessarily."

Marti felt relieved that his voice sounded stronger. He was in the Cardiac Care Unit. She could see the leads that were hooked up to the monitors. But he looked and sounded much better.

"She said she was going to call the housekeeper to come stay with her," Marti told him.

"Good. She didn't tell me that." He hesitated, then said, "Officers, she did not mean any harm to anyone yesterday. She hardly ever raises her voice. That mess that poor girl made of her hair? She didn't even call to complain."

"Why do you think she felt she needed to threaten the patriarch with that gun?" Vik asked him.

"For some reason that I don't understand myself, she felt very desperate. She was worried about how she would survive without me. It isn't as if we need the money, whatever the manuscript and jewelry is worth. She's well taken care of, always will be."

"Has she ever worked?" Vik asked.

"Of course not."

"Does she have any job skills?"

Newsome thought for a moment, then said, "None that I know of."

"Maybe she needs to have some money set aside in her own name," Vik suggested. "Something she can see is her own."

"Why? My mother never did." He was silent, then said, "I can take care of that. She takes quite good care of me. She's an excellent cook. And she's accepted my son Tom's death and those two miscarriages better than I ever will."

Vik took a chair on one side of the bed. Marti sat in one by the window. It hadn't warmed up much yet. According to the weatherman it was the coldest spring in five years. But the sun was out, and it shone through the window and made rectangular patterns on the floor.

"Now," Vik said. "About that gun."

"I didn't even know it was in the house."

"Do you know who it belonged to?"

"It must have been my father's, or perhaps even my grandfather's. We never went hunting, were never taught how to use guns or even bows and arrows. Whatever we did do, even fishing, Dad always made sure we learned from professionals. I'm not even sure Dad knew how to use a gun. I don't know where Harriet could have found it. Was it a real gun?"

"It was real," Vik told him. "Could it have belonged to your oldest brother?"

Newsome shook his head. "Warren Junior thought the best thing about being in the Army was learning how to fire a rifle and whatever other weapons they used in the war. He didn't know how when he enlisted."

Vik looked at Marti and raised his eyebrows. She took over.

"Do you know where the jewelry came from?"

"No, but my guess is that Warren Junior found a way to send it home."

"Would he have done something dishonest to get it?" she asked.

Newsome pushed the button that elevated his head before he answered her. "That would have been half the fun. It wouldn't have seemed wrong to Warren, just daring, another adventure, another opportunity to play the hero."

"Was the jewelry in the box all of the jewelry your father received?"

"I have no idea. That's all that has been in the box since he died. If he gave any away before then, I wouldn't know. I can't think of anyone he would give it to either."

Marti took out her notebook. "Does the name Savannah Payne-Jones mean anything to you."

Newsome shook his head.

"Sara Tamar Jones?"

"No."

"Tamar Greathouse?" These were the names of Savannah's daughter and mother, according to the articles Holmberg had found.

Again he shook his head.

"How about Jerry Payne?" That was Tamar's husband.

"No. I'm sorry. Those names mean nothing to me."

"They are all African American. Could they have been employees of your father or mother?"

"No, we didn't have any African Americans working in the house when I was growing up. The household help came from Poland and lived in. There could have been someone paid out of pocket to do handiwork or odd jobs outside, but not a woman."

"Did you ever observe an African-American male working on your property?"

"No. I never did."

"Would there be any employment records to indicate if someone did?"

"Probably not, but check that out with the owners. We did keep extensive records."

As they stood to leave, Vik said, "Will you be going home anytime soon?"

"Sometime today. But I do want to thank you for bringing me here. I feel much better now that they've run all these tests and not found anything wrong with me. I don't even have any clogged arteries. The chest pain is just caused by stress."

"I'm glad to hear that," Vik said.

There was something likable about Thomas Newsome and Harriet. Marti didn't know what it was, but she felt much the same way as Vik.

"So," Vik said, when they returned to their car. "I think it's a safe bet that all of the jewelry got here through this Warren Junior, but as far as we've determined so far, there's nobody still living who can tell

293

more about that than we already know. There's nobody who can tell us exactly how it got here, or who it was given to. Maybe someone stole the gold and zirconia pieces from Warren Senior. Maybe he gave the jewelry away."

"Let's follow up with the current owners of the business, see if they have any record of the names we do have. And let's give Harriet a call. Maybe she'll remember something Newsome didn't. And Holmberg might come up with something when he comes in this afternoon. He's out on patrol with Lupe right now."

CHAPTER

36

Delilah watched from the window as a car pulled up and a woman who had to be Laura Hunt got out. Asher's cousin, if that's who she was, didn't look nothin' like she remembered. Had her hair pressed with a hot comb back then. Now she looked like she was wearing a wig what with all them braids. Delilah had the door open before the woman reached the porch steps.

"I've come to see Mr. Jefferson."

Them braids made her look younger than Delilah thought she was. That and all that makeup.

"He'll be over soon as he sees you're here." When Cornelius came back from talking to her at Sadie's, he said Laura had been calling Sadie off and on for years, asking about Tamar and Asher.

Delilah led the way down the hall. The paper with Savannah's picture was on the table.

"Coffee?" she asked.

There was no answer. Laura was reading the article.

"That's Tamar's daughter," Delilah told her. "Not that I have to tell you that."

"Is this why you wanted to see me?"

"I wanted to see you because she's wearing Tamar's jewelry. That old clunky stuff that Asher gave her. You come here and took that watch from Cornelius. I wondered at the time why you just had to have it. Me and Cornelius, we don't neither of us know what we're looking at, do we? But you do. I was goin' to ask you how Asher got it, 'cause I didn't want no shame attached to Tamar's name. But I think I just might of figured that out."

"Figured out what, old woman?"

"Old woman! Who you calling old? Tamar would have been seventy-two if she was still living. You was older than her first time you come here. Better watch who you callin' old, girl. There's us who can deal with our age."

"I'm not Laura," she said. "I'm Jenny, Laura and Asher's daughter. Laura's dead. God only knows what happened to him. They never married anyway, so I really don't care. And fifty-two isn't old."

"You need to do yourself a favor and wipe off some of that paint you got on your face and get rid of that wig."

Jenny came up behind her. Before Delilah could turn to face her, the girl grabbed her arm, pulled her over to the table, and pushed her down in the chair.

"You shut your mouth, old woman," she said. "And stay there," she warned.

Delilah sat very still. Jenny stood with her back against the sink and her arms folded.

Cornelius picked that moment to come in. He came into the kitchen smiling. "Laura, you looking good, girl."

"Hah. That ain't what the old woman thinks." She picked up a knife off the counter. "And you just sit your old ass down at that table with her."

Delilah watched as Cornelius stopped smiling and sat down. "Laura," he began. "You remember—"

"I am not Laura. I'm Jenny. Laura and Asher's daughter."

"Asher's daughter? No wonder you looking so good," Cornelius said. He sounded confused.

"Shut up," Jenny told him. She was holding the knife like she meant to use it.

In as quiet a voice as she could manage, Delilah said, "Why you really come here, girl?"

"That old man wanted to know where Asher's cuff links were, what they had to do with the jewelry Asher gave Tamar. He asked too many questions. How Asher got it, where it came from. I knew what those questions were about as soon as I saw you had a copy of this newspaper article."

"You knew Tamar had a daughter?" Delilah asked.

"No, stupid. Tamar. Tamar. Who gives a damn about her? It was the jewelry. You two have found out what it's worth, haven't you? I know you didn't think I would give it to you, or did you?"

"You have Tamar's jewelry," Delilah said. Officer Torres hadn't said anything about the jewelry. But if Jenny had it . . . "Savannah didn't just drown, did she?"

"That jewelry was mine!" Jenny said.

"Of course it was," Delilah told her, not that it was true.

"Don't you try to placate me, you old bird."

Now what did placate mean? It had to be something insulting. Delilah almost had to bite her tongue. She looked at the knife before she opened her mouth and decided not to say nothin'. This would teach Cornelius not to keep sharpening her kitchen knives on that old razor strop of his. She glanced at him and said, "You okay?" He nodded, but she could see he was more scared than she was.

C H A P T E R

37

"Whoa," Holmberg said as they drove past Miss Delilah's house.

"Keep going," Lupe told him. "Turn at the corner."

As soon as they were out of sight of the house, Holmberg pulled over.

"A dark blue PT Cruiser," Lupe said. "And the porch light is on. That means trouble. Run the plates. Wisconsin." She repeated the numbers.

She called in. Almost as soon as she said they had a possible hostage situation, Lieutenant Nicholson came on the line.

"A *possible* hostage situation, Torres?" she scoffed. "Here, in Lincoln Prairie? When's the last time that happened?"

"I've got one, possibly two senior citizens, in a house in Bullfrog Bog." She gave the exact location and intersecting streets. "There's a car parked outside that could be connected with the Jones homicide."

"You're basing a hostage situation on that? Did anyone see anything?"

"Not that I know of."

"The sergeant says nobody has called in a complaint."

"The porch light is on," Lupe told her.

"The porch light?"

"Yes, they know that if they have a problem during the daytime they put it on, and if it's at night, they turn it off. We set that up last year as a signal when we were having those home invasions."

"I wasn't here then," said the lieutenant. "We don't have a hostage team, Torres. I'd have to call the sheriff's office. I suggest you get more substantial information before you ask me to authorize a thirty-man team to go out on a 'possible' hostage situation. I'll be waiting to hear from you." The last thing she said was, "Porch light. If someone that old lives there they probably forgot to turn it off this morning."

Lupe didn't bother to tell her that most of the people who lived here had to watch their utility bills to keep their gas and electricity from being turned off. It had taken a lot of convincing to get them to leave a light on at night. She put a call in to Marti and Vik.

"We'll be right there," Vik said. "Don't do anything until we get there. Did you run the plates?"

"Car belongs to a Jennifer Hunt Cooper," Lupe told him.

Marti shook her head. The name meant nothing. "That's one that's not on our radar," she said. "If this is the same car, and the same woman, what on earth is she doing there?"

Lupe told them about making a copy of the *The People's Voice* article that Elroy had e-mailed and leaving it with Delilah and Cornelius. "Bullfrog Bog was where all the black folk lived in the forties. These two are neighbors. Both of them were young and recently married back then, but not to each other. I thought the photo might jog their memory. I didn't expect anything like this."

"I'm going to have Vik talk to the lieutenant again. Sit tight; we're on our way."

When Marti and Vik arrived, Slim and Cowboy were with them, along with two TAC officers.

"Nicholson made one hell of a call," Vik said. "Insists that we don't have a witness or anything substantial enough to warrant deploying a thirty-man hostage team. Technically, she's right. It just pisses me off that she doesn't think you're street-smart enough to make the right call. I don't want anyone to get hurt, but if something goes wrong here, it's her ass, not ours."

"I want to go in," Lupe said. "If anything is wrong, Delilah and Cornelius will need a familiar face to keep them calm. They trust me and Delilah's smart enough to follow my lead and kick Cornelius in the shins if he doesn't."

"You think they're both in there?"

"All they've got is each other. Evenings she likes to listen to the radio and he likes to watch TV, but during the day they are all the company they've got."

The TAC team gave Lupe a few instructions. "Do not focus on the hostages. Give the subject your entire attention. You want to try to figure her out. What gets her excited, what calms her down. Play with it, test it, and bring her up and down. Remember, you're in charge. She only thinks she is. Do not take your weapon with you. She might be in a position to disarm you. Once you go in there, all you've got is guts, instinct, and common sense."

"You've done a couple of those hostage-training weekends," Marti reminded her. "Remember what you practiced."

"Draw me a floor plan," the TAC officer told her. "Show me the windows and the doors."

Lupe drew a quick but detailed sketch. "My guess is

300

that they are in the kitchen. That's where I always find them if they're not sitting on the porch or working in the garden."

"How are you going in?" the TAC officer asked.

"If she's done what I told them to, leaving that light on, the door isn't locked. I'm just going to walk in, call out that it's Lupe from the visiting nurses come to see how they are. They'll catch on and not let anyone know I'm a cop."

"Sounds like a plan," the TAC officer agreed. "If it is a hostage situation and the front door is not in their line of vision, I'm going in right behind you. I'll stay in this front room as backup until I can figure out what's going on. Do not focus on anyone but the hostage taker," he cautioned. "Whoever it is, you've got to hold their attention and figure out how to play them."

C H A P T E R

38

Delilah's back was beginning to hurt from sitting so still. Cornelius looked like he was about ready to pass out, and that woman was still standing there holding that knife on them. It seemed like she had been here for hours. Delilah kept hoping that Officer Torres would drop in again, but it didn't seem like she was coming back, at least not today. Cornelius swayed in the chair.

"Put your head down!" Delilah told him. He did. "Why you come here and threaten us like this?" she asked. "We don't mean you no harm. You know we just a couple of old folks. Don't nobody pay attention to old people no more. Why you got to be different?"

"I told you to shut up."

Delilah could tell the woman was thinking, trying to figure out what to do. She figured that if she could hold her attention, without making her mad, it would take that much longer for her to decide.

"You know, don't you?" the woman said.

"Know what?"

"Know about that jewelry, about what happened to that woman in the newspaper. All of it."

"No," Delilah said. "No, I don't. You ain't told me nothin'."

"I didn't have to. Unfortunately, as old as you two are, you are not stupid." She pointed the knife at Delilah. "Him, he's oblivious to everything right now. But not you." She took a step closer. "Not you. You've got it all figured out, haven't you, you old biddy."

"Don't you be disrespecting me!" Delilah pushed back the chair and started to stand up. "Your momma didn't teach you no better than that?"

The woman lunged at her and Delilah felt a sharp pain in her stomach and then something sticky and warm, as she fell to the floor.

Lupe could see that the door was ajar. She listened, but couldn't hear anything. She pictured what she would see when she went inside. She would see the kitchen table from the doorway. She thought Delilah and Cornelius might be sitting there, but she didn't think whoever was with them would join them.

The woman would have to stand, be threatening. Maybe by the sink, maybe by the counter, or the stove, but away from the table. She touched the door. She couldn't remember hearing it squeak when Delilah opened it. She hesitated. God, if this was a mistake, a bad call. What if she wasn't doing the right thing? What if she caused them—Delilah and Cornelius—to be killed? She wasn't even armed.

The TAC officer tapped her on the shoulder. He had his weapon in hand. He nodded and she went in.

"Delilah, Cornelius," she called. "It's me, Lupe, the visiting nurse." There was no response. Cornelius was sitting with his back to her. His head was on the table. She continued down the hall. "How are you two doing, today?" As soon as she reached the kitchen she saw Delilah crumpled on the floor. Blood was pooling around her.

"Get your ass in here," a woman said.

Lupe turned and saw her standing with her back against the sink holding a knife. There was blood on the blade.

"Hostage down," she called. The woman rushed her, arm upraised, knife pointing. Lupe ducked low and head-butted her in the gut. The woman grunted, and the knife clattered to the floor as she doubled over. Her arms were wrapped around her stomach. She staggered back, then slumped to the floor, moaning.

The TAC officer was there as Lupe reached Delilah. She felt a pulse in her carotid artery, but was afraid to move her to check out the bleeding.

By the time she looked up, the woman had been taken out by Vik and Marti, and the second TAC officer was telling her to get out of the way.

"Ambulance coming," he said. "She hasn't bled out yet. Bleeding looks like it's slowing down. We might be getting some clotting. Don't move her. She's better off right where she is."

Lupe sat on the floor beside Delilah. "Be all right," she said, repeating something Delilah often said. "Be all right." She couldn't see Delilah's hands so she patted her shoulder. Delilah's face was ashen, her eyes closed. Don't die, Lupe thought. Don't die, old girl. "Fight," she whispered. "Fight, Delilah, fight."

"The old man looks like he's in shock," the TAC officer told her. "No wounds, and he's breathing okay."

Lupe and Holmberg followed the ambulance. Delilah

was rushed into a cubicle in the emergency room and, almost as quickly, taken upstairs. "Surgery, now," the doctor said.

"How . . ." They were gone before she could ask the question.

She asked the nurse where Cornelius was. He had an IV drip going and was on a heart monitor, but conscious. "I told Lila we ought to call you," he whispered. "She gonna be okay?"

"I don't know," Lupe admitted. "If I just went in a few minutes sooner . . ."

"She didn't keep nothin' from you deliberate," Cornelius said. "That actress in the picture, that was her granddaughter. Sara is her great-granddaughter. She just wanted to know the truth about the jewelry. She was going to tell you. She just wanted to protect her kin. That's all she got left, that one great-grandchild." He closed his eyes. Soon he was snoring.

Lupe wandered over to the surgical waiting area, and glanced at the clock, surprised that it was only a little past two o'clock. She had been having breakfast with Delilah not more than six hours ago. Holmberg brought her some coffee.

"Poor old thing," she said. "Poor old thing. If we hadn't wasted all that time with the lieutenant . . ."

"Things happen the way they're supposed to," Holmberg said. "We're just the ones who have to live with it."

"Hungry?" he asked a few minutes later.

"No. And if anything happens to her, I'll never eat a blueberry pancake again."

She caught Holmberg's puzzled expression, but didn't explain.

Vik and Marti sat in the room with the bolted-down table and benches. This time, Jennifer Hunt Cooper sat across from them. Cooper was smart enough to keep her mouth shut and demand to see an attorney.

"I know my rights. I don't have to tell you anything and I'm not going to tell you anything. How do I get an attorney?"

"We found the jewelry in your purse, the gold and zirconia pieces Savannah Payne-Jones was wearing in that PR photo," Marti told her.

Cooper did not react.

"We also found the cuff links you showed that jeweler in Chicago."

That seemed to surprise her, but again she said nothing.

Marti looked at Vik. He scratched his chin. He didn't think they were going to get anything out of her either.

As they got up, Cooper asked, "When's my bail hearing?"

"Sometime within the next twenty-four hours," Marti said.

"Twenty-one hours," Cooper said. "I've been in custody for three hours already."

When the door to the interrogation room closed and locked behind them, Vik said, "Too much TV. A couple of days in the real world of jail should take care of that."

Their next stop was the state's attorney's office. The case had already been assigned to one of the assistant SAs.

"Cooper won't talk without an attorney," Marti told her. "And there are some things we need to know. We've got a couple of senior citizens in the hospital who might be able to help us eventually, but aren't able to talk with us now. Without them, Cooper's all we've got."

"I think she knew when she went to Delilah Greathouse's home that she was going to have to shut her up, as well as Cornelius Jefferson," Vik said. "Greathouse is still in surgery. Except for being scared half to death, Jefferson seems to be okay. As for Savannah Payne-Jones, Cooper could argue that it was not premeditated. We've got her for that because she had possession of Jones's jewelry. We've also got a couple of witnesses who can confirm that Cooper picked Jones up the night she died."

"What we don't have in the Jones case is a weapon," Marti explained, "or any proof that Cooper brought a weapon with the intention of committing bodily harm. The knife she used on Delilah was on the kitchen counter. Maybe, that night on the bridge, she picked up whatever came to hand. Right now we can't prove premeditation."

"You're suggesting a plea bargain," the assistant state's attorney said.

"That's your call," Marti told her. "There are a few things that we would like to know. And with those two in the hospital, unless someone else can tell us . . ."

"We will be asking that she be held without bail," the SA said. "That shouldn't be a problem with one homicide charge and right now the attempt on Greathouse. We can't find any major priors on her, but she was involved in two aggravated-battery cases, the first seven years ago, and again two years ago. Got probation both times. We'll see that she has ample opportunity to get an attorney as quickly as possible, if a public defender isn't assigned to the case. What do you need to know?"

Marti began with the jewelry. "We don't know how it came into Jones's family's possession. Savannah Jones's mother is the original owner. We also have a photo of the original owner with her husband. We'd like to know who he is, and if and how he figures in. These two people in the photo went to Massachusetts and reinvented themselves. Nothing on their marriage license is accurate. And, there's a connection between the jewelry Cooper had in her possession, not only with Jones, but also with the Newsome family."

The ASA looked puzzled.

"Their company did the renovations that bricked in the windows and sealed off the second floor in that building where those skeletal remains were found last year," Vik explained. "Cooper, Jones, and Newsome all have jewelry made by a Prussian named Otto Von Weiss; he never left Eastern Europe."

"You think that a fifty- or sixty-year-old homicide is connected with this?"

"Maybe just indirectly. But it's no coincidence that they all have jewelry made by the same person."

"So, Jennifer Cooper could possibly tie up some of those loose ends. Okay. I see where you're coming from. I'll see what I can do. But I'm going to call you before I make any deals, or you call me if you get these questions answered without her. At this point, I don't know of any mitigating circumstances other than the issue with the weapon. I'd just as soon charge her with Murder One."

"Hospital?" Vik suggested, when they got back in the car.

"Might as well," Marti agreed.

They found Lupe and Holmberg in the surgical waiting room.

"They're still operating on Delilah," Lupe said. "It's been three hours now."

"What about Cornelius?"

"He's on a heart attack and stroke watch. His blood pressure and heartbeat are erratic. No visitors until they get it under control."

Marti could see that Lupe was upset. "Look," she told her. "We followed procedure and everything went down fast. She could have lain there and bled out."

"But if we went in even a few minutes sooner . . ."

"What happened, happened. The one thing we cannot do is second-guess. We're cops. We had one shot at it. We took it. We did it right. That was not a situation where we could risk playing cowboy."

Lupe nodded. Marti looked at her for a few moments, decided what she said was sinking in. She was getting ready to leave when a doctor entered the room and walked toward them. He was wearing surgical scrubs. A mask dangled from his neck and he was still wearing a white cap.

"What?" Lupe asked.

"Mrs. Greathouse made it through surgery. She's in intensive care. All we can do now is wait."

"Can I see her?" Lupe asked.

"Come up in about half an hour."

Lupe turned to Marti when he left. "The granddaughter," she said. "That actress's daughter."

"Delilah's great-granddaughter, Sara."

"Delilah's a fighter, Marti. Knowing Sara is here would really give her something to fight for."

"We'll get her."

Sara and Akiro were in the den watching television when Marti and Vik arrived at the pastor's house.

"We need to talk with you," Marti said.

Akiro turned off the television.

"You have a relative here, your great-grandmother."

"That can't be true," Sara protested. "Ma would have told me."

"Not if she didn't know." Marti explained about Savannah's PR photo being in *The People's Voice*. "Someone saw it and either recognized the jewelry or realized who your mother must be because of her eyes, or both. In any case, your great-grandmother finally saw that picture today and knew who it had to be. She contacted the woman we are charging with your mother's death. That woman came to her house and stabbed her."

Sara got very pale. Akiro rushed over and put his arm around her and led her to the sofa.

"She's dead, too?" Sara whispered.

"No, but she had to have surgery and she's in intensive care. We think that if she knows you're there, and you know who she is, it might help. She's in her eighties, but she's got a fighting chance of pulling through."

"Let's go," Akiro said. "We'll follow you. I've rented a car."

He helped Sara to her feet.

"I'm okay," she said. "I'm okay."

41

Sara listened as the nurse explained the serious-ness of Delilah's condition, then followed her into the room to see her great-grandmother. The old woman looked so tiny. Machines clicked and beeped. Something wrapped around her legs inflated and deflated. Sara wasn't sure what she should say, what she should call her.

"Grandmother," she said. "It's me, Sara, your great-grandchild. I'm Savannah's daughter and she was Tamar's daughter. She didn't know about you. Neither of us did. She would have come to you years ago if she knew. I would have come, too."

She was so little, so still. Sara looked at the nurse, who nodded.

"I'm going to stay right here at the hospital until you wake up and can talk to me. Please don't leave me. You're all the family I have."

She touched the old woman's face, stroked her hair. "Don't leave me, Grandmother. You don't know me, and I don't know you. There is so much you can tell me that I don't know. There's so much that I want to tell you. Please wake up. Please talk to me."

The nurse said, "Mrs. Greathouse, your great-grand-daughter, Sara, is here. We're going to let her come in every hour for ten minutes to see you. She's not going to leave until after you wake up and talk to her."

The nurse led her out of the room. "We have no idea of what people can hear post-op," she explained. "Sometimes they tell us things they heard us say. Sometimes they even tell us things that were said in the operating room. So we talk to them and we want you to keep talking to her. But she needs rest more than anything. Ten minutes every hour. I'll come and get you."

"And if . . ."

"She has a strong heart and good lungs. She was in good health when she came in. She's old. She lost a lot of blood. She's had almost three hours of surgery. That's a lot of trauma to recover from. It depends on whether or not she can handle the stress from the injury and the surgery. It might be a while before she wakes up. Sometimes even when we know the anesthesia has pretty much worn off, they still need to sleep. Be patient."

Akiro came to her and held her. "A great-grandmother!" he said. "You have a great-grandmother, Sara."

"She doesn't know that."

"Who can say? Maybe she does."

"Perhaps," Sara said, but she didn't think so. Akiro was always the optimist. She didn't think the old woman could hear her, but how she wished that she could.

"Let's sit here together," he said. "It could be a long while yet before she wakes up."

"I wonder if she's anything like Ma. They don't look alike. She's so tiny."

Akiro smiled. "And you're not."

"So I get my height from her. But she looks so small, Akiro, and so helpless. And Ma didn't know. She was so close to her and she didn't know it."

"But you do."

"Fate, Akiro?"

"Who knows," he admitted. "Things happen that seem strange to us that might not be so strange after all."

"What if she dies without ever waking up? I've lost Ma. If I lose her without even knowing her . . ."

"Tell her that the next time you go in."

"The nurse says they don't know if she can hear me, that sometimes they remember, sometimes they don't."

"So just talk to her. Say whatever it is that you feel. You know how it is with my grandmother. She calls sometimes and tells us things like, 'Be careful when you are driving today,' or 'Don't go to the grocery store today.' We don't know why she does that. We listen and do as she says so we'll never know if there's anything to what she tells us. Does she know something we do not? Or does she just like the attention? What's the difference? It's like having a sixth sense who lives four blocks away. Some of us humor her. Some of us believe her."

"I want to hear this grandmother speak," Sara said. "My great-grandmother."

She didn't think she would really believe that was true unless the old woman was able to tell her that herself. Then she would find out about Tamar, and she could talk about Savannah.

C H A P T E R

42

Marti felt exhausted. Ben and the boys were outside shooting baskets when she pulled into the garage. She went into the house, gave Momma a kiss on the cheek as she walked through the kitchen, took note of the garlic-and-basil aroma of Momma's spaghetti sauce, and headed for her recliner in the den.

When she woke up, Ben was sitting on the couch.

"The test," she said, sitting up.

"I go in for surgery Wednesday morning."

Marti's stomach began churning. "That's not enough time to . . ."

"Think about it?" he asked. "I don't want any of us to think about it. Let's just get it over with and know for sure what's what."

"What did the doctor say?"

"My PSA went up half a point. If you want to talk with him we can see him tomorrow afternoon. He won't be able to tell you any more than we know now until after the surgery."

She felt the acid bath begin. She was going to have

to see a doctor about this pretty soon. "When do you want to tell the boys?"

"Tonight. After supper. We'll have to tell Joanna, too. Momma already knows."

They waited until Theo and Mike finished their homework.

"Surgery?" Mike said. "On purpose?"

"The doctor says I should do it now."

Both boys were silent for a few moments; then Mike said, "This isn't like when you were in the car accident, is it?"

"No, it isn't."

"Are you going to stay asleep like you did then?" Theo asked.

"No. Not as long."

"Good. That was scary."

"This is scary, too," Mike said. He looked ready to cry.

"Do you get to stay home like you did when you had the accident?" Theo asked.

"You'll have to put up with me hanging around for about six weeks."

"Good!" Theo managed a lopsided grin. "We need to get some work done on our Boy Scout badges."

Marti wanted to hug Theo. She knew he was trying to make Mike feel better.

"Dad," Mike said, "are you going to be okay after the surgery, like you were after the accident?"

"I don't think I'll be as sore," Ben said. "Everything

316

hurt after that accident."

They waited. When there were no other questions, Ben said, "Now, Mom will decide when you can see me. It might be Wednesday night. It might not be until Thursday or even Friday. She'll tell you how I'm doing and if you have to wait to see me, she'll tell you what's going on. You two okay with that?"

Both boys said yes.

"And if you think of anything else you want to know, either one of you, I'll be home all day tomorrow."

That done they went up to Joanna's room. She had cleared a place on the floor by throwing her clothes into a corner and was sitting on the floor, surrounded by books.

"Homework?" Marti asked.

"A report."

"Due tomorrow?"

"No. Today. The teacher's been out sick since Thursday. Infected wisdom tooth. I figure I'll turn it in to the sub before she comes back."

"Good thinking," Marti said. She moved a stack of books and sat on the floor beside her.

Ben sat on the unmade bed.

Joanna looked up at him. "You've got it, haven't you?"

"Surgery's day after tomorrow."

Joanna burst into tears. "Baby," Marti said, holding her. She hadn't expected this. It was several minutes before the crying subsided to sobs, then hiccups. "You

317

okay now?" Marti asked.

"No! How can I be okay?" She turned to Ben. "What if something happens to you? What do I do then? You can't just . . . you can't. You can't . . ." She began crying again.

Ben came over, helped her up, and held her. "It'll be okay."

"You don't know that."

"I know you'll be okay."

"No!" Joanna said. "If anything happened to you, I'll never be okay again."

Marti knew just how true that was.

By the time she had showered and was ready for bed, Marti was wishing tomorrow was Wednesday. How would they make it through the day? How would she help these children if the outcome wasn't good? She wanted to scream, "Why, God?" Instead she said the Jesus prayer, got into bed, put her head on Ben's chest, and cried, too.

C   H   A   P   T   E   R

43

TUESDAY, MAY 18—LINCOLN PRAIRIE

There was a message from Thomas Newsome when Marti went upstairs after roll call. "Those windows were bricked up and that false ceiling put in on May twenty-ninth to the thirty-first, nineteen-forty-four," she told Vik.

"I'll make a note of that," he said. "Put it right in with all of these other miscellaneous notes."

She called the hospital. "Delilah has come out of the anesthesia, but she's still sleeping. She's holding her own. The nurse will talk to Cornelius's doctor when he comes in and let us know when we can see him."

Slim and Cowboy had come and gone. Vik brought her a cup of coffee. "What's the word on Ben?"

"Surgery tomorrow," Marti said. Tears sprang to her eyes as she said it. She wiped at them.

"I'll let the sergeant know we won't be in. If anything comes up he can reach me at the hospital and I'll handle it. What time are they admitting him?"

"Six A.M."

"How are the kids?"

"Not good."

"Waiting's the hard part. Knowing is easier."

That sounded similar to what the patriarch had told her, but Vik would know that better than anyone. She said the Jesus prayer again. Such a simple prayer, but the patriarch was right, it calmed her.

"Marti," Vik said, "you check your in-box yet?"

"No."

"Check out the ballistic report on the gun!"

She found it. "Well I'll be damned," she said. It was the gun used to fire the bullet that killed the body in the closet.

"We should talk to Newsome," Vik said. "But I

don't think he knows anything."

"If we just had a little more information . . ."

"I know. I know."

"So what do you want to do?" Marti was feeling so lethargic she didn't feel like doing anything.

"Let's wait, talk to Cornelius. Those two know a lot more than they've been able to tell us. And Delilah can't tell us anything right now."

Marti checked her e-mail. Lieutenant Nicholson hadn't sent her anything since she told her off last week. She wondered if she should worry about that and decided she had enough on her mind already. To hell with the lieutenant. Vik was still sending reports for both of them.

It was a little before noon when Vik got a call from the hospital. The doctor said they could speak with Cornelius. When they got there, they went up to Intensive Care to ask about Delilah first.

Sara came over to them. "She's not talking yet, but she does open her eyes sometimes."

Marti gave her a hug. "How are you doing?"

"I'm okay as long as she is. Akiro went to get us some lunch. I'm not leaving until I know for sure that she's going to make it and she's awake enough to see me and know who I am. The doctors are not making any promises, but the nurses say she's improving. Lupe is in with her now. She stayed here with us last night."

Marti waited until Lupe came out. She looked

exhausted, but she was smiling. "She looked at me," she told Sara. "I'm sure she knew who I was."

Marti knew she should caution Lupe against getting so emotionally involved, but she did that herself. Instead she hugged her, gave Sara a hug, and went to the elevator.

Cornelius Jefferson was sitting up in bed when they got there. He had an IV drip with a smaller bag of medication attached, and was hooked up to a monitor. He looked so tired Marti felt bad about having to bother him.

She showed him the picture of Tamar and her husband.

"They was married?" Cornelius asked. "You're sure?"

"Do you recognize him?

"That's Edmund Newsome."

"The youngest son?" Marti asked. "The one who went missing?"

"Yes. I thought she must have married Asher."

"Back up," Marti said. "First, how would Tamar know Edmund Newsome?"

"He'd come by to pick up Asher sometimes, or drop him off after work. They talked. I can't say they knew each other that well. But that is Edmund Newsome in the picture."

"And who's Asher?"

Cornelius was silent for a moment. "He was just a boarder at my house. But my wife, and me, we didn't have any kids. We kind of got close." He closed his eyes.

Marti sat down beside the bed. Vik took the chair by the window and sat there scowling with his chin in his hand. His expression said, "Here we go again. More useless information."

"Take your time, Mr. Jefferson," she told him. "We've got all day. Don't tire yourself out."

"Asher was twenty-eight," he said. "Tamar wasn't but sixteen. Lila got married and pregnant at fifteen. Her husband was ten, twelve years older than she was. We both thought Asher and Tamar made a good match. We encouraged them. I think Lila just wanted Tamar to be safe, protected. Tamar was kind of willful. Me, I just didn't want Asher to leave. He was as close to having a son as I ever got."

He stopped talking again, closed his eyes, and rested for a few minutes.

"Soon as Lila got them to set a wedding date everything went wrong. October tenth, they was supposed to get married. All of a sudden Asher got this job offer in Michigan. He left in February, came back toward the end of May. Then he left again. That's the last we ever saw of him. First time he left, he wrote Tamar just about every day. This time there was nothin'. Two months later Tamar was gone, too. Never did see her again either. She left her mother a note. Lila never did tell me what she said."

He popped an ice chip into his mouth and closed his eyes. Marti had a lot of questions, but he sounded so tired she was afraid to ask them.

She got up. "Mr. Jefferson, we still need to talk with you. What if we leave now and come back in a couple of hours?" Eyes closed, he nodded. He was snoring softly when they left.

"Have you eaten today?" Vik asked.

Marti hadn't.

"It's lunchtime. I'm hungry. Let's let the old man rest for a few hours. Did you note what he said about this Asher? We have to nail down the year, but the guy left the end of May. That building was bricked up the end of May. And he was twenty-eight, same as our skeletal remains."

Marti nodded. She had caught the age, but hadn't paid attention to the dates.

She ordered her usual at the Barrister, shepherd's pie, but she just picked at it. Her stomach was churning. Vik watched her, but said nothing until they were back in the car.

"Best to keep busy," he told her.

"The old man's probably still sleeping," she said. "He needs to rest. Let's take a quick drive to the lake."

She sat and looked at the water, blue near the shore, gray in the distance. "The sun's out," she said. She hadn't noticed until now. The lake always soothed her. She had spent hours watching it after Johnny died. But Ben, he was going to be all right. He was. She watched the seagulls as they ran along the sand, sailed in wide circles above the water. When her stomach calmed down, she said the Jesus prayer again, then turned on the ignition.

Mr. Jefferson was awake when they returned. He seemed glad to see them again.

"Are you going to be here long?" Marti asked.

"For a couple more days at least. Going to be late getting the tomatoes in this year. Nurse says I can see Lila, maybe tomorrow or the next day. You seen her?"

Marti nodded.

"How's she doin'?"

"Much better."

"I know they ain't tellin' me everything. What happened to her?"

"Nothin' much," Marti lied. "She needed a little surgery. They're watching her real close because of her age, same as you."

He nodded.

"I need to ask you a few more questions about Asher."

"I sure wish that was him in that picture. Hard not knowing what happened to him." His voice sounded stronger than it had this morning.

Marti took the chair by the bed again. Vik returned to his seat by the window. He had his notebook out this time.

"What year was it the last time you saw him?"

"Nineteen-forty-four. Just before D-Day."

"Do you know how tall he was? What he weighed?"

"He was about five feet nine inches. Not sure what he weighed. One sixty, one seventy. Hard to say, lot of muscle. He did odd jobs for Mr. Newsome at the construction sites, carrying stuff around, loading stuff. Hard work other folks didn't want to do. Got paid half what white folks did, but money's money."

"Was he mixed?" Marti asked.

"Said his daddy was a white man. Didn't come from here, came from up in Wisconsin. Came to Lincoln Prairie looking for work. Lot of coloreds living in the Bog back then. He asked around for a room to rent; folks sent him to me." Cornelius smiled. "Good Christian man he was. Knew the Bible well as I did and my daddy was a preacher." He stopped smiling. "At least that's what I thought until yesterday."

He was silent, sipped some water. "That Jenny. We was expecting Laura, his cousin. Least that's what she told us. Seems she wasn't. Asher already had a child by her while he was courtin' Tamar."

"Jenny?" Marti asked.

He nodded and was silent again.

"What about the jewelry?"

"Oh, that." It came out like a sigh. He closed his eyes.

"If you're too tired . . ."

"No. It's got to be said." But it was several minutes before he spoke again. Marti and Vik just waited.

"The jewelry," he said finally. "Only way Tamar could have got it was from him. He gave me a pocket watch just before he left. Laura and Asher come and got it. They said she was his cousin. We didn't know nothing about them having no child."

"Do you know how he got the jewelry?"

"Don't want to know, probably do. Asher got these packages from Warren Junior. The packages came to my house, he took them in to work, gave them to the old man. A couple of packages came after Warren Junior got himself killed. 'Fore he left, Asher was sportin' these cuff links, big green stones, flashy just like the ring and the earrings Tamar's daughter was wearing." The old man sighed and closed his eyes. "I didn't want to know. You know how it is when you don't want something to be true? You make like it ain't. But I knew. I did know. Even then. Wasn't that much of a surprise when Asher's daughter showed up yesterday. I just didn't want to know, is all."

"Just one more question, Mr. Jefferson: Why did Jennifer Hunt Cooper come here yesterday?"

"Because I called her. She kept in touch with Sadie. Old Sadie lives right down the street from us. 'Course when she come we thought she was Laura. Didn't know then there was a child between Laura and Asher. Lila wanted to know what Tamar knew about how Asher got the jewelry, if Tamar was involved. She didn't want Tamar's daughter or granddaughter to be tainted by nothin' Tamar did."

"And this Jenny knew that?"

"I tol' her on the phone. Used Sadie's phone, ask her."

He was quiet then. Marti looked at Vik. He nodded.

326

They knew all they needed to know for now.

"Mr. Jefferson, is there anything we can do for you?" she asked. "Anything we can bring you?"

"Don't need nothin'. But the company is good. I'm just tired is all. Has Lila seen her granddaughter yet?"

"Sara's been here since yesterday. Spent the night."

"Sara," he said, and smiled.

"What about Thomas Newsome?" Marti asked on the way to the precinct.

"We know enough to put things together. We've got enough to close the case on the skeletal remains. There are no surviving eyewitnesses. There's time to decide what to tell who."

"And we can call the assistant state's attorney," Marti said. "I don't think we'll be needing a plea agreement. Cornelius and Delilah know too much. Cooper knew when she came here that she was going to have to kill them. I do wonder why she went after Savannah though. Maybe she thought she knew something, too. Maybe she thought Jones would hand everything over. She had no way of knowing about the gambling."

"Maybe she just decided that since her father stole that jewelry, it belonged to her, so she took it anyway she could."

"Maybe she did," Marti agreed.

Marti heard from Josef that afternoon.

"We want to thank you for helping us recover that jewelry."

327

"Your boss had that situation well in hand before we got there," Marti told him.

"Yes, but it was a relief to him to have someone to give that gun to. I did want to tell you what I found out about the jewelry before we returned to Bucharest."

Marti was curious.

"According to a knowledgeable source in Romania, Otto Von Weiss was commissioned to make this jewelry by people who did not expect to see their homeland again. That's why he used the gems that he did. I am not sure that we will ever be able to identify whom they belonged to, but they are of historic significance."

Marti thought about Tamar's zirconia. Josef didn't know about that. She would explain this to Sara, let her decide what to do.

"Thank you for telling me. It was puzzling. Oh, and please thank your boss for me."

"For what?"

"He'll know. My husband will have surgery tomorrow."

"It is good that you told me. We will keep him in our prayers."

"Thank you." She was beginning to appreciate what Vik had once told her about how difficult it was to be there for Mildred, to watch and wait.

The call from the bank about her credit card came in just as Marti was getting ready to go home.

"Am I speaking with Marti MacAlister?"

"Yes, you are. Detective Marti MacAlister."

"Well, that's interesting. I've got someone on another line who claims to be you. She says she lost her credit card, knows the credit card number and your Social Security number but can't remember the PIN number. She wants me to issue another card, but send it to a post office box in Chicago."

"You've got to be kidding."

"No, ma'am. I'm not. She thinks I'm on another line trying to get my supervisor to authorize sending it to a post office box."

"Good. I am going to put you through to the Identity Theft Division of the state's attorney's office. Here's the direct line in case we get disconnected."

"I'll be damned," she said when she hung up.

"What was that all about?" Vik asked.

"I *was* a mark," she admitted, incredulous. "At the library. They left everything in my purse and copied down the information."

Vik came close to smiling. "That was about the only lucky break we got on this one," he admitted.

"What do you mean?"

"It got you focused on that jewelry, and the jewelry was the key to it all."

Marti remembered Josef's call. She had forgotten to tell Vik what he said.

"Guess what—" she began.

WEDNESDAY, MAY 19—LINCOLN PRAIRIE

Everyone was in the waiting room with Marti. Vik, the pastor, Momma, Theo, Mike, Joanna, and Ben's partner, Allan. Lupe, Holmberg, Cowboy, and Slim were on duty, but in and out. Ben's doctor was smiling as he walked toward them.

"Everything went just as we expected," he said. "It was totally contained, early stage one. Once he recovers it will be as if he never had this procedure. Everything is going to be fine."

They all hugged. Joanna cried. The doctor smiled. "He'll be in recovery for an hour or two and then we'll take him to his room. He might not feel great for a few days, but you should all be able to spend a few minutes with him by this evening. Marti, you can come with me now."

Smiling through her tears, Marti gave everyone another hug and went with the doctor.

Delilah sat on the front porch in a well-cushioned wicker chair and put her feet up on the hassock. Sara covered her with a cotton throw even though the sun was shining and the weather was warm. Cornelius was out back with someone that Sara had hired to help him with the garden this summer.

"You don't have to plant anything, Grandmother," Sara said. "I am going to see to it that you are both always well cared for."

Sara would be here for the summer. Then she would be returning to Los Angeles to marry that nice young man, Akiro. She had promised that Delilah and Cornelius would have a cleaning woman. A cleaning woman! She had already remodeled their bathrooms and had railings and new fixtures put in so they couldn't fall and hurt themselves.

Delilah reached out and took Sara's hand. "You know, child, just having you here, that's more than enough for me. Just having you here. You don't got to do all of this for us. Just stay the summer. That's more than I ever thought I would live to see."

"Oh, no. You're the only grandmother I have, the only family I've got. If you two think you're being spoiled now, just wait. I'm going to take real good care of you. One thing Ma always told me was that when you got a gift you always showed your appreciation. You and Cornelius are a gift I never would have expected."

Delilah smiled and closed her eyes. All that excitement and that surgery had sure tired her out. And poor Cornelius had been so absentminded for a while. He was getting more like his old self every day though. Being out in the garden was good for him. A man needed something useful to do, even when he was old. As for her, she was going to listen to this great-granddaughter of hers and start takin' life easy. Sara looked so much like Tamar it was almost like having her with her again. She would let the child go when she had to, but for now she was thankful each day she was here.

C   H   A   P   T   E   R

45

SUNDAY, JUNE 20—LINCOLN PRAIRIE

Marti was glad that summer had finally arrived. It was Vik and Mildred's twenty-eighth wedding anniversary. The weather was perfect, sunny, seventy-six degrees. Vik had set up a canopy in his backyard, beneath which were tables and chairs. He hired a caterer and a band. Roses and late bulbs were in bloom. A gardener had put in borders of annuals. A three-tiered wedding cake was on one of the tables surrounded by vases of cut flowers. Mildred was lovely in a nile green dress and Vik was wearing a suit.

When the band began playing "I Love You Truly," Vik took Mildred by the arm, guided her to the grassy dance area, and took her in his arms. Their dog, Maxie, followed, close behind. As they waltzed, staying pretty much in one spot, Maxie, always watchful of Mildred, circle-danced around them.

Marti reached for Ben's hand. One day, they, too,

would share a moment like this. For today, all was well.

When the song ended, all of the guests applauded. Ben leaned over and kissed her.

E P I L O G U E

WEDNESDAY, JUNE 30—LINCOLN PRAIRIE

Lieutenant Gail Nicholson looked at the chief of police in disbelief. She had come expecting an outstanding evaluation as well as a recommendation to at least one of the chief-of-police positions she had applied for.

"As I said, you have done an excellent job in terms of updating our computer capabilities—equipment and programming. We're real state of the art now. However, Gail, you just don't have the people skills to deal effectively with our detective force. So, I'm offering you a lateral to an administrative position with supervisory responsibilities for the appropriate office and technical personnel."

He handed her the copies of the applications she had filed with the other departments. "I cannot recommend you for either of these positions." Then he opened a manila file she had given him with her reprimands of MacAlister for his signature along with a recommendation for her demotion. "As for this, I would shred these if I were you, before I toss them out."

"But she—"

"MacAlister and her partner are the best homicide detectives not just in the county, but in the state. You've brought them into more compliance in terms of reporting than I expected, but this has gone too far. I can't replace either of them. Nor can I replace my best vice detectives." He hesitated, then said, "So if a replacement became necessary, they would not be the ones to go." He handed her the folder. "Make sure you shred this, then get rid of it," he repeated. "Effective tomorrow, Deputy Chief Dirkowitz will temporarily assume your current responsibilities and you will report to your new administrative command."

Gail Nicholson returned to her office, looked around. At least there wouldn't be much packing. She shredded the incident reports she had kept in the manila folder, not because she cared who read them, but because she didn't want anyone to know how humiliated she was. How dare he choose MacAlister over her. How dare he.

She wanted to leave. She wanted to walk out the front door and never look back. But nobody had ever done this to her before, and nobody would ever do it to her again. MacAlister would pay big-time for this. She would stay long enough to make sure that MacAlister paid. Payback was something she had gotten very good at over the years. Achieving it was the best high in the world. She smiled. MacAlister had gotten it all wrong. Marti MacAlister's ass would be hers. She would see to that, and soon.

Center Point Publishing
600 Brooks Road ● PO Box 1
Thorndike ME 04986-0001 USA

(207) 568-3717

US & Canada:
1 800 929-9108